AIRS AND GRACES

AIRS AND GRACES

A Charles Patterson Mystery

Roz Southey

CRÈME de la CRIME

This first world edition published 2012
in Great Britain and in the USA by
SEVERN HOUSE PUBLISHERS LTD of
9–15 High Street, Sutton, Surrey, England, SM1 1DF.
Trade paperback edition first published
in Great Britain and the USA 2012 by
SEVERN HOUSE PUBLISHERS LTD.

British Library Cataloguing in Publication Data

Southey, Roz, 1952–
   Airs and graces.
   1. Patterson, Charles (Fictitious character) – Fiction.
   2. Musicians – England – Newcastle upon Tyne – Fiction.
   3. Great Britain – History – George II, 1727–1760 –
   Fiction. 4. Detective and mystery stories.
   I. Title
   823.9'2-dc22

ISBN-13: 978-1-78029-017-1 (cased)
ISBN-13: 978-1-78029-521-3 (trade paper)

All Severn House titles are printed on acid-free paper.

Severn House Publishers support The Forest Stewardship Council [FSC],
the leading international forest certification organisation. All our titles that
are printed on Greenpeace-approved FSC-certified paper carry the FSC logo.

Typeset by Palimpsest Book Production Ltd.,
Falkirk, Stirlingshire, Scotland.
Printed and bound in Great Britain by
MPG Books Ltd., Bodmin, Cornwall.

For Lynne

WITH THANKS . . .

. . . to everyone at Severn House – always helpful, friendly and a pleasure to work with.

. . . to my agent, Juliet Burton, for her support, unfailing enthusiasm, and excellent advice.

. . . to Lynne Patrick for her continuing belief in me. Without her, Patterson's career would never have got off the ground. And she cooks a mean chocolate-orange tart too.

. . . to Matthew and Anne, for their patient endurance of all the insults flung at Handel.

. . . to Jackie, Laura and Anu, who encouraged me to persist with my writing.

. . . to my family, particularly to my sisters, Wendy and Jennifer, and brother-in-law, John, for their continuing support. To Sonia, for reading Patterson during the sleepless nights caused by two babies. To my father-in-law, Ron, and to my late mother-in-law, Joan, for being generous with their praise.

. . . and of course, to my husband Chris who puts up with last minute panics, ferries me to and from murder mystery evenings and crime-writing conferences, keeps me supplied with tea, and even laughs at my jokes . . .

One

Philippe, let me encourage you to come to England!
The women here are delightful beyond imagining!
[Letter from Louis de Glabre to his friend Philippe
Froidevaux, 16 January 1737]

'Watch out!' Esther cried.

I ducked, and my feet went out from under me. I slid in the snow, flailed wildly and ended up flat on my back. The snowball flew over my head.

Fat flakes of snow pattered wetly on to my face and clogged my eyelashes; blinking, I looked up at the dark night sky. Perhaps this hadn't been a good idea.

Esther was giggling as she bent to help me up. Her fair hair was coming loose under her hat, and her greatcoat was splattered with patches of snow where my aim had been better than hers. My wife; my *lady* wife, with generations of stern ancestors behind her, and a reputation as a sensible, middle-aged woman, was scandalously wearing breeches, and throwing snowballs. And I'd worried over the twelve years' difference between us, thinking she'd find me a callow youth!

'Are you all right, Charles?'

I sat up, feeling the wet soaking through my coat, and my shirt and my breeches. Even in the swirling blizzard, I could see the heightened colour in Esther's cheeks, the excited glow in her eyes. I was relieved; she'd not been feeling well recently.

'No,' I said grumpily. 'I'm not all right.' How would the ladies and gentlemen of the town – my customers – react if they saw me at this moment. Respectable musicians do not roll in the snow like children. I scrambled up. 'Why did you throw a snowball and then tell me to duck!'

'*I* didn't throw it!' she said, with laughing indignation. 'Hugh did!'

The flakes were coming down faster and thicker, veiling

everything around us with a thick curtain of white. Obscuring the deserted Key: the tall buildings, the chandlers' shops, the taverns and the brothels, the printing office. Ships at the wharves had snow on every line of the rigging, and were sitting in a thin layer of ice as the River Tyne froze at the edges; the tidal flow kept the centre running though sluggish. The bell of All Hallows' church struck midnight. Sunday. That made it worse; Sunday is supposed to be a day of pious restraint.

I couldn't see Hugh anywhere. Hugh Demsey, dancing master, who'd just put me on my back in the snow. This expedition had been his idea. We'd originally intended to spend a quiet Saturday evening at home in Caroline Square, over dinner and wine, with music and conversation afterwards. My wife, myself, and my closest friend. Comfortable, cosy entertainment for a cold January night. But that was before Hugh glanced out of the window and said, 'Good Lord, it's snowing!'

In the week or two since Christmas, we'd had an entire week of heavy frosts, and temperatures so cold no one wanted to venture out of doors. The snow had been bound to follow. 'Let's go out and have a slide,' Hugh said enthusiastically. Looking at the gently falling flakes, I'd remembered the winters of childhood, sledging and sliding and skating, and throwing snowballs . . .

I spotted Hugh at last, a dark shadow in the blizzard; I grabbed up a handful of snow and squeezed it hard. I'd have to be careful; Hugh was standing at the edge of the river and I didn't want to knock him in. I sauntered up to him, arm behind my back. If only Esther didn't give me away with her giggling!

Hugh swung round. His hat had come off and his black hair slapped about his face. Even the voluminous greatcoat couldn't disguise the handsome figure the ladies so admired – dancing masters rarely get fat. 'Look at this!' He pointed down into the river.

It must be a trick; I said, 'No, you don't get me that way!' but he'd already turned back. Esther peered over his shoulder into the driving snow that obscured the water below. I kept a safe distance, just in case, and followed their gaze.

The tide was out, exposing ice-crusted mudbanks below the wharfs. Two lanterns burned in the darkness, apparently hanging in the middle of the river. In reality, they were on the shops on the Tyne Bridge of course; I could just make out the bridge's high arches and the dark hulks of the houses. Snow swirled in again.

'The second arch,' Hugh said. 'There's something hanging down.'

He was right. A faint whitish line seemed to be written on the bridge, dropping down the pier from one of the shops to the mudflat below. A rope – and someone was climbing down it.

'An elopement!' Esther said, delighted. 'I had half a mind to do something similar myself, Charles!'

Esther and I have been married five months now and society is, just, beginning to accept the situation. An alliance between a man of twenty-seven and a woman of thirty-nine is bound to be frowned upon, particularly when the woman has money and status, and the man is a mere musician. No one, apparently, believes that it can be a matter of love. There was a time when I set my mind against all idea of marriage, for fear of the damage it might do to Esther's reputation. She herself was equally determined to marry me.

The matter hadn't required an elopement to settle it, however. Ours was a 'forced' marriage; my patron found us in a compromising position. That is to say, we were standing decorously a good six feet apart, but the room was a bedroom, which makes all the difference. I have long been extremely glad of the way matters turned out.

'We ought to do something,' I said, uneasily eyeing the figure on the rope.

'Don't be such a prig, Charles!' Hugh said. 'You're spoiling the romantic moment!'

Esther cautiously strained to look down at the mud flats. 'I cannot see an earnest lover.'

The snow danced in closer, blowing into our faces, obscuring our view. I squinted against the flying flakes, at the figure sliding down the rope. A woman, wearing skirts and struggling with them. She should have copied Esther and opted for a pair of breeches. The figure hung for a moment by one hand, then let go, dropping the last few feet to land on hands and knees on the mudbank.

'Mud is not romantic,' Esther said regretfully.

The woman scrambled to her feet, hauling up her skirts. She looked lithe and active, obviously young, and certainly not weighed down by anything as prosaic as luggage.

The thick snow swirled in again. 'We should do something,' I said uncertainly. I caught glimpses of the figure struggling through the mud towards the landing steps up on to the Key. There was no impatient lover in sight. 'It might not be an elopement. She might be a thief – stealing from one of the shops on the bridge . . .'

Esther and Hugh broke into protests at the same time. Hugh grabbed my arms and turned me round, away from the bridge. 'No, no!' he said. 'Not a thief.'

'This is *not* another crime,' Esther said, firmly. 'Or, if it is, it is a small one, and we need not worry about it. Time to go home.'

'That's right,' Hugh said. 'Go home. Have a nice sleep. Forget all about it.'

'Yes,' Esther said, wickedly. 'Sleep – just what I was thinking of.'

I sighed. Over the past two years, I've somehow become embroiled in five murders – not in the least my fault – and now Hugh and Esther persist in thinking I see death and disaster everywhere. 'I'm not thinking of taking a hand in it myself! We could call out the Watch.'

'They won't come out!' Hugh said. 'Not in this weather! Besides, do you want them to see your wife in her breeches?'

'Alas,' Esther said, 'my reputation would never be the same again.'

'Then,' I pointed out, 'you should stop wearing them.'

'I will,' she agreed cordially. 'When we get home . . .'

Hugh roared with laughter, slipped on the snow and almost went down. I grabbed at him to prevent him falling in the river, but he recovered almost immediately, dipped and snatched up a handful of snow. Esther shrieked, and dodged for the shelter of a pile of barrels. I seized snow from the top of the barrels—

And heard the screams of a frightened child.

The screaming was coming from the bridge. I swung round, slipped, regained my balance and started running. In the wet dance of snow, I could see barely a foot in front of me, but the flickering lights on the bridge led me along. Shadows shifted in the blizzard, a large dog pattered away from me, leaving deep footprints.

On the slope up on to the bridge, the cobbles were icy and I went down on to my knees. Hugh was at my shoulder, helped me up. Shops and houses clustered on both sides of the bridge; to the left stood a group of four shops. The door of the last stood open, a haze of light seeping out . . .

The screaming went on – the panicking desperate fear of a young child.

Hugh and I reached the door together. The upholsterer's shop. I glimpsed the elegant interior in uncertain candlelight – fine striped wallpaper, elegant chairs, gilt mirrors gleaming. An occasional table had been knocked over, a small clock lay beside it on the floor.

The child was at the back of the room, standing by the counter. Staring down at something behind it.

We bolted for her. Six or seven years old, in her nightgown, with a candle in her hand and her dark hair in a braid down her back. She was screaming, mouth wide, face red and tears streaming down her face. Esther pushed past, took the candle from the child's hand and put her arm round the thin shoulders. The child turned into her embrace, hiccupping and sobbing.

We looked down on the body behind the counter. A young man, an apprentice, lay on the mattress that had been his bed. A blanket was pulled over him and he looked as if he was curled up in sleep.

Except for the blood pooling around him. Blood that was still liquid. I bent to touch him. He was as warm as in life.

'Esther,' I said. 'You'd better get the child out of here.'

She nodded, understanding at once I was afraid the murderer might still be here. She gave me the candle and said briskly, 'Take care.'

The shop had been open so the murderer had probably already escaped, but I was taking no risks; I looked round for a weapon and picked up a heavy candlestick.

'More blood,' Hugh said. He was standing at the door into the interior of the house. Stairs climbed straight up from the door; a small bloody footprint was imprinted on the bottom stair.

'It's the child's,' Hugh said. 'But it's coming *down* the stairs. She had blood on her feet *before* she saw the boy.'

I looked up into the darkness at the top of the stairs. I didn't want to go up to whatever horror awaited there. But there was no choice. Hugh took hold of another candlestick and we climbed by the light of the child's candle, following a trail of bloody footprints.

At the top of the stairs was a dark living room and another flight of steps. The bloody footprints came down the upper flight and in silent agreement, Hugh and I went up to a tiny landing whose boards creaked horribly.

A door on the right stood open. In the thin light of the candle, we saw a woman lying in bed, a woman in her fifties, long grey hair in a plait over her shoulder. She lay on her back, hands resting on the sheet, a red stain covering her breast. Her husband lay on his side, turned away from us; I edged through the narrow space between the bottom of the bed and the wall, and held the candle over him. His blood was still dripping on to the floor.

I went back on to the landing. A tiny stair went up again just outside the door, to the attics presumably. No blood on those stairs. We turned to the only other room on this floor. A smaller bedroom, with frivolous draperies of white and pink. A girl lay huddled on the bed, dark hair tangled, her back a mass of blood.

'They were all killed in their sleep,' Hugh whispered. He cleared his throat. 'At least they'd have known nothing about it.'

I was looking at the bed on which the girl lay. It was wide, and she was on the nearer side of it. On the other side, a second pillow was dented with the mark of a head; the blankets had been thrown back. There was no blood on that side.

I lifted my gaze to the far wall. The window was open. Snow swirled outside over the dark river, drifted in the casement and settled on the floor.

'Damn,' Hugh said.

We had not witnessed an elopement. We'd seen a murderer making her escape.

Two

The ladies will simper at you, and blush, and lower their eyes becomingly, but they are game for anything, my friend, I promise you.

[Letter from Louis de Glabre to his friend Philippe Froidevaux, 17 January 1737]

I went down the stairs in a wild rush, into the dark shop. Esther and the child were at the door and half a dozen people with them, neighbours in nightshirts and nightgowns, dressing robes and shawls, holding up lanterns and straining to see in. Esther had positioned herself to block their entrance; as I pushed past, I heard her say, 'We've sent for the constable . . .'

Outside, I nearly went head over heels on the slippery cobbles and slowed, breathing heavily. Injuring myself wasn't going to help catch the killer. It was probably too late anyway – the girl would be long gone. We might even have passed her; in this blizzard we might have come within three or four feet without seeing each other.

The snow swirled around me. The girl must have come ashore by the landing steps just upstream from the bridge. I stumbled along to the steps; on the Key at the top were the dog's tracks again and a man's, close together. Then another set of prints. Pointed toes, and small heels – the marks of a fashionable female shoe.

Not ideal for running in and the wearer had been trying to move too fast – after only a few steps she'd measured her length in the snow. I saw scuff marks where she'd hauled herself up again. The tracks angled across the snow; she'd skirted the Sandhill, where the smart buildings of the town are, and turned west, heading for the shabby streets on either side of the broken-down town wall.

I staggered on, head down against the blizzard. The wind blew the snow directly into my face, tugged at the skirts of my greatcoat. The streets were silent and empty. The prints of man and dog crossed towards the tumbledown town wall; the girl's footprints carried straight on to the narrow streets and alleys beyond the wall – the haunts of less than respectable people: inns and lodging houses for sailors, shops selling secondhand clothes and taverns dispensing gin.

The woman had slipped again as she came up to the first houses but not fallen. I followed her footprints along the front of a shuttered tavern, to an alley that looked derelict. I stopped, cursing. The alley was narrow and the buildings on either side had kept out the snow; the footprints disappeared.

A female voice above my head said, 'And what do you think *you're* doing?'

I looked up. In the driving snow, it was difficult to be certain of anything but I thought I saw a gleam high up under the eaves of a house at the entrance to the alley. A spirit. And plainly an unfriendly one.

My heart sank. Every living person must come to this sooner or later; death claims us all. After death, the spirit lingers on in the place of death, for eighty or a hundred years, before final dissolution, and fate is kinder to some more than to others. Those that die in the comfort of their own homes can enjoy the company of friends and family, almost as if they still live. That is my ambition, as it is of every living man or woman.

But there are all too many who die alone and angry, and who grow angrier by the day. By the sound of her voice, this spirit had been a young woman; anyone dying in an alley like this was likely to have been less than respectable in life. And the weather could only make things worse – spirits don't like the cold; it bleeds the strength out of them.

But it's never wise to offend spirits; they possess a surprising ability to do harm, if only by spreading malicious tales. I said in as friendly a tone as I could manage, 'I'm looking for a woman . . .'

'I wager you are,' she said. 'That's all any man thinks of!'

'She may be in danger—'

'Yes,' she said, stridently, 'And I know who from! Well, I can do for you, sir!' And she shrieked at the top of her voice. 'Help! Rape! Help!'

No one came in response, no one poked their heads out of

the broken windows in the abandoned houses. Her cries became ever more shrill.

There was no point in staying to argue; my quarry was long gone. I turned back for the bridge. The blizzard was behind me now and blew me along, almost faster than I wanted to go. Ahead, on the bridge, lanterns blazed; shadows moved between the snow-shrouded shops; pools of light glimmered on the river and on the snow around the landing steps. Something gleamed where the woman had fallen.

A coin. Tarnished and old, badly misshapen and thinned by years of use. I turned it over and saw an effort had been made to shine it, revealing an unfamiliar design, a strange shaggy head. A foreign coin, no doubt, brought in by a sailor. I dropped it in my pocket. Had she been a thief after all, looking for the shop's takings? This foreign coin could have been among them.

The bridge was crowded with people. All the neighbours, and whores and sailors who'd run up from the taverns on the Key. Esther and the child were nowhere to be seen. A watchman, big and burly, stood at the door of the shop to keep people out; he smelt of beer, and turned a bleary eye on me as I came up, obviously knowing who I was. 'No luck, eh?'

I shook my head.

He let me in and closed the door behind me. Several branches of candles had been lit in the shop; I blinked against their brilliance. The only occupants were Hugh and the new constable of All Hallows' parish, Mr Philips, the brewer. Philips turned as he heard me come in; his face was sheened with sweat and he was trembling visibly, despite being fully dressed and covered with a heavy greatcoat. Hugh gave me a speaking look.

'Mr Philips is not at all well, Charles,' he said. 'I was trying to persuade him to get back to his bed.'

Philips coughed, a hack he obviously couldn't control. He shook his head, croaked, 'My duty—' More coughing. I brought one of the ridiculously delicate chairs and insisted he sit.

He broke into another coughing fit. I whispered to Hugh, 'Where are Esther and the child?'

He jerked his head towards the stairs. 'They've gone up to the drawing room. You didn't catch her then?'

'Lost her in the alleys outside the town wall.'

Footsteps on the stairs. A great hulk of a man stepped down into the room: James Fleming, the stationer, who has the shop next door. He was in his nightshirt and dressing robe, and the nightcap still clung crookedly to his bald head. He said bluntly, 'It's Samuel Gregson all right. And his wife. The girl's his youngest daughter, Sarah. Sixteen years old, she was.'

Hugh swore.

'And the lad?' I asked.

'The apprentice, Ned. Sixteen, maybe seventeen.'

A watchman came down the stairs behind Fleming, with an opened bottle of brandy and several glasses. He looked startled to see us but we weren't in the mood to complain about petty depredations; Hugh took the brandy and poured a large glass for Philips, and another for me. Fleming shook his head. The watchman went back upstairs.

I sipped the brandy and felt warmth creep back into me. 'Tell us about the Gregsons.' I suddenly remembered Philips' presence – he had the authority here – but he waved a hand at me to carry on, still struggling to control his cough.

Fleming pursed his lips judiciously. 'I've lived next to them nigh on thirty years. Gregson was a decent man. Hardworking, thrifty.'

This sounded faint praise to me. 'How old?'

'Fifty-five last All Souls' Day.' Fleming drew himself up with a sigh. 'His wife, Sophia, was a year or two younger. Good house-keeper but there was always something wrong with her world. Too cold, too hot, too few customers, too many – you know the kind.'

I nodded. 'And the daughter who died?'

'Sarah? A gentle girl. Wouldn't hurt a soul.'

'The apprentice?' Philips managed, hoarsely.

'Good lad. Bit shy.'

'And the child?' I asked.

'That's the granddaughter, Judith. Her mother died when she was born and the father couldn't be bothered with her, so the grandparents took her in.'

'She sleeps in the attic,' Hugh said. 'I've been up there while you were away. Little cubby hole under the roof. Nice dolls, pretty clothes.'

'They idolized her,' Fleming agreed.

'Just before the child screamed, we saw a woman climbing down a rope from the window over the river,' I said. 'She ran off into the town and I couldn't catch her. Do you know who she might be?'

Fleming said heavily, 'She killed them?'

'She certainly has questions to answer,' I said, then relented my evasiveness. I said, 'The victims have only just died, and she was seen fleeing from the house. Who is she?'

'The other daughter,' Fleming said. 'The one from London.'

The Gregsons, according to Fleming, had ten children of whom five had survived to adulthood. Even these had evidently been too many for Gregson's purse; two of the older children, a boy and a girl, had been packed off to Mrs Gregson's childless elder brother in London; another daughter was sent to Bristol to a cousin. The woman I'd seen running off was Alice, the daughter who'd been brought up in London.

'Mrs Gregson's brother died,' Fleming said, 'and there was nowhere for the girl, except to come home to her parents.'

'When had she last seen them?'

He pursed his lips. 'Probably not for twenty years or more. She left when she was three.'

I wondered how Alice Gregson had felt about coming back to live with people who must have been complete strangers. We paused for Philips to splutter over his brandy; Hugh trimmed a guttering candle.

'She arrived on Tuesday,' Fleming said. 'Less than a week ago. A little fair thing with ringlets and a simper. Petticoats worth a fortune on her back.'

The watchman came down the stairs again and said, somewhat unnecessarily, 'The surgeon says they've all been stabbed, sir. More than once too. Except for the boy.' The watchman made a point of shuddering. 'Stabbed the old gent five times and the woman four.'

I glanced at Philips but he was huddled round his brandy glass and made no effort to ask questions. 'Does it look like there's anything missing? Any sign of robbery?'

'There's some jewellery upstairs that's been left – trumpery stuff. But there's an empty box in the cellar that mebbe had money in it.'

Fleming frowned. 'There won't have been much. Samuel wasn't one for keeping money in the house. He invested it with local coal owners almost as soon as it came in. He was worried about those burglaries we had last year.'

I remembered those – a couple of local lads had netted a surprisingly large amount of money before being caught; they're presumably now robbing the residents of the Colonies. And from the way the woman had moved, I couldn't think she was carrying anything particularly heavy, like a bag of coins.

'Surely it doesn't matter whether Gregson kept money here or not,' Hugh said. 'It only needed someone to think he *might*.'

'It must have been a burglar,' Fleming said. 'How could a girl murder her parents? It's not natural.'

I poured myself more brandy. 'Did she get on well with them?'

He shook his head. 'She wanted to go back to London. Nagged her father all the time over it, no matter who else was present. I heard her myself.'

Philips moved convulsively. We had to wait while he got over another coughing fit. 'Need an inquest. Swear in a jury.'

'You're in no state to do anything of the sort, sir,' Fleming said bluntly. 'In any case, we can't do anything on a Sunday. Put a guard on the door and get home to your rest.'

Philips staggered up. 'Mr Patterson, Mr Demsey – you'll be on the jury of course?'

Hugh looked alarmed; I said, 'As witnesses, I think it would be better not.'

Fleming turned Philips firmly to the door. 'I'll sort out your jury, Mr Philips; the neighbours'll be more than willing. Now *get you home!*'

Philips spluttered into his handkerchief. His shoulders sagged. He was on the verge of giving in; Fleming hastened the process. 'The girl's been in the town only four days, sir. She doesn't know the town. She'll be in custody before morning.'

She was not, of course.

Three

Mind you, all the grand ladies and gentlemen can be as prosy as anything when it comes to their pet subjects: religion, and the rule of law.

[Letter from Louis de Glabre to his friend Philippe Froidevaux, 17 January 1737]

'The child saw nothing,' Esther said as we strolled along the Key towards All Hallows' church the following morning. The snow was thick and crisp and we had to concentrate on keeping our footing. I'd suggesting hiring a chair, but Esther was feeling unwell again and wanted fresh air. We were early of course, as I was playing the organ for the morning service. At least it had stopped snowing, although the sky was still grey.

'She was sleeping in the attic,' Esther continued, 'and woke thinking she heard someone calling her name. She thought it was her grandfather – he often cannot sleep, apparently.' Her face darkened. 'She's young, Charles, but she knew straight away they were dead.' She nodded at an acquaintance in a carriage.

'Did she tell you anything else of interest?'

'She heard the front door open but cannot remember when. It could have been much earlier, when she first went to bed. And she didn't like her aunt – Alice evidently sneered at her for being silly.'

All Hallows' church stands on a hill raised above the Key, approached either by a steep hill or a flight of steps, both very slippery on this day. Esther stopped to take a breather, and a young couple with a baby passed us.

'I do not understand,' she said. 'What in heaven's name could make a girl stab her parents, her sister, and an innocent boy!'

Alice was twenty-three years old, I reflected, hardly a girl. 'For the money, I presume. To get back to London. What puzzles me more is how she found the strength to do it. And why in the middle of the night? Why didn't she wait until this morning when everyone went off to church? She could plead illness, stay at home, take the money and be away an hour or more before anyone got back.'

'She is plainly a silly spoilt young woman.'

'No one can be *that* silly,' I protested. 'Why kill at all? They were all *asleep* – no threat whatsoever!'

The congregation in church was plentiful, although the weather had plainly kept the invalids and elderly indoors. Hugh sat at the back of the church and winked as we walked past. A tall thin man of about thirty years old sat beside him; Esther whispered, 'Is that the architect?'

'For the new Assembly Rooms? I think so. Hugh's looking after him while he's in town.'

Fleming was in a pew halfway down the church, with the little girl, Judith, between him and his wife. The child looked bewildered and confused; Mrs Fleming kept patting her consolingly on the shoulder. And that was another mystery – why kill everyone else without pity but leave the child? She'd nearly foiled the killer's escape. I left Esther in our pew and climbed the stairs to the organ loft, to play the voluntary while the rest of the congregation came in. And to brood.

At the end of the service, Esther waited for me inside the church porch as usual; by the time I'd collected my music together and negotiated the worn steps down from the organ loft, she was conversing with Hugh and the London architect, whose name, I gathered, was John Balfour. He was a stiff man, with a stiff bow; he wore his own mousy hair loose and his clothes were neat rather than in the latest fashion.

'Is this the first time you have been in Newcastle?' Esther asked.

Balfour bowed. He looked strained, as if he hadn't slept properly.

'Staying at the George,' Hugh said, 'courtesy of the Directors of the Assembly Rooms. Had a dreadful journey north. Came by boat to Shields.'

Hugh sounded rather too cheerful about this; I said diplomatically. 'I'm sympathetic; four or five years ago, I had a rough sea journey coming back from London.'

Balfour cleared his throat. 'The weather was inclement.' His voice was light and a little hoarse.

'I hope you were not *too* indisposed,' Esther said.

'In bed two days,' Hugh said with indecent relish.

'But you are better now, I hope?'

Balfour bowed.

'Everybody's very much looking forward to the new Rooms,' I said, wondering if it would simply be better to let Balfour retreat to his bed. First Philips, now Balfour – and Esther was sickening too. Winter is always an unhealthy time of year. I glanced at Esther's pale face. She had not been eating very much recently, and had complained of feeling queasy. Perhaps I ought to insist she consult an apothecary?

'Except for Charles.' Hugh said to Balfour, 'Charles is the musical director of the concert series.'

Balfour looked surprised. 'I'm not sure the rooms will be suitable for concerts.'

'My point exactly,' I said, dryly.

'The design's based on the Rooms in York, apparently,' Hugh said.

'Oh, *they* are very elegant,' Esther said, in admiration. 'Do you know them well, Mr Balfour?'

'I had the honour of being the assistant architect, madam.'

'We're lucky to have him,' Hugh said. 'Nearly said no!'

'I was unwell,' Balfour said, reddening. 'But I changed my mind. I thought it was better to have something to occupy me.'

Only, of course, to be struck down again by the journey north.

Esther was starting to shiver; I made our apologies and led her out of the church. Thankfully, it was still not snowing. A swift farewell to the curate, and we started down the churchyard path, only to be accosted by a boy with a note for me. I gave him a penny for it and he dashed off, happy.

The note was from Philips the constable and said:

Honour'd Sir,

I would be grateful for the Pleasure of your Company as soon as you judge it practical, to discuss the unfortunate Deaths of Mr Samuel Gregson, Upholsterer, and his Wife and Daughter; also the Death of Edward Hills, Apprentice. If you could see your Way to paying me a Visit this Day, despite it being the Day of Rest, I would remain, Dear Sir, Your Obed^t Servt

E. Philips

'They obviously still have not found the girl,' Esther said, reading the note over my shoulder. 'He is anxious and wants help. I think you have another investigation on your hands, Charles.' And she looked at me with a mixture of good humour and exasperation.

Balfour had been accosted by the curate; I put Esther into Hugh's care and started down the snow-covered steps.

Philips lives on the Side, the steep and winding street that leads from the Sandhill to the upper reaches of town where more genteel people reside. To reach it from All Hallows' church meant slipping and sliding down Butcher Bank, and in two or three inches of snow that wasn't an attractive prospect. But I negotiated the bank safely, and a maid of no more than fourteen opened Philips's door and showed me into his study.

The constable sat in front of a fierce fire, wrapped up in three blankets and a rug, and was still shivering. Yet sweat was pouring off him. I began to think I'd not been sensible in coming here. I kept as far back from Philips as was polite.

His teeth battered together audibly. He managed to get out, 'You see how I am.'

'Won't go to his bed,' said a woman coming in behind me. She looked of an age to be Philips's daughter; I knew him to be a widower. 'Insisted on talking to you.'

'Got to catch her,' he said through gritted teeth. 'A woman like that – kill her own parents and sister. Abomination of nature! God knows what she might do next.'

He jerked his head at his daughter and she gave me a speaking look before going out. Philips reached with shaking hands for a key that lay on the table beside him, amongst all the paraphernalia of illness: papers of powders, jugs of weak ale, dry bread. He held the key out. 'I know what I'm asking, Mr Patterson, sir – it's not the sort of thing a man of your station in life ought to have to do, but I don't have much choice. Can hardly keep my feet.'

I frowned. 'You want me to supervise the watchmen?'

Philips shook his head and I had to wait until he coughed himself hoarse. 'No need for that. McLintoch's the man in charge. Has all his men out looking – they're willing but they've not got much sense. I want the girl found, Mr Patterson, and I need someone capable to do it! I leave you to decide how to go about it. I know you have experience in these matters.'

'I don't see what I can do. It's surely just a question of searching the town. The watchmen will know the sort of places she might hide.'

He ignored me. 'The jury's sorted, Fleming's done that, and the inquest is tomorrow. Noon. In the Golden Fleece. Lawyer Armstrong is the sitting coroner.' He seized my arm as I offered him back the key. 'I need a man of sense to keep an eye on things for me, Mr Patterson!'

It was pointless to deny him; he was frustrated at not being able to do things himself, and would rest easier if I agreed. 'Certainly I will, if you think it will help.'

He subsided into his blankets with a sigh of relief. 'Nothing much to be done anyway. Not for three days.'

I knew what he meant. The spirits of the dead do not separate from their bodies until around three days after death. Sometimes it can take even longer, and on rare occasions it has never happened at all. Presumably, Philips hoped that the Gregsons would be able to throw light on their murderer's identity; I doubted it, given they'd been killed in their sleep.

The daughter came back in again and hinted she wanted me off. I went back on to the Side; desultory flakes fluttered down from the heavily-clouded sky. Above the houses, I glimpsed the tops of buildings on the bridge. I thought of Alice Gregson, bending over her sleeping father and bringing the knife down again and again, then calmly climbing out of the window to make her escape . . .

It's been a good ten years since my own father died, and at times I can hardly remember his face. We had the coldest of relationships; he was never abusive, or violent, or offensive in his language, but at the same time, he made it plain he didn't think much of me. I can't remember why. We were on the worst of terms, yet never at any time did I consider doing him injury. But a mere girl – a 'little fair thing' according to Fleming – had struck her own father not once but five times and then proceeded to murder three others.

I wanted to know why she'd done it. What had turned her relations with her family to such dramatic violence?

The key to the shop was cold in my hand. I turned for the bridge.

Four

Everyone has a story of terror to tell, about the time they were robbed on this road or that; no one feels they have lived until they have been held up by at least one highwayman.

[Letter from Louis de Glabre to his friend Philippe Froidevaux, 17 January 1737]

A watchman stood at the door of the shop, enjoying a chat with a maid from one of the other houses on the bridge. The bodies were still inside of course, awaiting the viewing by the inquest jury before they were moved; at least the freezing weather would preserve them in a reasonable state. A second watchman was the centre of an eager knot of sightseers who were trying to bribe him into letting them into the house. The sightseers had plainly, by their clothes, just come out of church; the watchman was enjoying the attention but, as far as I could judge, resisting all blandishments.

Standing a little back, on his own, was John Balfour.

He was staring at the shuttered windows of the shop, ignoring a spirit trying to attract his attention. He started in surprise when I spoke to him and flushed, the colour two bright spots on his white cheeks. Despite his thick greatcoat, he was shivering violently. 'You must think me a vulgar sightseer like all the rest,' he said.

I said diplomatically, 'It's natural to be shaken by such an occurrence.'

'Yes,' he said, then, with an effort and a sudden rush: 'My father was stabbed to death.'

I was taken aback. Balfour didn't wait for me to respond. 'He was a clergyman. A wealthy man, with everything one could hope for – a good living, a respectful family, a position of some consequence in the neighbourhood. But he could never leave well alone!' He was staring at the house, but I fancied he didn't see it. 'It was a silly quarrel over a scrubbing brush. A neighbour had borrowed it, he thought it had been stolen . . .'

I said, more sympathetically, 'Did you witness the quarrel?'

He nodded, lifted his right arm; I saw a white scar on the back of his hand. 'I tried to stop them.' He thrust his hand back into his pocket. 'The neighbour was a butcher and had a knife in his apron. When my father said unforgivable things about the man's wife, he flew into a fury – and my father reaped the whirlwind.'

The snow drifted down; the sightseers admitted defeat and moved off. Balfour gestured helplessly. 'How do these things happen? In one moment the world is turned upside down, everything destroyed.' He said passionately, 'How can anyone do such things!'

I could give him no answer. We stared at the shop in silence.

'She did do it, I suppose,' he said at last.

'We saw her.'

'You saw her do it?' he echoed incredulously.

'We saw her running away.'

'They say she climbed down into the river. Is that possible?'

I nodded. 'It was low tide. She clambered across the mud flats and up some landing steps. Risky – but she accomplished it successfully.'

'And she killed them for money?'

'There's some missing, certainly.'

Another couple strolled up to the watchmen, coins for the bribe openly in their hands. They were middle-aged, respectable-looking tradespeople, not the sort you'd think would regard dead bodies as a pleasant diversion on a Sunday morning after church. Maybe they were thinking of the moral lessons to be drawn: the transience of life, the bitterness of ingratitude, the ungratefulness of children . . . I doubted it.

'And she didn't have help? A girl killed four people on her own?'

'They were asleep,' I said, 'and therefore didn't struggle. There's no evidence to suggest anyone else was involved.' I was starting to shiver too; I said, 'Forgive me. I need to look in the house and my wife's expecting me home before too long.'

I got out the key to the shop as I spoke and Balfour glanced at it in surprise. 'Do you have authority here? Are you a Justice of the Peace?'

'I'm helping the constable – he's ill.' It seemed necessary to have some reason for going in. I added, 'I just want to check everything's in order.'

'May I come in with you?' He forestalled my instinctive refusal. 'I promise not to touch anything.' He inhaled deeply. 'It's just . . . I've had such imaginings – it rouses such memories. It would help to see the reality.'

I doubted that. But the house had been fully examined and the surgeon had looked at the bodies; it could do no harm. 'Very well.'

One of the elderly watchmen had gone off with the disappointed couple. His colleague clearly already knew about my deputizing for Philips. Informed by one of the spirits, no doubt – the efficiency of the spirits' message system is legendary. He stood back to let us in with merely a quip or two: 'Mind yourself, sir, they're a dangerous lot in there. Don't knock anything over – they'll charge you!'

Balfour came in after me, hesitantly, as if he was already having second thoughts. With the shutters fastened, the house was pitch-black but a branch of candles and a tinderbox stood on a shelf by the door. I lit the candles and held them up. The house, unheated, was ice-cold and the metallic stench of blood was almost overwhelming. Rats scratched in corners.

Balfour looked around in the flickering candlelight. 'It's very elegant,' he said, almost at random, as if he wanted to break the silence.

I shared the feeling. Something about the still, empty house made me shudder. 'Gregson must have decorated it himself, as an advertisement. He was the best upholsterer in town – he painted and decorated many of the shops and houses. His wall-papers were well thought of.'

'And he had charges to match his reputation, no doubt,' Balfour said with a ghost of a smile. He took a few steps forward, saw what lay behind the counter and grabbed blindly for support.

I should have known this would happen. I started towards him, but he shook his head and drew himself up straighter. 'I'm all right. It was just the shock.'

'I need to look around,' I said. 'Stay here if you wish.'

He shook his head, decisively.

We climbed the stairs to the living room above. The fire was laid but unlit, the room chill. A psalm book lay on a small table; I opened it and read Mrs Gregson's name inside. She must have put it ready for Sunday service.

Balfour watched me from the door. 'Are you looking for anything in particular?'

There was one thing I should have thought of before. 'The girl must have brought a travelling trunk from London but she would have had a smaller box too, for her trinkets – jewellery, ribbons, letters, a journal perhaps. She might have written something that might help us.'

We went up the next flight of stairs to the bedrooms. Balfour stood on the landing, his handkerchief to his mouth, as I hesitated on the threshold of the room belonging to the two girls. The younger girl's body still lay on the bed, facing away from me, as if curled around a stomach ache. I was glad I couldn't see her face.

It was a very small room, barely large enough to accommodate the bed, a wash-stand and a chair. Alice Gregson had slept on the far side; she would have had to crawl across the bed to reach the door. 'She must have killed her sister first, else she would have woken as Alice clambered across the bed. Then she must have gone into her parents' room and stabbed them.'

Balfour was breathing heavily.

'Which means she must have had a knife hidden on her own side of the bed, under the mattress or the pillow.'

I didn't like the look of that bed but there was no help for it – I half-crawled, half stumbled along the bottom of it, trying to avoid the bloodstained linen and the body. On the other side was a narrow area of bare floorboards. The window had been closed and the rope of sheets that had formed the girl's escape lay curled in a bundle on the floor. The sheets had been torn, and the strips tied together with a knot I hadn't seen before; when I tugged, the knots merely tightened.

'This would have taken some time to make.'

'That's what must have disturbed the child,' Balfour said. 'Sheets don't tear quietly.'

'She wouldn't kill, then calmly sit down to tear up a sheet,' I said. 'She made this earlier.'

He stared. 'You think she *planned* the killings?'

I checked under the bed but there was no box and no loose floorboards where one might have been hidden. Nothing under the pillow either, and it was difficult feeling under the mattress while not disturbing the body that lay on top of it.

We went up another floor, to the attic. The stairs were narrow and the steps shallow for a grown man's foot. The attic was divided into two by a low partition wall, as in a stable. The near end was a cosy, cheerful little space with a small bed and bright bedding, thrown back as if the occupant had just got up; a toy cat sprawled across a pillow, a book was laid neatly on the table beside the bed.

The other end of the attic, beyond the partition, appeared to be storage space. Stooping low under the sloping rafters, I made my way into it. The candlelight flickered over a travelling trunk, obviously recently deposited there, with not a speck of dust on it. The key was in the lock; I threw the lid open.

The smell of roses came out in great wafts. Balfour sneezed. Dresses, virginal white, comparable in quality, even to my inexperienced eye, to the dresses Esther wore. The aunt and uncle in London must have had plenty of money to spend. Wraps and slippers, a pair of dancing pumps, ribbons laid carefully flat. And a small box hidden under an embroidered nightgown.

I opened the box and found a fine piece of lace, faintly yellow with age. A necklace of cheap bright stones, the sort a child might like. More ribbons. A few newspaper cuttings and a letter.

I unfolded the letter. Balfour peered over my shoulder at the impeccable copperplate writing.

> It's no use, you can rail as much as you like but you should know by now you cannot have your own way by wheedling and whining. It's about time you mended your ways and learned to behave as a young woman should. You're coming back and there's an end on it.

It was signed, coldly: *S. Gregson.* No *your loving father* or anything of that affectionate sort. The kind of letter my father might have written, in fact.

'No wonder she was angry,' Balfour said.

I refolded the letter and put it and the cuttings in my pocket to look at again later. 'Nothing particularly helpful,' I said, resigned. 'Hardly surprising.'

'I wonder if there are any other papers.' Balfour glanced around.

'She'll have taken anything incriminating with her,' I said 'Another reason to believe she planned this.'

We went downstairs again, to the shop with its blood-splattered wallpaper samples and spindly chairs. Balfour looked about. 'I don't know now why I wanted to see the place. I was looking for – *something*. Understanding, I think.'

I nodded, knowing exactly how he felt. 'Would you care to to dine with us? It can be lonely in a strange place where you know no one.'

He was plainly tempted. 'Will your wife not object?'

I laughed. 'My wife, sir, is capable of dealing with anyone and anything, no matter how short the notice!'

I put the branch of candles back on its shelf. The shutter on the window by the door was loose; I pushed at it then realized that one of the brackets holding the bar was broken. I pulled half of the shutter open to give me room to fix the bracket—

For one moment I saw gloomy daylight and a thin snow drifting down; the next there was a flash of darkness that made me start. Then I saw lantern light, outlining the figure of a woman, cloaked and hooded, standing in the middle of the bridge. Her face was hidden by her hood but she seemed to be staring at the house . . .

Five

The working sort of man is a very dull fellow indeed, always talking about his home, or his work, or his gin. But some of the gentlemen have a sense of adventure. Some indeed have been as far as Calais.

[Letter from Louis de Glabre to his friend Philippe Froidevaux, 17 January 1737]

I flung the door open. The coldness of a winter's night cut into my bones. Stars glittered like ice in the pitch-black sky; a sliver of moon hung over the bridge. There was no snow but frost sparkled on the cobbles.

I knew at once what had happened. Strange though it may seem, our world is not alone. Another world lies beside it, as close as pages in a book. The two worlds are recognizably the same, and our own selves live in both; I once met my counterpart there and we were as alike as twins. But there *are* differences: some people do not exist in this other world. Esther does not; others are different – Hugh's counterpart, for instance, is twenty years older than he is. Most importantly, there are no spirits there.

It is possible to move between the worlds, to *step through* from one to the other, if you know how; great coldness, and a moment of darkness are the signs that *stepping through* is taking place. I came upon the knowledge by chance, and at times have not known whether to bless or curse the ability. I feared it greatly at one time; more recently it has begun to intrigue me. But one thing is very clear: when the gap between the worlds narrows and allows me to *step through*, it's a time of crisis. Like now.

The woman was staring at me. She was tall and held herself arrogantly. But her hood was close around her face and in the night on the unlit bridge all I could distinguish was a dark strand of hair fallen loose over her shoulder.

She turned on her heels, towards the Gateshead end of the bridge. I called, 'Stop – please! I want to talk.'

She walked faster. 'My name's Patterson . . .' Now she was picking up her skirts and running. I started after her, but she was already too far off to catch, dashing into the trees on Gateshead bank.

Cursing, I came to a halt. She was gone and there was no point in lingering on the deserted bridge. I must get back to my own world, and quickly. The two worlds do not quite run in step; a few minutes here can correspond to several hours in our own, or vice versa. I once stepped back to find I'd lost twelve hours, and half the town was looking for me. Was Balfour even now wondering what had happened?

I turned back to Gregson's shop and saw a large notice adorning the window.

> Matthew Ellison, Successor to S. Gregson. Mr Ellison wishes to inform the Public that he has taken over all the Stock of the late Mr Gregson and will do his Utmost to supply the Ladies and Gentlemen with all the latest Fashions in Furnishing, Chairs, Tables &c. and all at London Prices. Carriage free.

I fingered the notice. The corners were torn, and coming free of the glue that had fixed them to the window. It wasn't new – Samuel Gregson must have died some time ago in this world. I wondered if he'd died a natural death.

Taking a deep breath, I stepped forward, shivered, blinked. Ice suddenly underfoot made me slip; I put out a hand to the wall of Gregson's shop to steady myself. I was back in my own world.

I walked back into the shop. Balfour glanced up from a scrutiny of a rather dull landscape on one wall. 'Did you manage to fix the shutter?'

I could hear voices in the street outside: the watchmen and some sightseers. Obviously, I'd been absent for a very short time. The relief was almost overwhelming. 'No. The catch is broken.'

Balfour gave me a weak smile. 'Well, it's given me time to consider – and I've come to the conclusion this is none of my business and I'd do a great deal better not to think of it.' The smile settled more securely. 'What's done is done. I can't dwell on it for ever. With relation to my father, I mean.'

We walked up Westgate together; the snow was still crisp underfoot, hardly trodden down at all. The sky was looking heavier, the cloud layer thicker. Balfour, in pursuit of his good intentions, abandoned the subject of the Gregsons and quizzed me instead on my marriage. Was my wife of a very old family? Did we have any children? He had a fine line in tactlessness. 'She's a very wealthy woman, I hear. You were lucky to catch her. Of course, she's not in the first flush of youth.'

In short, he was suggesting Esther had been old enough to be grateful for whatever she was offered, and I was after her money. Not the first time those accusations had been made; I swallowed my annoyance.

My wealthy wife was in the drawing room, entertaining Hugh, who lounged in a chair with a glass of our best wine. He gave me a grin. 'No need to tell us! The spirits already know you're standing in for Philips; the news will be all over town by now!'

Esther wasn't in the least annoyed by my inviting Balfour; she greeted him graciously and offered him wine. He liked our drawing room. I saw him look approvingly at the simple stylish vases Esther favoured, the long mirrors, the framed landscapes between the windows. Some of the drawings were Esther's own and Balfour was soon excitedly recognizing the places they depicted: palaces of medieval princes, an ancient bridge in Florence, long-ruined temples in Rome.

'You've been to Italy?' He was a different man in his enthusiasm, bright and engaging. 'I went there with my master to study all the antiquities. He made me measure and draw and analyse the old temples day after day. Wonderful places. All the carved stones, the statues – beautiful!' He peered closer. 'These aren't too bad at all.' He jabbed a finger at one of the drawings. 'Although you don't quite have the trick of perspective. See here . . .'

Hugh opened his eyes wide at me. I have only the haziest idea of what perspective is, but in my opinion Esther's drawings are not deficient in anything. She took the criticism well, however, listening courteously as Balfour undertook to explain how she could improve her drawing technique, and even smiling – a trifle fixedly – when he said paternally, 'But these are very well as a beginning.'

It was as well, I thought, that Balfour had never seen Esther with a pistol, facing down a villain. If he had, he'd have run a mile before patronizing her so casually.

We went in to eat. Being Sunday, of course, the meal was cold, left for us by the servants before they went to church and their day off. We served ourselves, and Balfour tucked in approvingly. Esther complimented him on his designs for the York Assembly Rooms; he modestly disclaimed the credit, smiled indulgently, said that such things were dreadfully boring for ladies, then turned the conversation to the latest London fashions.

I made a mental note not to invite him again.

'Which reminds me,' Hugh said, intervening smoothly. 'We need to look at the proposed site for the new Rooms. Is tomorrow suitable, Charles? You're not teaching, are you?'

I was preoccupied with watching Esther, who was merely pecking at her food. 'You don't need me, surely.'

'You know the Directors want your opinion on the musical aspects of the room.'

'They know my opinion already,' I said tartly but sighed. If spending a few minutes on a building site would keep the gentlemen happy and ease my life as musical director of the concerts, it was a small price to pay. I agreed to go whenever they wished, having the day much to myself. I don't teach on Mondays but set it aside for composition, regardless of the fact I've not composed anything since long before my marriage; I usually find myself arranging someone else's music for the concert band.

'It will take only a few minutes,' Balfour said. He was drinking too much wine, and had a high colour in his cheeks. 'What about ten o'clock?'

He'd obviously realized I wasn't a gentleman, despite having married a lady. Gentlemen rarely rise before noon.

'Very well,' I agreed. 'As long as I've time to reach the Fleece for the inquest. And assuming it doesn't snow again.'

'Nonsense!' Hugh said. 'It'll be fine tomorrow. This has just been a wayward shower or two. We won't get any more snow now.'

'I might come too,' Esther said blandly, and was rewarded with a splutter and a stammer from Balfour.

'Oh – really – I don't think it will interest a lady . . .'

Esther smiled sweetly.

Hugh bore Balfour off to his lodgings, and Esther and I were alone at last. We repaired to the drawing room, lit candles to dispel the gloom of the overcast afternoon, and poured more wine. Esther sighed and sank on to the sofa. 'What an odd man! At times he can be engaging, at other times I want to hit him over the head with the nearest candlestick!'

I sat down beside her. Outside, in the garden, the soft snow was falling in a desultory fashion. I pondered on whether to comment on the fact she'd eaten almost nothing, decided against it, reluctant to spoil the moment.

'So,' she said. 'What happened?'

I should have known Esther would realize something untoward had occurred – she has a knack of reading me aright. I sat back with relieved weariness. The exertions of the previous night were catching up with me – too much excitement and too little sleep.

'I stepped through to the other world.'

Out of the corner of my eye, I saw her stiffen; Esther knows of that other world and doesn't particularly like it, in view of all the untoward things that have happened to me there. But she merely said, 'Go on.'

I told her of my encounter with the mystery woman. 'It was definitely not Alice – she had dark hair. But she must have had something to hide – why else should she run?'

Esther sighed. 'Charles, it was dark, she was on her own and a strange man steps out of a house and accosts her – believe me, any woman would have made her escape under those circumstances. Although,' she added, 'I do wonder why she was out alone at night.'

'It can't have been a mere chance unconnected encounter,' I protested. 'Whenever this has happened before, there's always been some connection with the murder I was investigating.'

'There's a first time for everything,' she pointed out. She sipped her wine. In the gloom, the candlelight flickered on her pale hair, casting golden glints. I put out a hand and fingered the soft strands. She smiled. I was glad to see her looking better and said so.

'Just a touch of cold,' she said, and stifled a yawn. 'I am getting too old for disturbed nights.'

'Nonsense!' I said fondly and took advantage of the moment

to kiss her. She emerged a little ruffled and inclined to giggle. I love Esther's giggle.

'Charles,' she said, drawing a finger gently down my cheek. 'You do enjoy making things much more complicated than they need to be! The daughter killed her family and for nothing more than a few pounds to help her get back to London. It is very simple.'

'Yes,' I said, leaning in to kiss her again, 'of course – you're right. Very simple.'

Six

Of course, there are uncharted regions, where the legends read *Here be dragons!* And believe me, Philippe, these dragons, who go by the name of respectably widowed gentlewomen, are formidable indeed.

[Letter from Louis de Glabre to his friend Philippe Froidevaux, 18 January 1737]

I didn't sleep well. Alice Gregson drifted into my mind as I started to doze and wouldn't drift out again. What made a girl do such horrific things? What turned commonplace dislike of her family into murderous rage? Could it have been mere selfishness, a resentment at being made to leave London? Surely there had to be more.

I was bleary-eyed at the breakfast table and so was Esther. She listlessly picked at a piece of dry toast.

'I do not think I will visit the Assembly Room site today. I have some letters to write. And I have received a note to say I will not be needed at the inquest.'

I was grateful for that, although Esther could probably have given her account of the evening without revealing she'd been dressed immodestly. But it worried me to see her still unwell, particularly with Philips in my mind's eye; I wondered again whether to suggest she see an apothecary. I knew she'd reject the idea out of hand; she was expert in preparing cordials and remedies

for the small illnesses of life – indigestion and so on – and was
no doubt dosing herself with something. But one more day of
this and I would definitely insist on her taking advice.

A bright gleam shot across the floor and climbed the leg of a
chair. Esther was sighing before the spirit reached the table top.

'Mistress—'

'Not now, George,' she said.

George Williams was once my apprentice, and my interference
in affairs that were not my own indirectly got him killed, a year
or more since, at the age of twelve. That, rather oddly, didn't
affect his loyalty to me, but marrying Esther did. George had a
boy's infatuation with Esther, and a hatred of anyone else she
paid attention to. Which has made him difficult to live with. But
there's no way to get rid of a spirit once they've died in a house,
short of demolishing the building or setting it on fire, which
means we all have to live with him. Somehow.

George's enmity includes not only myself but also Tom, our
young manservant whom Esther trusts too much for George's
liking. I glanced towards the door and sure enough there was
Tom, trying hard to hide his annoyance.

'George,' I said. 'Remember what I've told you – it's Tom's
job to deliver messages, unless they come from other spirits.'

The spirit flared green, always a sign of annoyance. 'Visitor,
Mistress,' he said, ignoring me entirely. 'For the master.'

'Good,' Esther said briskly. 'Thank you for telling me, George.
Goodbye.'

'Mistress . . .'

'Go, George!'

I'd not had a taste of Esther's temper; indeed, I'd grown used
to the idea she didn't have one. But the snap in her voice sent
the spirit fainter and smaller at once. 'Yes, Mistress,' it said hurriedly,
and slipped out of the room without further ado.

There was a moment's silence. Tom said deferentially, 'There's
a visitor for you, sir. I've put her in the drawing room.'

Her? 'I presume she gave a name?'

'Mrs Fletcher, sir. She says she's a daughter of the late Mr
Gregson.'

I gave him a smile to compensate for the annoyance he'd had.
I lived in fear he'd decide he'd had enough of George and take

himself off to a household where the spirits were more friendly. He was young – barely nineteen – but efficient and hard-working. We'd find it hard to replace him.

'Something will have to be done about George,' Esther said, after Tom had retreated. 'I will not have the household disrupted like this!'

After a moment, I said, 'I'll speak to him . . .'

She melted into rueful laughter. 'Oh, Charles, you know he will never take any notice of you!'

'I'm not master in my own home,' I said with deliberate melodramatic emphasis. I was rewarded with a mischievous giggle.

Mrs Fletcher was standing by the banked-up fire in the morning room. In her mid-twenties, perhaps, but the way she wore her brown hair, drawn back tightly under her cap, made her look older. She was dressed like a tolerably well-off tradesman's widow, in decent, but drab, clothes. She looked as if she'd been sizing up the quality of our furniture.

She inclined her head coolly. 'Mr Patterson? I am Sophia Fletcher. The spirits tell me my parents have been murdered and I understand you know the details.' She had a hard voice, as if she was more used to commanding than pleading. A woman who had a number of servants kept under firm control, I guessed.

'I'm sorry you weren't informed directly. I wasn't told there were other family members in town.'

'I'm not living in town,' she said, 'I walked in from Cherryburn this morning when I heard the news.'

She'd been lucky to get through the snow. I indicated a chair and she sat down, very upright. I took the chair opposite. 'Forgive me, I'm not entirely clear on your family's history. You're the third daughter?'

'The second. And the fifth child. The one that was sent to Bristol. In the course of time, I married and was widowed.' She gave me a long look. 'I've been to see the constable but I'm told he's ill, and you're dealing with the matter in his stead.'

I started to offer my sympathies for her parents' deaths but she waved them away. 'I can't say I ever had any fondness for my parents, Mr Patterson. It's difficult to love someone who gave you away. Be so good as to tell me what happened.'

'As far as we can tell, your sister Alice stabbed everyone in the house before fleeing the scene. The watchmen are looking for her, but haven't found her yet.'

'And what do you presume her reason to have been?'

'There was some money missing – probably not a great deal, but perhaps enough to get her back to London.'

Her lip curled; she said, after a moment, 'She was always a spoilt brat, thinking of nothing but her own pleasure. But I find it difficult to imagine her a murderer.'

'You know her well then? Despite being brought up in different households.'

'We have met. And Sarah frequently wrote to me about her.' She paused, said, 'She can be engaging but has a will of her own. I had a letter only a day or so ago from Sarah, relating her home-coming. She was intolerable, apparently. She refused to do anything to help about the house and shop, wanting to know why there were no servants.'

That was unusual – I'd have expected the Gregsons to have at least a maid. Mrs Fletcher's gaze was intent on my face. She said, 'I take it you never met my father? He was not a man to spend more than he had to – he had a wife and daughter to do the work, after all. He was always mean, in spirit and in deed.'

Her tone held such contempt that it nearly took my breath away. My expression must have betrayed my feelings; she said bluntly, 'I despised my father, Mr Patterson – his petty-mindedness, his narrow vision and his joyless spirit.'

Which was comprehensively damning. 'Do you know if your father kept much money in the house?'

'He might have. He never let a penny go unless he was forced to. I've seen him strike my mother for buying a ribbon.'

'He was violent?'

Her lip curled again. 'A man has the right to chastise his own wife, does he not?'

I wondered if the late Mr Fletcher had dared to take similar measures.

'Well.' She brushed down her skirts. 'At least some good will come of it. There are only three of us left to inherit: my brothers in London and Exeter, and myself. My mother left me her jewellery and the household goods. I would like to retrieve the jewellery as soon as possible.'

So we came to the real reason for her visit. At least she was direct.

'We could go down to the shop now,' she said, adding, as an afterthought, 'If it's convenient.'

I shook my head. 'Nothing can be done until after the inquest. The bodies are still in the house, and the jury need to view the premises.'

'After the inquest, then?' she persisted.

'I understand,' I said carefully, 'that the will is in the possession of Lawyer Armstrong. I have to follow his wishes in this matter.'

She looked at me long and hard, then rose to her feet. I rose too, of course.

'I think you take a great deal on yourself, Mr Patterson,' she said. And she swept out without another word.

I went back to the breakfast room, amused rather than annoyed. Esther was finishing off her toast and looked rather better; she listened to my account of Mrs Fletcher without much sympathy.

'So she was only interested in her inheritance? And she criticized her father for his interest in money? Like father, like daughter, clearly!'

I bent to kiss her cheek. 'I must go or I'll be late meeting Hugh and Balfour. Enjoy your letters.'

She looked almost cheerful. 'No, I have decided to tackle the accounts for the Norfolk estates. Some of the tenants are being remarkably recalcitrant in paying their rents – a bad harvest, apparently.'

Esther's estates in Norfolk and Northumberland supply us with the greater part of our income. Technically, after our marriage, they belong to me, but Esther has such experience of managing them that I have decided to leave the matter to her. I've agreed to take an intelligent interest, however, but so far all I've learned is that it's a very complicated business and that tenants are usually obstreperous.

'I thought it was a good harvest last year.'

She twinkled at me. 'It was – except, apparently, in Norfolk.'

I stopped on the doorstep as I stepped out of the house, looking across the expanse of the street to the railed gardens in the centre of the square. Hugh had been right in his prediction; the weather had improved markedly. The sky was blue and almost cloudless;

a bright sunshine glittered on the thick snow carpeting the street and lining the tree branches. It was still very cold but the sunshine lifted my mood immediately.

I had time, before meeting Hugh and Balfour, to fit in a visit to the Watch. They have their room in a small building, little more than a hut, behind the Printing Office at the far end of the Key. Someone was coming out as I got there; he held the door for me and I was hit at once by a wave of warmth. A huge fire was burning at the other end of the room; the room was saturated with the smell of smoke, beer and hot meat pies.

There were only two men in the room and I knew the chief of the watchmen at once – I'd seen him once or twice in passing. A thickset Scotchman, with bowlegs from his years on board ships plying between Newcastle and London, carrying coal to the capital.

He bowed. 'Abraham McLintoch at your service, sir. You must be Mr Patterson, sir.' He had the thickest of Scotch accents. 'Mr Philips sent me a note, sir. Saying he's given you the keys to the shop. Said you would be in charge, sir. Until he was better. Nothing to worry about, sir. Everything in hand, sir.'

The excessive politeness was a means of defence, I guessed, until he felt he'd got the measure of me; there was a keen considering look in his watery eyes.

'I came to ask if there'd been any sign of the girl.'

He looked gloomy. 'Nothing, sir. I've got all the men out, and the spirits are looking too.' He explained, 'We've a gang of spirits, you know, keeping us in touch with what's going on. No one better for knowing things than spirits. Sir.'

'And they've heard nothing?'

His gloom deepened. 'Nothing to worry about, sir. We'll get her, sir. Bound to. No one can hide from us for long, sir.'

'No,' I said. 'I'm sure.'

On the Key again, the snow crunched beneath my feet, the seagulls screamed, the sailors loaded the boats with much shouting and swearing. Something was wrong. Alice Gregson was a young girl who'd been in the town no more than four days; she couldn't know it well enough to hide from watchmen who'd been born and brought up here. Under other circumstances, I'd have been anxious for a pretty young woman who'd gone missing – there

were all too many people ready to take advantage of the defenceless. It would be ironic if something had happened to her.

Although of course, a woman who'd just killed four people
could hardly be described as defenceless. Anyone who tried to
take advantage of her would probably regret it very quickly.

But I was beginning to wonder if there was another reason
she couldn't be found. What if she was not in Newcastle any
longer? Not *this* Newcastle at any rate.

Seven

I had nearly forgot! At all costs bring a good wine with you
when you come; here there is only beer, which is tolerable,
and gin, which is not.
            [Letter from Louis de Glabre to his friend Philippe
                                    Froidevaux, 18 January 1737]

I passed the bridge on my way up to the George where I was
to meet Hugh and Balfour. There was still a watchman on guard
outside the shop; he was reconciling his duty and his inclinations,
by refusing to let sightseers into the house but charging them for
a look through an unshuttered window.

I walked up the Side, passed St Nicholas's church and cut off
into the Clothmarket, from which an alley led to the George
Inn. Hugh and Balfour were waiting for me in the inn yard.

'I told you the snow would go!' Hugh said triumphantly. 'That'll
be it for the winter.'

'I hope so,' Balfour said. He looked cold and subdued.

'Come on then!' Hugh said. 'Got to make sure we're finished
before the inquest.' He grinned at me. 'Had a message this morning
to say I wouldn't be needed.' He nudged me in the ribs. 'Lawyer
Armstrong says he trusts you to give an accurate account of what
happened.'

'I don't think I'll go,' Balfour said.

'Very wise,' Hugh agreed. 'Bound to be a crush. Half the
town'll be there.'

Now, *that* was a cheering thought.

The proposed site for the new Assembly Rooms is in the Groat Market, separated from the Clothmarket by a block of houses and shops. The place was easy to find. Six months ago, on one of the hottest nights in June, a fire broke out in a mercer's shop and within an hour the property was consumed, along with the empty house next door; the mercer's body was found in the ruins. What remained of the buildings had been considered too dangerous to leave standing and the walls had been pulled down, leaving only the remains of the cellar creating a deep hole in the ground crisscrossed by charred timbers. The timbers were now under a layer of snow, showing here and there as black smudges in the white. The mercer's spirit must have evaporated in the fire.

Balfour looked at the ruins with a jaundiced eye. 'The space occupied by both properties is to be used?'

'Robert Jenison, the director of the Assemblies and the Concerts, owns both. He's willing to donate the sites to the town.'

Hugh leant over a wooden fence that had been put up round the ruin, to prevent anyone falling in. Footsteps in the snow suggested that several people had climbed the fence this morning and gone down into the cellar pit. 'What on earth were they after?'

'Wood. Free fuel for the fire.'

'Break their necks,' Hugh said with a grin.

Balfour was shivering, although it seemed warm to me in the sunshine. He searched his pockets, took out a measure, and asked Hugh to hold one end of it while he plodded up and down, muttering under his breath. He seemed to be making a great show of it, as if wanting to impress us with his efficiency – surely he must have all this information already. But he'd worked on the new Assembly Rooms in York, so he must be competent. And I knew from experience how a good performance can inspire confidence in an audience.

What he found didn't seem to please him. He muttered, 'Not really long enough. Or wide enough for that matter.' The site was only one property deep; on its far side ran a narrow alley covered in snow. Balfour scowled. 'Is there any chance of *that* property being incorporated?' He waved a hand at the tavern next door.

'I think Jenison owns that too,' I said, not entirely certain. 'But you won't be popular pulling down a tavern.'

Hugh was still peering down into the hole. He swung his leg over the fence. I grabbed his arm. 'What are you doing!'

'I can see something shiny down there. Look – under the far bank.'

Cautiously, I peered over the edge. 'It's probably just a dropped coin.' *Just*? A few months ago, before my marriage to Esther, I'd been an impecunious musician and every penny meant a great deal; I'd have been thinking of climbing down there. How quickly things change. 'Hugh, it's dangerous!'

'Nonsense!' Hugh said with magnificent inconsistency. 'Half a dozen people have already been down there!' And without more ado he launched himself down the slope.

I stopped talking; distracting him would only make it more dangerous. Besides, he wasn't after a dropped coin. He was after a little excitement; Hugh was not a sit-at-home man – he liked to be always *doing*.

Inevitably, his feet went out from under him; he waved his arms wildly for balance, slid a foot or two then righted himself. He put down a hand to one of the large snow-covered timbers and it shifted. A faint waft of charred timbers drifted up. Hugh bent down, took off his glove, and with white fingers tried to dig something from the frozen earth. He had to work at it but at last eased it loose.

Something caught the sunlight.

We helped Hugh clamber back up the slope; his boots were encrusted with snow and thick smudges of it adorned his great-coat. He opened his hand, grinning.

A ring, mostly tarnished and blackened, lay on his palm, with just a trace of brightness on one edge. An oval stone was attached to the ring. Hugh rubbed with a thumb, cleaned off some of the dirt. A greenish cameo slowly emerged, with a figure engraved on it; we peered at a woman in flowing draperies, holding what might be a tambourine. A graceful nymph, dancing.

'Looks like it's been there since before the fire,' Hugh said, prising earth from the loop of the ring itself.

'It must have belonged to the mercer.'

Balfour shook his head. 'It's very old.' He took the ring from

Hugh's cold fingers. 'I've seen things like this in London.' I've rarely seen such pleasure on a man's face. 'It's Roman.'

We contemplated the ring, as Balfour turned it this way and that. Its age and provenance were not particularly surprising. This is a very old town; the bridge is on the site of a Roman predecessor and from time to time, when the river's dredged, ancient pieces of stone or metal are pulled out. The churches are full of bits and pieces that were allegedly part of some older building, an arch here, an engraved stone there; now and then, pieces of human bone are even found.

'Quite nice,' Balfour said, nonchalantly. 'If you don't want it, I'll take it.'

The casualness of this remark made me look at him sharply. But Hugh merely took the ring back, saying, 'No, no. I like it. A dancing nymph seems an appropriate possession for a dancing *master.*'

'I'll give you a guinea for it,' Balfour said.

'You should show it to Heron,' I said. 'He'll know how old it is.' My patron, Claudius Heron, is a collector of all things ancient. He's also a wealthy gentleman which means he can afford to indulge his fancy; his house is full of antiquities, usually rather dull and battered. It all seems a waste of money to me.

'I wonder if there's anything else down there,' Balfour said, peering over the fence.

Hugh looked up from his contemplation of the ring. 'There could be, couldn't there?'

'You can't be intending—'

It was too late. They were already eagerly scanning the pit in the hopes of seeing something else glint in the sunshine.

'It's very cold,' I said, knowing they wouldn't listen. 'Why don't we go into the tavern and warm up?'

They climbed over the fence.

If they wanted to freeze themselves to death in search of trifles, I wasn't going to stop them. I've known Hugh since our charity school days, and have long since realized that any opposition merely makes him more obstinate. But how two grown men could work themselves into such excitement about grimy tarnished bits of metal, I couldn't comprehend. Heron is the same. Amazing.

Warmth slapped at me as soon as I pushed open the tavern

door. A huge fire roared in an ancient fireplace and filled the room with smoke. So this was where most of the timber from the burnt-down houses had gone.

I accosted one of the serving girls, ordered a beer and slumped into a chair in a corner. Water dripped from my boots on to the floor and started to steam. The tavern was moderately busy; a group of colliers gambled in one corner, a sailor sat morosely on his own. High above the fire, lights clustered in the corner where wall meets ceiling – five or six spirits, keeping warm.

The girl who brought my beer confirmed that Jenison owned the tavern. So it might indeed be possible to add this property to the new Assembly Rooms, particularly as I knew Jenison thought the poor drank too much; he might think it his civic duty to address the problem of riotous behaviour. Alternatively, he might think he was getting a nice rent, thank you very much, and that civic duty sometimes has to take a back seat.

A spirit dropped down on to my table to talk.

'Still snowing, is it?' it asked.

'No, a nice bright sunny day.'

The spirit flickered. 'It won't be nice till spring comes. I hates the cold.'

It was a friendly spirit; the living man clearly had had wit and cheerfulness and knew a good few jokes, some of which might even have been repeatable in front of ladies, if they'd been broad-minded. All in all, conversation with him made the time pass very agreeably, as I drank my beer and warmed my freezing toes.

'Just passing, sir?'

I shook my head. 'We're examining the site next door – they're proposing to build Assembly Rooms there.'

'I heard that, sir. Bad luck if you ask me.'

I cocked an eyebrow at the bright gleam. 'Oh yes?'

'Stands to reason after what happened.'

'The fire, you mean?'

The spirit slid closer, said confidentially, 'Well, we all know it wasn't an accident, don't we?'

I stared. 'Do we? I mean, I've heard nothing.'

'Money troubles,' the spirit said with some relish. 'Never had any sense, that fellow.'

'The mercer?'

'Had his house and shop all done out – beautiful it looked, all in the latest London fashions. Spent a fortune on it. Said it would attract customers. Silly fool – spent so much he couldn't afford to buy his stock!'

'You think he set the fire himself?'

'Was going to do a runner!' the spirit said with glee. 'Take the valuable stuff with him, sell it off, keep the money for himself and to the devil with his creditors.'

'But the fire caught him.'

'Some people are just plain incompetent,' the spirit said philosophically.

I finished my beer and went back outside. Hugh and Balfour were still down in the cellar, tramping about in the snow and ash and apparently having the time of their lives. I wondered if I was getting a bit old and staid – after all, I was married now. The idea was lowering.

I called down to them. 'I have to go to the inquest.'

Hugh didn't even glance up. 'Fine. Fine.'

I left them to it.

A private coach stood in the yard of the Golden Fleece, the luggage being unloaded from its top. The paint was freshly scraped along one side and a footman was recounting tales of disaster to the Fleece's ostler. The party had set out before the snow started, got caught in the blizzard, spent the night in a barn. Despite his constant protestations of how awful it had been, the footman had plainly enjoyed himself. 'Well nigh impassable on Gateshead Fell,' he said with relish. 'Any more snow and you'll not get through!'

Well, at least that meant Alice Gregson couldn't leave the town.

The inquest was being held in the Long Room on the first floor, and the stairs were crowded. I was about to push my way up when I heard my name called. Glancing round, I saw a slim figure in the passage that led to the tap room. Even muffled up in greatcoat and hat, my patron, Mr Claudius Heron, was unmistakeable.

Heron's a gentleman born and bred, in his forties, and he looked on the general populace crowding the inn stairs with a jaundiced eye. He jerked his head at me, and I followed him back out into the yard, stood shivering on the cobbles as Heron seemed to breathe more deeply away from the *hoi polloi*. He's fair-haired, and this morning the cold had turned his pale skin to pure white.

'Not a pleasant business,' he said. 'I hear you are directing the search for the girl.'

I shook my head. 'The watchmen have that in hand. She's hiding well.'

'She will long since have left the town.'

'If she has,' I said, looking at the scratched paintwork of the coach, 'she'll be frozen in the snow by now.' I wondered if I could tactfully steer Heron inside again, out of the cold.

'Not a mystery then?'

'Not at all. Except for her motive in killing them.'

A faint smile touched his lips. 'I know better than to think it will be that simple when you are involved.'

Heron has intimate knowledge of my recent adventures – he's been involved in one or two of them himself.

There was a stir in the inn; someone called out that the jury were returning from the Gregsons' shop. 'I suppose you give evidence?' Heron said, turning for the inn again. 'I thought I might call in to see what was decided. I was sorry not to make the meeting with the architect this morning. I had an appointment with other shipowners.'

'You missed very little,' I said, as we came into the crowded passageway. 'Except for a great deal of measuring.'

'I have heard good things of Balfour. He has extensive experience in this type of building and his correspondence makes him sound a sensible man. I was glad he changed his mind and came after all. Though I did not expect it – he was quite adamant when he wrote that his health was not good enough.'

'He was greatly incommoded by the journey.'

'I think it is a more deep-seated matter than that,' Heron said.

We were back in the crush of bodies again, but Heron has an effortless way of cutting through crowds. Something to do with his look – his raised eyebrow, particularly. The crowds parted before him and we climbed the stairs unobstructed. In the Long Room above, a table and chair had been set out for Armstrong the coroner, and a few seats for the elderly and infirm around the walls. A thick press of people milled about.

'Do you have time to give me a violin lesson?' Heron said, surveying the crowd. 'I would be obliged if you could come up to the house, tomorrow morning.'

I bowed my agreement; I had little choice – patrons must be kept sweet. Heron nodded and went off to exchange a few words with an acquaintance.

Lawyer Armstrong strode into the room.

Eight

They are proud of their law – all the questions and enquir-ings. But oddly, the people with the final say as to whether this person is guilty or that, have no qualifications in the law whatsoever!

[Letter from Louis de Glabre to his friend Philippe
Froidevaux, 18 January 1737]

All eyes were on the members of the jury who filed into the room behind Armstrong. Everybody knew they must have come direct from viewing the bodies, and were on the lookout for signs of horror. They were not disappointed; the eight men, all sensible no-nonsense tradesmen, were white-faced and plainly shocked. It cannot have helped that they were all neighbours of the Gregsons and must have known them well.

The jury shuffled into their chairs and Armstrong spread out his papers on his table. I glanced round for people I knew. Fleming was on the jury, of course, and his wife was sitting comfortably on a sofa in a window embrasure, with the little Gregson girl beside her, playing with a rag doll. Just in front of her was Heron, talking to his manservant, Fowler, who was bowing deferentially. Not even Heron can think it necessary to bring his manservant to an inquest, so I presumed Fowler must have come on his own account, out of mere interest. Gregson's surviving daughter, Mrs Fletcher, stood alone at the back, severe as ever.

Armstrong sat down. He has the lined face of a man, but is

lanky as a boy; when he folded himself under the table, his knees knocked against the underside of it.

Formalities over, the first witness was called. Myself. 'Mr Patterson?' Armstrong said. 'Could you tell us what happened on Saturday night? Sunday morning, I should say.'

I told them, omitting the snowball fight, saying merely I'd been walking on the Keyside with my wife and friend. The story of the figure climbing down the makeshift rope caused great excitement, as did our discovery of the bodies and the blood – I've never had such a gratifying audience reaction in the concert hall. Armstrong wanted to know if I'd seen the escaping girl carrying anything and I said I had not, although she might have had something in her pocket, but nothing very heavy.

Armstrong moved from the musical profession to the medical, calling Gale the barber-surgeon. Gale, an unprepossessing figure, slight in stature and round in face, is a man who likes to think he is master of all things medicinal, and has offended both the apothecaries of the town and the physicians by his wide-ranging activities. There is no questioning his competence, however, and he made an even bigger impact than I had, with his detailed description of the wounds. 'All but the apprentice had been stabbed many times,' he said. 'Mr Gregson five times.'

Someone made a play of fainting noisily in the crowd and was borne up and helped to a chair. Heron watched in grim contempt; his servant, standing behind him, caught my gaze. Fowler's lean sardonic face was harsh and angry. Whatever had Heron said to him?

Armstrong asked for the little girl, Judith Gregson. In the sensation caused by the appearance of the child, Balfour slipped into the room. He reddened when he saw I'd noticed him and, under cover of the noise, said awkwardly, 'I thought I'd just see how things were going.' A pity; I thought he'd have been much better keeping away.

Mrs Fleming brought up the child and she stood in front of Armstrong's table, clutching her rag doll to her thin chest. Armstrong has no children but he does have a kind way with them and he coaxed her delicately. 'You sleep in the attics, I hear. Is it warm and cosy up there?'

She nodded dumbly.

'And your doll lives up there too? Does everyone else sleep downstairs?'

Another nod.

'Including your Aunt Alice? Did you like your Aunt Alice?'

She said nothing, which was eloquent in its own way.

'Do you like your Aunt Sarah?'

'She plays shops with me,' she said shyly.

'I'm sure she does.' Armstrong twinkled. 'Now, I'm very sorry, Judith, but I'm going to have to ask you about last Saturday. Do you remember going downstairs in the middle of the night?'

She started crying.

In the end, with the exercise of a great deal of patience, he got the information from her. She'd thought she heard her grandfather calling and went down to see him. But he'd been in bed and she couldn't wake him. She couldn't wake her grandmother either nor Aunt Sarah, and Aunt Alice wasn't there. And the shop door was open. And she was scared, and wanted someone to come. So she screamed.

Several ladies openly wept.

Armstrong thanked her, said she'd done very well and he was very pleased to have met her, and Mrs Fleming bore her out of the room talking of lemonade.

Two watchmen gave evidence, which interested me rather more. Abraham McLintoch told of discovering the knife that had obviously done the dreadful deed, near the body of the apprentice, in the shop. A hubbub followed this revelation and McLintoch had to wait for it to subside. The knife was probably from the kitchen, he added, a very sharp knife, more than capable of inflicting severe damage.

The second watchman told how he'd searched the house. He couldn't see that anything had been stolen, at least the house hadn't been ransacked or turned over. Most of it looked undisturbed. There was jewellery upstairs and some nice candlesticks. But in the cellar he'd found a money box, open but not forced – the key was still in the lock. There was nothing left in the box except a receipt for some money Gregson had been paid. He'd searched everywhere, he said, but found no more money.

Fleming then heaved himself up from the jury chairs. His description of how he'd woken to screams on the night told me nothing new, but I was interested in his information on Alice Gregson. Her father had evidently sent his apprentice, Ned, down to meet her at the Fleece on the Tuesday evening before the murders; Fleming had seen them walk up the bridge together. 'She was a little thing,' he said, 'dolled up in the London fashions – all thin petticoats, and feathers in her hair. And her nose in the air, as if she smelt something she didn't like. Looked like she couldn't make the effort to put one foot in front of another. One of your city girls who's never done a stroke of work in her life.'

Heron shifted impatiently; he glanced at me and raised his eyebrows.

Alice Gregson had been in Newcastle only four days but Fleming had seen a great deal of her, in more senses than one. The assembled crowd muttered in shock when he described her flimsy London dresses, how low they were cut, how many ribbons and how much expensive lace she had on them. She'd usually stood staring out of the window, as if looking for someone, or hoping for some diversion. She'd yawned a lot, and said she wanted to go back to London. She'd even said she thought Newcastle *barbaric*. This produced outraged gasps of horror.

Armstrong cut through the noise and asked if Gregson had kept much money in the house.

'His recent takings only, I believe,' Fleming said.

'But there might have been enough to take the girl back to London?'

Fleming nodded. 'There might have been.' He added scrupulously, 'I don't know for certain.'

'But in view of the burglaries last year, Gregson might have *said* he had no money even if he had?'

'I suppose so, yes,' Fleming said, doubtfully.

There was never any doubt of the jury's decision. The four deceased were pronounced to have been murdered by Alice Gregson, aged twenty-three. Heron was at my elbow seconds after the pronouncement. 'Nellie's coffee house,' he said peremptorily.

'It doesn't make sense.' Heron threw himself back in his chair. An acquaintance nodded to him in passing; half the town seemed to have repaired to the coffee-house once the inquest was over

– the male half at least. 'I don't doubt the girl killed them, but the evidence is totally unsatisfactory. Armstrong should have asked more questions. For one thing, the neighbours say she was a slip of a girl, who did not have the strength to walk a hundred yards. But she apparently had the strength to stab four adults and then climb down a makeshift rope dangling above a deep river.' He signalled to one of the serving girls. 'It is not easy to stab a man.'

Heron's a swordsman and not merely in the practice rooms. I've seen him fight in anger; I'd wager he knows from experience exactly how hard it is to kill someone.

He paused to order coffee from the girl. 'Secondly,' he continued, 'there is the question of the knife.'

'Found near the apprentice,' I agreed. 'Which logically means he must have been the last victim. Alice was in her room, probably pretending to sleep. She must have killed her sister first because she would have woken as Alice crept over her. Then she killed her parents, went downstairs, killed the apprentice. So far, so good. But then she made her way back upstairs in order to flee down the rope. That's not logical. Why did she not simply walk out of the front door?' I stopped to allow the girl to put the two dishes of coffee on the table. 'And why leave the child unharmed?'

Two elderly gentlemen accosted Heron, enthusing about the price of coal. I hunted in my pocket for some money to pay the girl and nearly gave her the foreign coin I'd picked up from the snow. I waited until Heron extricated himself from the two gentlemen. 'And why did she choose the dead of night to steal the money?' I asked. 'She could have taken it while everyone else was in church on Sunday. She'd have had a free run of the house, and been away several hours before they got home. She didn't *need* to kill those people. Even if for some reason she *had* to steal the money at dead of night, they were asleep – they weren't threatening her.'

Heron reached for his coffee but didn't comment.

'And what happened to the money?' I worked through a possible sequence of events. 'The box was opened with a key which presumably Samuel Gregson kept close. As an inmate of the house, Alice could have had easy access to that. But only the money was taken – the box was left. So she must have put the coins in a bag, or in her pocket. But that means she would have been carrying them when she climbed down the rope – and she wasn't running like a woman with a heavy burden.'

'Perhaps there wasn't much in the box.' Heron nodded at yet another acquaintance.

'Then why murder for it? Surely she'd have made certain in advance it was worth the effort?'

'Perhaps there was no money at all – perhaps it was government stocks? Or Mrs Gregson's best jewellery.'

'There's no suggestion Mrs Gregson had expensive jewellery. Gregson was evidently not a generous man.'

Heron sipped coffee. 'Then she moved the contents of the box *before* the crime.'

I thought of the rope of sheets. 'If she moved the money earlier, and took her time to make the rope, as she must, then it was all planned in advance – though the theft would have to have been at the last moment, or Gregson might have missed the money. But if she already had the money, there was even less reason to kill them.'

Heron paused for a moment. 'Then only one answer comes to mind.'

I nodded. 'She *wanted* to kill them.'

We sat in silence as the noise of the coffee house raged around us. Almost everyone, it seemed, was discussing the murders. More than one gentleman bemoaned the fact he'd never set eyes on Alice Gregson. She was christened an Amazon, a doughty warrior. Gregson, it seemed, was not regarded with a great deal of sympathy; he'd apparently not been entirely aboveboard in some of his financial dealings. Several gentlemen mentioned grossly inflated bills they'd received from him.

I set my head back against the chair. 'Alice had only been here four days – she hardly knew any of them. What had they ever done to her?'

A spirit slid down the wall, hesitated on the edge of the table as if unwilling to interrupt us. It was an old spirit, rather faint. It said, 'Pray excuse me, my dear sirs, but I have a message for Mr Patterson from Lawyer Armstrong. Would he oblige Mr Armstrong by visiting him in his rooms as soon as possible.'

Heron permitted himself a small smile. 'There must be a problem with the will.'

'I don't see why it should involve me.' I got up nevertheless. Armstrong is a sensible man, who wouldn't inconvenience me for no reason.

Heron said, 'Is there any point in telling you to be careful? You do, after all, now have a wife to consider.'

That brought to mind other occasions on which he'd told me to take care – and when I'd taken no notice of him and paid the price.

'I'll try,' I said.

He raised one elegant eyebrow.

Nine

If there is one thing the English enjoy more than anything else, it is a good family argument; they can cosset these with the greatest enjoyment for decades.

[Letter from Louis de Glabre to his friend Philippe Froidevaux, 18 January 1737]

Lawyer Armstrong's house stands in Amen Corner behind St Nicholas's church, not far from the head of the steep Side. A brisk short walk from the Fleece, snow crunching underfoot and sunshine warming my back. Armstrong was waiting in the sunlit outer room of his office; he greeted me with a smile that had a great deal of relief in it, and thanked me for coming.

'I have Mrs Fletcher with me. We've been reading the will.'

We went into the inner office, a room lined with books and boxes; dust motes floated in the sunlight. Mrs Fletcher, in her severe cap and neat practical dress, turned a look on me so expressionless it was daunting. We sat down, Armstrong cramming himself into the small space beneath his desk.

'To reiterate,' he said, 'Samuel Gregson left all his property to be divided equally between his children, with arrangements made for the upkeep of his wife should she outlive him. There are three surviving children, two sons, in Exeter and London, and Mrs Fletcher.' He nodded at her in acknowledgement. 'There are strictly four surviving children but of course Alice cannot profit from her murderous acts.'

'Assuming she did kill them,' Mrs Fletcher said.

Armstrong said sharply, 'The inquest has come to that verdict.'

'The jury were fools,' Mrs Fletcher said contemptuously.

Which was tantamount to saying that *Armstrong* was a fool. I hurriedly intervened. 'Why do you believe your sister may be innocent?'

'Look at the evidence! Alice is a slight girl who has never done a day's work in her life, yet she's supposed to have killed four people in a particularly brutal manner.' She lifted her head in the face of Armstrong's obvious annoyance. 'It's plain someone else was involved. Obviously, she disturbed a burglar and fled in fear.'

'And what happened to this burglar?' Armstrong said.

'He ran off when he heard the child's screams. With the money, and whatever else was stolen.'

This was patently not the first time the subject had been raised, and was, I suspected, the reason I was here. 'There is nothing to suggest anything else was stolen,' Armstrong said, with an obvious effort to be civil.

'*I* will be able to tell you if that's true,' Mrs Fletcher said, 'when I've had a look at the house and its contents.'

'I have already said—'

'My mother had some jewellery which would attract a thief.'

'The watchman who searched the house said the jewellery was still in your mother's room,' I pointed out.

She smiled grimly, the sun catching her hard profile. 'My mother had some trinkets which are no doubt still there, but she also had more valuable pieces, inherited from her mother.'

'The house must be inventoried,' Armstrong said firmly. 'I will send one of my clerks to do it. Moreover, your brothers must be informed of what has happened before anything can be moved.'

'And in the meantime the house could be broken into and the jewellery stolen!'

'No one is to be allowed inside that house,' Armstrong said sharply. 'I have it in trust for *all* the beneficiaries.' He turned to me. 'You, of course, may go in and out of the property as you see fit, Mr Patterson, but Mrs Fletcher does not have my permission to do so.' He glared at her. 'I trust I make myself plain.'

Mrs Fletcher's mouth set in a long hard line. Dust motes floated around her head. She held Armstrong's gaze for a long moment, then got up. 'Good day, Mr Patterson,' she said, and swept out.

Armstrong leant back, sighing. 'Just like her father – *he* was headstrong, would never be guided. Forgive me, Patterson, but I thought it best we confront the issue directly. Else she'd be at your door trying to sweet-talk you into letting her see the shop and you'd not know whether it was appropriate or not.'

'I quite see your point.' I hesitated. 'You say you knew Gregson well. Would you describe him as a violent man?'

Armstrong pursed his lips. 'Argumentative, certainly. He never raised a hand to me, or to anyone else in my presence, but a man will often behave differently in the bosom of his own family.' He was being remarkably frank; I suspected he wouldn't have said so much if he'd not already had some concern over the matter. He looked at me from under his bushy eyebrows. 'Violent or not,' he said, 'Samuel Gregson should not have been murdered. His life was unjustly taken from him, and that is indefensible, in both legal and moral terms.'

I nodded. 'I was hoping for some understanding of the girl. If Gregson was violent towards her, that might, in some part, explain what she did.'

'Would it explain killing her mother and her sister? And the apprentice whom she hardly knew?'

'No,' I said. 'That's the problem.'

The sky was clouding over as I stepped out of Armstrong's office into the shadow of St Nicholas's church. A few flakes of snow drifted down; it looked as if Hugh's weather prediction was wrong after all – there would be more snow. The first concert of the year was due next week and I was beginning to doubt it could go ahead.

I decided to go home. I was still worried about Esther. She had been unwell for some days now; she really ought to see someone. If the illness developed into something like Philips's, I would never forgive myself.

I turned into Westgate, the street where genteel folk live, in large houses and extensive gardens, above the fogs and smoke that drift up the river. Trees hanging over the walls were lined with white; a crow stood on a branch and cawed mournfully. The snow had been worn down into slush and I kept to the edge of the road, where the walking was firmer. The street was almost deserted, only one man, muffled in greatcoat and hat, hurried towards me, slipping as if his boots heels were worn and had no grip. He came abreast of me—

And with one swift moment, swung his arm.

I ducked out of his reach, slipped and fell. I hit the ground with a thump that knocked the breath out of me. As I foundered in the snow, I heard him grunt, saw his fist heading for my face. I jerked back – and hit my head against a house wall . . .

Ten

An Englishwoman's home is a stage; she invites all her acquaintance in to see the china and the tea and the little knick-knacks she herself has made.

[Letter from Louis de Glabre to his friend Philippe Froidevaux, 18 January 1737]

Somehow I managed to stagger up Westgate. Through the pain in my head, I could think of only one thing – getting to Hugh's rooms near the top of the street above the clockmaker's. The shop was shut; I stumbled down an alley to the side door, dragged myself up stairs that seemed endless . . .

Hugh's dancing schoolroom is directly over the clockmaker's. I fell against the door; it gave way beneath my weight and I toppled in. At the far end of the long polished floor, Hugh was sitting at a small table, scribbling.

'What the devil!' He leapt up, seized hold of me and pushed me down into a chair. 'Stay here! I'll get brandy.'

He dashed out. I leant back against the wall, winced, sat upright again. There must be a bruise on the back of my head as big as the Tyne Bridge. At least it wasn't bleeding. I put my head in my hands. Hugh came back with a bottle of brandy and poured me a glass. I downed it, squinted against the pain.

'I was attacked,' I said, thickly. 'A fellow at the bottom of the street. Rifled my pockets.'

'Did he get much?'

Grunting with effort, I hunted in my pockets. 'I had a few shillings . . .'

'House key?'

'Don't carry it.'

'Nice to have servants to let you in,' Hugh said without rancour. 'Careful!' He moved something from the table under my elbow – the ancient ring. 'Is money all he got?'

'No,' I said, with foreboding. 'He got the key to Gregson's shop.'

Hugh poured more brandy, dragged up another chair and sat down astride it. 'Was there a label on the key?'

'No – but if he didn't know where the key was for, why should he have taken it?'

'He might have known you,' Hugh pointed out, 'and thought the key was for your own house. Plenty in there to steal.'

The brandy was having a beneficial effect; I drank more. 'There's no sense in taking the key to my house. He couldn't use it till dark, and by then we could have all the servants on watch and the locks changed.'

'Thieves don't always think sensibly.'

I stirred wearily. 'I'll have to go and look at Gregson's shop.'

Hugh pushed me back. 'Nonsense! Have more brandy.'

'Philips entrusted me with that key! The least I can do is check no one's broken in.'

Hugh sighed and gave in. 'I suppose I'd better come with you.'

'Haven't you got lessons?'

'Finished for the day. I'll get my greatcoat.'

It took more effort than I'd anticipated to get down the stairs to the street, but once I was out in the cold fresh air, I felt better. Hugh strolled with me down Westgate in the gloom of the early winter evening, stopping where I'd been attacked and looking round. The snow had been scuffed and the place I'd fallen was very obvious.

'He was audacious,' Hugh said. 'Or mad. Attacking you in broad daylight, in the street, where anyone might have intervened!'

'Hugh,' I said. I rubbed my aching temple. 'Why should he want the key to the shop?'

'He knows the place is empty and wants to rob it.'

'What if it's more than that? What if this wasn't a casual robbery? What if he's connected with the murders?'

'Nonsense!'

'Mrs Fletcher thinks her sister didn't kill them.'

Hugh made a derisory noise.

'She thinks Alice fled from a violent burglar. Presumably she now daren't come forward and say so, because she'll be apprehended and charged.'

'You're tired, Charles,' Hugh said soothingly. 'Get home to bed. You'll be better in the morning. It was a common thief who just happened to see you in the street.'

My head was throbbing and I could hardly think straight, but I was absolutely certain I was right. 'He's connected with Alice, I know he is,' I said obstinately.

'If he's the killer,' Hugh said patiently, 'why should he want to go back to the shop? If it was me, I'd get as far away as possible.'

'Maybe he left something there.'

'It would have been found by now.'

'Perhaps it was, but we didn't recognize its significance.'

Hugh sighed.

The snow was coming down in a more determined fashion by the time we got to the bottom of Westgate; negotiating the steep Side was difficult and we both slipped several times. On the Sandhill only a few people were about, mostly hurrying for shelter. The Key was busier, with sailors still loading ships, but there was none of the idling that is usually to be seen – everyone was doing what they had to, then getting inside again. Hugh shivered melodramatically. 'I hate winter.'

We climbed the slope to the bridge; a horseman came the other way, a burly man on an ugly chestnut horse. The man's coat and hat were dusted with snow; he looked weary as he reined in the horse.

'Gentlemen.'

He was a rough but handsome man of forty or so with a weather-beaten face like a sailor's. I was struck by an odd feeling of familiarity, as if I ought to know him.

'Can you direct me to a good inn?' he asked. 'Clean but not too expensive?'

I gave him directions to the Golden Fleece. Hugh said, 'Have you come over Gateshead Fell?'

'Don't know what it's called,' the man said. 'It was damned unpleasant. Nearly didn't get through.'

We watched him ride off in the direction of the Fleece. 'Londoner,' Hugh said, dismissively. 'Soft.'

'I'm sure I know him,' I said. 'But I can't place him. I haven't seen him recently, I know that.' Maybe it had been in London; I was there four or five years ago, studying and gaining experience, playing in the opera orchestra and such like.

We turned for Gregson's shop; I took hold of Hugh's arm. 'The door's open.' We looked for a moment at the thin line of darkness between door and jamb – it looked as if someone had meant to shut it, but not quite caught the latch. I cautiously pushed at the door. It swung, creaking. We hesitated; Hugh said, 'If it is a thief, he won't still be there surely.'

Cautiously, I ventured in. The house was pitch-black; I groped on the shelf by the door, hoping the candles and tinder box would still be there. They were; I lit a candle and held it high.

The shop had been ransacked, the furniture turned over and smashed, pictures thrown on to the floor in showers of glass, wallpaper samples torn up and scattered. We stood, staring at the mess. 'The key's in the lock on the inside,' Hugh said.

I turned on my heels, fighting the ache in my head. At least the bodies had not suffered – they had been removed after the inquest. 'The thief must have come in, locked the door behind him; with the shutters closed, no one outside could have seen him. When he'd finished, he simply unlocked the door and walked off, leaving the key.'

I put the key in my pocket, relieved to have it in my possession again so quickly. We avoided the debris and climbed the stairs to the drawing room above. That too had been turned over; cushions had been ripped and the stuffing thrown out, ornaments swept from tables.

'Looking for valuables,' Hugh said.

'Then why leave the candlesticks?' I pointed to the mantelshelf. It was the same tale upstairs, in the bedrooms. The stained bedding had been torn off the beds and the mattresses slashed, feathers lying in little drifts about the floor. Gaudy ribbons, almost the only sad remains of Sarah Gregson, were trampled and dirty on the floor. Upstairs in the attic, the little girl's bed had been overturned; beyond the partition, Alice Gregson's trunk had been emptied, and the contents scattered over the floor: the stylish dresses, dancing pumps, cobweb-thin lace, handkerchiefs, night-gowns . . .

I frowned at the tangle of clothes. 'He was obviously looking for something but I'm damned if I know what.' I glanced at Hugh; he shrugged. I sighed, scrubbed at my eyes. 'We'd better be thorough and look in the cellar. I haven't been down there at all – there didn't seem any point last time I was here.'

We went back down the stairs to the shop, found a door that led to a narrow stair built into the structure of the bridge. Unsurprisingly, the cellar below smelt damp; I held the candle higher in an effort to see into the dark corners. Hugh took a branch of candles from a table in the middle of the room and lit them from mine; the room brightened.

It was a moderately-sized room, full of boxes, and furniture in various states of repair. The boxes had been disturbed, although not, in most cases, completely turned out; it looked as if the thief had merely glanced in and lost interest when he found china tea-sets and painted shepherdesses. On the table stood a moneybox, with the lid thrown back, empty except for a scrap of paper. A receipt: *Rec'd £112 11s 6d of William Threlkeld*. The signature was Gregson's. Threlkeld: that name was familiar too. But my head was throbbing ever more fiercely, and I was beginning to long for sleep with a rare passion.

Something caught my attention – a gap on a shelf. 'This is presumably where the box was kept.' The shelf was dusty and the place where the box had stood was obvious, a rectangular clean spot. With another identical space next to it.

'There were *two* boxes,' I said.

Hugh inspected the shelf. 'Maybe our thief took the other one just now. There was probably more money in it.'

I shook my head and winced. 'The watchman at the inquest said he'd searched the entire house and there was no money left anywhere. This must have been taken at the time of the killings, or before.'

'Maybe Gregson moved the box himself.'

'That would be a coincidence, and I don't much like coincidences.' I looked at the empty box on the table. 'Alice could have emptied one box into the other, leaving the empty one behind.'

'That sounds more like it.'

'But Fleming said Gregson didn't keep much money in the house and in any case there's no point in having two money boxes unless one is full. And if one *was* full, she couldn't have emptied the other one into it.'

Hugh sighed. 'It's probably not in the least important.'

'I still say she wasn't weighed down by anything heavy when she fled.' That reminded me of the foreign coin Alice had dropped; I reached into my pocket. 'Damn it, he's taken that as well!'

'Charles,' Hugh said with heavy patience. 'The fellow was a common thief – he took everything he could find.'

'No, he didn't,' I retorted. 'I've still got my neckerchief and my coat. Any thief worth the name would have taken as many of my clothes as he could manage.'

'He was disturbed,' Hugh suggested, 'and had to run off.'

'Maybe. But surely anyone disturbing him would have come to my aid.'

Hugh gave another sigh. I shook my head in an effort to clear it. 'Let's say Alice took the missing box, but didn't have it on her when she slid down the rope. That means she must have removed it from the house *before* the murders but not long before, because Gregson might have missed it. Supposing she came down here, took the box, passed it to an accomplice—'

'Wait, wait!' Hugh interrupted, eyes wide. 'An *accomplice*? Where did *he* spring from?'

'The man who attacked me.'

'He was a common thief! And you were talking about a burglar before, not an accomplice.'

'No, *Mrs Fletcher* was talking about a burglar, but that plainly doesn't make sense. The rope, Hugh, think of the rope! Alice made that in advance, and she couldn't possibly have anticipated she'd need to escape a chance burglar. This was all planned, Hugh!'

'Any accomplice or burglar,' Hugh pointed out, 'must have made his escape at about the same time as Alice. We'd have seen him.'

'Not necessarily. He had time to run off while we were watching

Alice slide down that rope. And, in any case, the snow was so thick, I could hardly see a yard ahead when I ran on to the bridge.'

I walked about the cellar, restless and frustrated. 'And now he's come back. He must have thought there was something that would implicate him. If only we'd found it!'

Hugh repeated, 'It was an opportunist thief, Charles. He'd heard you had the keys of the shop and was looking for valuables.'

'Who'd know I had the keys?'

'The watchmen. And Philips could have told half a dozen people.'

That was true enough. I gave in to the pain in my head. 'I'm going home. I need sleep. Hugh – don't tell anyone about this. Not at least until I've had time to tell Philips and Armstrong what's happened. They ought to know first.'

He nodded and blew out the branch of candles. Shadows gathered around us. With the single candle, we climbed the stairs to the shop. I checked the shutters, particularly the one with a broken bracket, then locked the door behind us. I couldn't resist glancing about the bridge in case I saw the woman from the other world again, but there was only the snow, falling steadily now, and a passing dog that gave us a curious look.

I wished I could rid myself of a growing suspicion we'd accused the wrong person of the murders.

Eleven

In the homes of the poor, you will see many old things, still used out of necessity. In the houses of the rich, you will see many old things, displayed for their antiquity, which is often great, and their beauty, which is often non-existent.
[Letter from Louis de Glabre to his friend Philippe Froidevaux, 19 January 1737]

'It's a long way from being robbed in the street, to believing in an accomplice,' Heron said, running his fingers over the stem of his wine glass. We were sitting in the elegant Chinese beauty of his newly redecorated library; looking at the flawless taste and quality of the wallpaper, the vases and the little statuettes, I knew for certain that Samuel Gregson's hand had never come anywhere near it; Heron had had London men up to do the work. Gregson had been good but not up to gentry standards.

After a tolerable night's sleep, my head still ached, but I felt a great deal better. Esther had been exasperated when I arrived home, muddy and thick-headed; she'd gone straight to a cupboard for one of her cordials. I drank it under her eagle eye and felt compelled to apologize.

Esther laughed. 'I knew when I married you that you would never live a quiet life.'

'I do *try* not to get involved into anything untoward,' I said meekly.

She sighed. 'Yes, I know. Charles—'

'Yes?'

But she shook her head and said merely, 'Do be careful.' I wondered what she'd been about to say – and why she'd changed her mind.

I sent messages to both Armstrong and Philips about the robbery and gathered from the extreme politeness of the replies that neither was very pleased. Heron, in his library, had listened in near silence, interrupting only to clarify some small points, but went at last to the core of the matter.

'An accomplice?' I sat back in my chair. 'There's no definitive evidence, I agree, but there are some suggestive points. Several people have said Alice was watching for someone, for instance. You yourself said that she's an unlikely murderer from the physical point of view. And Mrs Fletcher, who seems to know her better than anyone else, thinks she wouldn't be capable of it.'

Heron considered this for a moment in silence, tapping a finger against his glass. 'Nothing was taken from the shop?'

'Not that I could see, but I can't be certain. I don't know the house well enough.' I'd probably end up applying to Armstrong for permission to take Mrs Fletcher round the premises. 'He must surely have been searching for anything that might incriminate him – papers and the like.'

Heron stared absently at the roaring fire. 'Are you sure your attacker was not the girl?'

I was startled. 'Alice Gregson?'

He raised an elegant eyebrow at my incredulity. 'I merely wondered.'

'I was attacked by a man. In greatcoat and breeches.'

'Your wife dresses in breeches,' Heron pointed out.

'He was too tall. And I heard him grunt – it was certainly a man.'

Heron nodded, conceding the point. The gilded clock on the mantelshelf chimed; he put down his glass. 'Time to go.'

We'd agreed to meet with Balfour to talk over the plans for the Assembly Rooms. It was only a few streets to the George but Heron had ordered his carriage; he was not a man to relish walking in snow. We went out into the hall.

'The girl is not yet caught?' Heron asked.

'I suspect she will never be.'

Heron smiled slightly. 'I suspect she will. I know your obstinacy.'

I considered telling him where I thought she was; Heron knows about the other world; he has accompanied me there on occasion. But I was still unsure of my conclusions and by the time I'd dithered over the matter, the servants were around us. Footmen loomed; Heron's manservant Fowler hovered by the servants' door. Heron took his coat from the butler.

Outside, the snow was coming down in a light but steady shower. It was very pleasant to sit in the comfort of Heron's carriage with a warm brick under my feet, looking out on the less fortunate who had to walk. Like the horseman from the previous night, who caught my attention as we drove down through the Bigg Market. I remembered his name now: Joseph Kane. He was a sailor who had worked on the boat I came home on from London some years ago. We'd not been on good terms – Kane wanted vails and I had no money to give.

From the George's yard, we went straight to the warmth of a parlour. A fire was burning in the grate and a bowl of mulled wine steaming on the table, but neither Hugh nor Balfour were there. Heron, not a man used to being kept waiting, was not pleased and sent a servant in search of Balfour.

There was an uncomfortable silence while we waited. I said, 'We looked at the site for the Rooms the other day. Demsey found an ancient ring.'

Heron was interested at once. 'There were Roman buildings in the town just about there. A skeleton was found in the next street – oh, eighty years ago, now. What is this ring like?'

Trust Heron to know such things. I did my best to describe the ring – fortunately, just at that moment, Hugh came dashing in full of apologies. 'Sorry I'm late! A cart overturned on the High Bridge and it was absolutely impossible to get past!'

'I hear you found a ring,' Heron said.

Hugh had it with him; I left them exclaiming over it and went to see if I could find Balfour. The servant was in the passageway, looking embarrassed. 'He's – er – otherwise engaged—'

A door opened behind him and a woman swaggered out, grinning; I'd no doubt whatsoever of her profession. The servant gave me an apologetic grin. Cautiously, I pushed the door wider. There was another parlour behind it, with a large fire and a table loaded with the remnants of a substantial breakfast. Across the other side of the room, Balfour, in shirt sleeves, was just buttoning up his breeches.

His face lit up with pleasure when he saw me. 'Patterson, my dear fellow! Do come in.'

'I think not,' I said, trying not to look disapproving. I wouldn't deny a man some pleasure, but to keep Heron waiting while he took it was folly. As one of the Directors of the Assembly Rooms, Heron was Balfour's employer, and Balfour would be wise to keep him sweet. 'Mr Heron's here.'

Balfour grabbed a tankard from the table and gulped down beer. 'A man needs a little breakfast, Patterson!'

He was remarkably cheerful this morning. He grinned. 'I like this snow. No getting out of town at all now, the ostlers tell me. Good job there are so many attractions, eh?' He winked at me, then frowned. 'You have a bruise on your forehead.'

'Have I? I had an encounter with a thief last night.'

'Really!' He didn't look particularly shocked. 'Some shady rough?'

'I don't know – I didn't get a good look at him. Will you please come?'

He grumbled but reached for his coat.

'The plans?' I suggested. He looked round, puzzled, then spotted a roll of parchment on a sofa and swooped to grab it up.

I needn't have been so anxious. In the larger room, the wine had been neglected; Heron was engaged in examining Hugh's ring. He angled the cameo so he could see the figure more clearly. 'This is extremely valuable.'

Hugh was taken aback. 'I thought it was just a trinket.'

Heron shook his head. 'I'll give you twenty guineas for it.'

There was a moment's respectful silence. Twenty guineas was extremely generous. Hugh cast me a surreptitious look. 'Actually,' he said, a trifle nervously, 'I'd rather keep it. The dancing connection, you see.' I fancied I heard a distinct note of regret; Hugh's an excellent businessman and not in the practice of turning down large amounts of money.

Heron gave the ring back at once. 'If you change your mind at any time, let me know.'

The plans were unrolled and the proposed building was revealed in section, plan and other views I couldn't name, beautifully drawn, with annotations in impeccable copperplate. Balfour became enthusiastic and launched into explanations. I let the details wash over me, disturbed a little by Heron's demeanour; he was surprisingly distracted. I saw him glance at the window once or twice; following his gaze, I saw the snow was beginning to ease.

The servant came back in again and signalled to me. I went across and was treated to a voice lowered conspiratorially. 'Lady to see you, sir.' He winked.

Balfour's exploits had clearly given the servant erroneous ideas; I followed him to the yard with some trepidation. In the thinning snow, an ostler was bringing out a matched pair of horses. Beyond the horses, under the arch to the street, I saw, with some relief, Mrs Fletcher.

She waited for me as I walked around the edge of the yard to avoid the nervous horses. 'I wanted to tell you I've taken lodgings on the High Bridge,' she said as soon as I was in earshot. 'With Mrs Mountain. And to ask if you've heard anything more of my sister?'

No polite greeting, no *sir*, I noted; Mrs Fletcher was apparently contemptuous of the ordinary courtesies of life.

'No one can find her.'

She contemplated me for a moment. Snow drifted in under the arch. 'I've heard of the attack on you, Mr Patterson,' she said. 'And the raid on the shop.'

Well, the story had been bound to come to her ears; it was her inheritance at stake, after all. I told her what had happened.

Her lip curled. 'Was anything taken?'

'I don't know,' I admitted.

'Let me look,' she said. 'I'll tell you.'

There was no point in resisting any further. 'I'll ask Armstrong if he'll allow it,' I agreed.

She inclined her head; at least she wasn't triumphant in victory. 'I believe I know what the thief was after.'

The ostler led the horses in our direction, intent on taking them out into the street; we stood aside to let him pass. The horses' breath blew out in great clouds in the cold air. Mrs Fletcher reached into the folds of her skirt, to her pocket, and brought out a grimy sheet of paper, folded into the shape of a letter. 'This was brought to me this morning by a rogue. He said he found it in the mud by one of the wharfs on Sunday. He wanted a shilling for it.' She turned it over in her fingers then held it out to me. 'He seemed to be telling the truth as far as I could tell.'

The letter had been written on what had once been good quality paper and was addressed to Alice Gregson in London. It had been superscribed in a different hand *24 December 1736*.

'The date looks very like what I know of Alice's writing,' Mrs Fletcher said.

I unfolded the letter and blinked at the dreadful scrawl that spidered its way across the sheet. The lines were not straight even by comparison with each other; letters sprawled and tangled promiscuously. I could make out only a few words but those words were incriminating: *dearest Alice . . . in your arms . . . your kisses . . . leave . . . morning . . . heart aches . . . dear love . . .* The letter was signed with a single initial which might have been T or I or J or F or even, at a pinch, S.

'A love letter,' I said, refolding it.

'It's reprehensible,' she said tartly, drawing her cloak more tightly against the last flakes of snow. 'But then Alice was always easily led.'

'You've no notion who the sender might be?'

'None. But you must see this supports my contention that there was a man involved. A lover. He must have followed her north.'

'I thought you believed Alice fled from a burglar.'

'A burglar she may herself have let into the house! Perhaps they plotted together to rob my father. If this man knows the town better than she does, that would explain why they can't be found. You must see that I'm right! Alice did not commit this crime.'

I held the letter out to her; she took it back with a set face. I said, 'Rest assured that if there *was* someone else involved in this affair, I will find him. There's no point in hanging the wrong person and leaving the real killer running free.'

She contemplated me for a moment longer, then, as was her habit, walked away into the street without a further word.

I found it odd she should plainly have such a low opinion of her sister, yet still refuse to believe her guilty. But I couldn't deny that both the letter and my own experience of the previous day were inclining me to think she was right.

Twelve

The English are never in error. At least, that's what they tell me.

[Letter from Louis de Glabre to his friend Philippe Froidevaux, 19 January 1737]

When I went back into the inn, Hugh was asking questions about the practical aspects of the Assembly Room design: where was the supper room, the withdrawing rooms? How many sets would the room accommodate? Heron was still staring out of the window.

He said, 'I believe it has stopped snowing. We should look at the site.'

I thought it would have been much more convenient if Heron

had come on the expedition yesterday. Hugh went amiably enough, however, and Balfour, in his boyish enthusiasm of the morning, was happy for any jaunt. Heron, in any case, brooked no opposition and strode before us out of the room, waving away the servant who came to enquire if he wanted his carriage. 'Nonsense – we can easily walk!'

I tagged along, irritable and cold but resigned; there's no resisting Heron when he's in a mood like this.

Only two or three streets separated us from the Groat Market site and we were quickly there. Heron leant precariously on the fence, looking down into the snow-covered ruins. There was a mess of footprints down there, mostly covered by the snow that had recently fallen, but the jumbled timbers had obviously been turned over again recently in search of fuel. The tavern next door was probably extremely warm, which was more than I was.

Balfour started to talk about the plans; Heron interrupted him unceremoniously, looking at Hugh. 'Where did you find the ring?'

I huddled in my greatcoat while Hugh pointed out the place. A few flakes of snow drifted down again. 'Just under the bank on the far side,' Hugh said. 'Some of the earth must have collapsed and the ring slid down with it.'

Heron pulled one of the horizontal bars on the fence free. 'I don't think this is safe,' I said in alarm. He gave not the slightest sign of having heard me, he stepped over the remaining horizontal bar, stood for a moment looking at the ramp of snow that led down into the ruins, then decisively started down. Hugh, grinning, followed. Balfour jumped down after them.

I sighed. I ought to have realized Hugh's find would appeal to the collector in Heron. They were engaged in a treasure hunt now, and that sort of thing had never appealed to me. Who wants to dig around in snow-covered ground for dirty bits of ancient jewellery?

I sensed movement, looked around. In the snow-covered alley that ran along the back of the ruins was a woman, cloaked and hooded. The cloak was pulled tightly around her and I could see nothing of her features. She reminded me of the woman I'd seen in the other world, although she wasn't as tall. She gave a little flounce and turned away. I saw an elegant foot beneath her cloak, a hint of a thin white petticoat. A glimpse of improbably bright yellow hair.

'Alice!' I said sharply.

Devil take it, the empty site lay between us with its cellar pit and protecting fences – I'd have to go round the end of the street. By the time I'd done that, she'd be well away. She cast a look back over her shoulder; I saw her face, almost childishly young, impish, mischievous. She danced round to face me, retreating step by step. 'Catch me!' she called, and, turning, ran lightly off.

I bolted for the end of the street, found a passageway down the side of the tavern, raced out again into the alley. In the ruins, no one was taking the slightest bit of notice; they were all hunkered down, prodding at the frozen soil. Alice was at the far end of the alley, just turning into another. She seemed to taunt me, waiting at the corner until I came within reach. A sudden piercing cold stabbed through me; the woman's figure shimmered and flickered. Then she was gone.

She'd *stepped through* to the other world.

I had to react quickly; because of the difference in pace between the two worlds, a moment's hesitation might leave me minutes or more behind her. I took a deep breath and a step forward, felt cold stab, saw darkness flicker. Then I was staring at the same alley in that other world. Close by, a horse whinnied from what seemed to be stables.

Alice was already gone. And in the snow was scrawled a single word in huge letters: WRONG.

I stared at the letters. *What* was wrong? Did she mean she wasn't Alice? Or that she wasn't the killer? Did she mean my surmises about what had happened were wrong? How could she know what those surmises were? Devil take her – why did she have to be so enigmatic!

I looked about but there was no sign of her and I had no time to spare. I needed to get back to my own world. I concentrated on thinking of Hugh and Heron pottering in the ruins, took a step back, felt a wave of cold and darkness . . .

Heron was still poking at the frozen earth with what looked like a charred stick. Hugh glanced round, was obviously surprised to see I'd moved to the other side of the site. He got up and came across, held something up. I bent to peer at it. 'What is it?'

'Come on, Charles! It may be filthy and tarnished, but isn't it obvious?'

I took the small object off his palm, rubbed the earth away. The object was flat, and almost, but not quite, circular. A gleam of brightness showed through the dirt. And the curve of a distinctive hairline . . . A *coin*.

'Silver,' Hugh said. 'And there are a lot more like it in that earth bank. Someone must have buried his worldly wealth there centuries ago, to keep it safe, and never got back to retrieve it. Heron says they're Roman.'

'Roman?' I echoed. The coin Alice had dropped in the snow had been just like this – that hairline was unmistakeable. How could Alice have been in possession of a Roman coin?

I felt a sudden longing to talk to Esther. She has a calm way of looking at things that encourages me to be logical and methodical. Hugh was looking up at me expectantly; I handed him back the coin. 'Very nice,' I said. He looked indignant. Damn the thief that had taken the other coin from my pocket! Without it, I couldn't prove the two were the same. 'I must go. I've a lesson to give.'

Heron, for some mysterious reason, heard that. He glanced up, rose and picked his way across to me. Balfour took over digging in the frozen earth.

'Come up to the house tomorrow,' Heron said. 'We will have a look at these coins in more detail.'

I couldn't conceive why he should think I'd be interested. But Balfour was calling out he'd found some pottery, and Heron turned on his heel and went back. Hugh gave me a grin. 'Well, you've got to admit they're interesting, Charles!' He leant closer confidentially. 'Even if not *quite* as interesting as Heron thinks. And the only other thing I have to do today is to polish the dancing room floor!'

'Polishing the floor would at least have the virtue of being in the warm,' I retorted.

I left them before Heron could decide to enlighten me further on his finds, cut back to St Nicholas's church and thence along Westgate towards Caroline Square. All this exercise had made me hungry; I could snatch a bite to eat at home, talk to Esther, and still be in plenty of time for my afternoon lessons.

I passed St John's church and came level with the vicarage garden. Idle flakes of snow fell on to the dark sleeves of my greatcoat. Tonight the Gregsons' spirits ought to disembody; it was unlikely they'd have much to say about their deaths given they'd been asleep but they might be able to enlighten us as to Alice's motives, or might have seen her with a man they didn't know. At least one thing was now certain; Alice *was* hiding in that other world. Though why she should risk returning, I didn't understand.

Someone seized hold of my arm.

Thirteen

Every English person you meet wants to tell you their life history; I have found it best just to doze during these recitals – any attempt to divert them is perfectly useless.

[Letter from Louis de Glabre to his friend Philippe Froidevaux, 19 January 1737]

Not again! I swung round, raising my fist – and looked into the furious face of Fowler, Heron's manservant.

'Damn you to hell, Patterson,' he said, gripping my arm like steel. 'You're avoiding me!'

'*Avoiding* you?' I remembered him hovering in the hallway at Heron's house that morning; he'd had no reason to be there. Unless . . . 'You want to talk to me?'

He was in a savage mood. Fowler has never used the deferential servant's tone with me, but this was worse than usual. His lean sardonic face was white. 'Damn it, you can't even catch a slip of a girl!'

His grip on my arm was bruising; I said, as calmly as I could, 'I have been trying to find Alice Gregson, I promise you that. What's your interest in the matter?'

His face worked as he struggled to control his anger. Fowler was once a ruffian in the back streets of London and there's a part of him, under the surface civilization, that remains a ruffian. 'Ned,' he said thickly.

'Ned?'

'Edward Hills.' He looked impatient at my obtuseness. 'The apprentice! Slaughtered by that bitch while he lay asleep on his bed. The boy who'd only spoken to her twice and then only to say *yes, madam, no, madam*. The boy who never said a word against her and certainly never made any advances to her!'

I knew what that meant. Fowler leant forward and hissed in my face. 'She killed him, Patterson. She slaughtered an innocent boy and I want her. And if you've any sense, you'll not ask what I intend to do to her.'

I glanced up and down Westgate. The street was quieter than normal but there were still people within earshot. 'We need to find somewhere private to discuss this.'

I pulled my arm out of his grip; he let me go, his lean face twisting in derision. 'That's right, Patterson. Hide me in a corner somewhere, hide *Ned*.'

'You know I don't care about *that*.'

'He was just a boy,' he said bitterly, changing tack because he knew what I said was true. 'An apprentice. You know what apprentices are like – you know what roughs and toughs they are. Nothing like Samuel Gregson, a respected citizen with his business and his money, or his wife, with her hair and her clothes and nothing in her head. Good upstanding citizens, both! Mustn't let anyone get away with hurting *them*. But who cares about an apprentice?'

I hauled him into the nearest tavern, on the other side of the street. It wasn't the smartest of places but a huge fire was roaring in the grate and the straw on the floor was reasonably clean. I pushed Fowler on to a bench in a quiet corner and signalled for beer. He was losing some of the first flush of anger; he put his head back against the wall and swore at a spirit who came across to chat. I said, 'Just found out his wife has been *entertaining* the neighbour,' and the spirit chortled and withdrew.

Fowler's thin mouth twisted in derision. 'Not likely *that* will happen, is it?'

I've been acquainted with Fowler about a year now, and known his secret almost from the first. No woman is likely to find herself marrying him; his tastes run in entirely another direction. It's not information he gives out freely, given it could get him hanged. I've never considered it any of my business, any more than my marriage is any of his.

But the boy's death *was* my business. I said in a deliberately mild tone, 'Have you known him long?'

He shrugged. His voice was still sharp, his accent aggressively London, but he was calmer now. 'Six months maybe. Damn it, Patterson, he was seventeen years old – did his tasks well, never answered his master back. Trustworthy, honest and lighthearted. He talked of having his own shop. And all that taken away by a girl who never gave him the time of day! Why? Damn it, *why?*'

'I don't know,' I admitted. 'There was money involved but not enough to warrant killing four people.'

'Money? In the house?'

I nodded.

'That was something new, then.'

The landlord brought a jug of beer and two tankards. I paid him and poured it out. The spirit had joined two or three others singing in a corner – there are always drunken spirits in taverns; I was glad of the noise that covered our conversation. 'Did Gregson not keep much there, then?'

'Hardly anything, according to Ned. Just enough to pay his bills. The rest he invested.' Fowler bared his teeth at me. 'Heron has most of it – good investment, Heron. All that coal, all those ships. Gives four and a half per cent on every pound invested with him, just like government stocks!'

He was in the mood to mock everything and everyone, I perceived; Heron's the only man who's ever gained his loyalty and Fowler usually won't hear a word against him. Years ago, during that disreputable period in London, Fowler took it into his head to rob a mild-looking, slight gentleman. When he found himself at Heron's swordpoint, he must have expected a hempen end to his career, but Heron somehow saw possibilities in him that no one else ever did, and offered him an unlikely life as a manservant. It would be wrong to say Fowler has led a blameless life since, but his crimes have been small ones, and discreet. As far as I know.

'Did you ever meet Alice?'

'Saw her once in the shop while I was waiting for Ned. A wishy-washy little thing, with yellow curls. Dressed up as if she was going to a ball – I've seen countesses in London dressed simpler. Wide hoops, material worth a fortune over them. Lace and ribbons on her petticoats, and jewels on her shoes.'

He drank beer, poured more. With any other man, I'd have worried but Fowler knows how to hold his drink. 'Her father came in and said *Go and talk to your mother, Alice. She's got work for you to do.'*

'And did she go?'

'She turned to Ned, and said *Don't stand there being lazy, boy. Get me my cloak – I'm going out.'*

Defying her father, scandalizing his customers and insulting a harmless boy all in two sentences. 'And what did you say?'

'Nothing!' he said savagely. 'Nothing, damn it! What *could* I say? What was there to say that wouldn't draw attention to Ned all the more?'

That must have hurt. Fowler's not a man to do nothing. 'And then?'

'Gregson told Ned to serve a customer, took the girl's arm and marched her into the back of the house. Ned told me later there'd been a huge row. Screaming and shouting and swearing.'

'And this was when?'

'Thursday, about noon. Told me all about it Friday night when I saw him.' His mouth twisted. 'The night before he died.'

He took another long draught of the beer. His lean face was less flushed, more weary – he looked as if he'd not slept. Fowler's loyalty is rarely given and never retracted. He'd never have betrayed the boy in any way, and wouldn't let his death go unpunished now. The spirits sang on in their corner; a keelman in yellow waistcoat puffed out acrid clouds of smoke from a long pipe.

'She was always after getting back to London,' Fowler said. 'Ned thought she'd decided to annoy everyone so they'd get exasperated and send her back. Not that there was ever any chance of that.'

'No one left there for her to go to, I take it.'

'There was a brother but he wouldn't have her. Got a wife

and family of his own and she was always arguing with them, or
something of the sort. Besides, the other girl was getting married.'

'Sarah? The youngest daughter?' I was surprised.

He nodded. 'She was the one supposed to stay at home and
care for her parents in their old age. But one of the Baltic
merchants took a fancy to her – he's old but she liked the look
of him. And his money, no doubt,' he added waspishly. 'If she
married, Alice would have to stay at home.'

From what I'd heard of Alice, she'd not have liked that in the
least. I sipped my own beer. It was surprisingly good, and my
estimation of the tavern went up. 'Did she have a lover, do you
think?'

He nodded. This was the old Fowler, in control of himself,
perhaps even a little too much so. 'Ned said she was always on
the look-out for someone. Staring out the windows all the time,
glancing at the clock. She slipped away from the shop more than
once but he couldn't follow, of course, so he didn't know where
she went.'

He finished his beer and I poured more. 'When did you last
see Ned?'

'Saturday night.' Fowler met my gaze. 'If I'd kept him an hour
longer, he'd be alive now.'

'You couldn't have known that.' The spirits roared with laughter
over something the keelman said. 'Did he mention anything about
her demeanour that day?'

'There was another argument. Alice was supposed to take over
from Ned in the shop about noon, so he could have his afternoon
off. Sarah and her mother were shopping, and there was no one
else who could do it. But she went out late morning and never
came back, so Ned was stuck there. I went in to see why he
wasn't leaving the shop, and Gregson was in a foul mood. I made
some excuse about wanting his catalogue for Heron, and got out
quick. Ned said she didn't come back till teatime.'

'Did he know where she'd been?'

He shook his head. 'But she'd had a good time – she went
out all whiny and sullen, and came back insolent and laughing.
Seemed a different girl, he said. She got a message too – she had
three or four of them in the time she was there. Ned took one
from a boy and said he could hardly read the writing.'

I thought of the dreadful scrawl on the note Mrs Fletcher had given me. More and more, I was convinced Alice hadn't been acting on her own.

'She had it in mind all the time, didn't she?' Fowler said savagely. 'She was planning to kill them all from the moment she got here.'

I wasn't prepared to go that far. I sipped my beer. '*Something* was certainly planned. Alice probably removed a box of money from the cellar in advance and spent some considerable time knotting together a rope from sheets. But how long it was planned, or *what* was planned, I don't know. Perhaps she – they – only intended to rob the house and something went badly wrong.'

'*I want her,*' Fowler said again. 'And if this lover had something to do with it, I want *him* as well.'

'The killer goes to the Assizes.'

'The devil she does!'

'Heron didn't save your neck in London to have you run it in a noose now!' I said, exasperated. 'She'll not get away, I promise you that.'

As soon as I said it, I knew it was foolish. Alice had not one but two worlds to hide in. But I'd said it now, and I wasn't about to take it back. Fowler was right in one respect: Ned was the least regarded of those who'd died. The others had been respectable, fine upstanding citizens and Ned a mere apprentice, and, worse, an apprentice with a secret most people would regard with abhorrence. But he deserved justice as much as the others.

I finished my beer. 'I must go – I'll be late for my lesson.' No chance of seeing Esther now, I thought ruefully. 'Will you be there tonight, for the disembodiment?'

Fowler nodded. 'He'll be distressed – he'll need me.'

I hesitated. But Fowler didn't need telling to be careful; he'd been living with this secret all his life. I nodded farewell and left him sitting, dark and silent amongst all the jollity of the other customers, reaching for the last of the beer in the jug.

Fourteen

They have no literature of speak of, although they are always speaking of it.

[Letter from Louis de Glabre to his friend Philippe Froidevaux, 19 January 1737]

I spent the afternoon going from one lesson to another, from one giddy girl to another, rebuffing all attempts to drag the details of the murders out of me. Emma Blackett, the fourteen-year-old daughter of a very wealthy family, was typical of the breed. She spread the score out on the harpsichord music stand, wriggled herself comfortable on the stool, raised her hands melodramatically as if to strike the first chord, then looked winningly sideways at me. 'Were you at the inquest yesterday, Mr Patterson?'

'Play the piece at half speed,' I said. 'I want to make sure you get the notes right.'

She pouted and started off at least three times too fast.

'This is an *adagio*,' I pointed out. 'It's supposed to be slow and heartfelt.'

She fluttered her eyelashes at me. 'Was *that girl* so dreadful?'

'Very. Now . . .'

'She must have found Newcastle very dull after London. I'd love to go to London,' she added wistfully, 'but Mama says it's not suitable for a very young lady.'

'It's very noisy,' I said repressively.

She looked excited. 'Is it? Have you been there?'

A fraught few minutes ensued, while I attempted to redirect her thoughts from parties and balls and shops, to one of Mr Handel's best works. As soon as I'd lured her away from thinking of London, she was back on the subject of Alice Gregson. 'She can't be as bad as they say! She couldn't have killed *all* those people!'

Gossip had clearly given her a mistakenly glamorous view of Alice.

After an afternoon of conversations of this sort, I staggered back home, longing for peace and quiet. I could easily escape the starry-eyed curiosity of adolescent girls, but I couldn't escape the confusion of my own thoughts. I had to go out again for the disembodiment of the Gregson spirits too, and the thin snow was falling with more determination – a bad night to wait in an unheated house.

Esther was browsing through the latest edition of *The Ladies' Magazine* in the drawing room and looking bored. 'I was too tired to make the accounts add up,' she admitted, 'and the *Ladies' Magazine* is not what it once was.' She was pale again; I frowned and was about to comment, when she put her hand on my arm and said severely, 'Dinner, Charles, or the cook will leave!'

If anyone was running the risk of offending the cook, it was Esther. She picked listlessly though the fish and meat, although she attacked a syllabub with some relish. Which was odd; she was not usually fond of sweet things.

She hardly let me finish my soup before she murmured, 'So what have you found out?'

I could hardly tell her about Fowler but I did regale her with his tales of Alice's behaviour, saying merely I'd had them on reliable authority. When I'd finished, Esther said, 'So you are no longer sure Alice killed them?'

'There was certainly a lover.'

'A man would have the necessary detachment to kill.'

'Detachment?'

'It must be easier to kill someone you do not know. To kill the parents who bore you, the family that gave you life, is entirely a different matter.'

I helped myself to meat and bread; the bread was still deliciously warm. 'But Alice hardly knew them. They can't have seemed like family to her.'

She shook her head. I thought of the insolent, mischievous girl I'd seen today; could I imagine her killing her family, and in such a brutal way?

I had to force myself to leave the warmth of the house an hour or so later and the cold was deep in my bones long before I reached the bridge. A swirling shower of snow came out of the heavens as I climbed the slope towards the shop. I'd anticipated the only people there would be myself and Abraham McLintoch, with perhaps one or two of the other watchmen as support. There's nothing dramatic about these events; spirits generally disembody silently, often unseen – one moment there's nothing, the next you become aware of a faint gleam somewhere in the room, a sense of a presence that wasn't there before.

These spirits would be distressed, of course, and there would be some uncomfortable moments as everything was explained to them. But there was plainly a general expectation of some exciting revelation. There was a huge crowd. All the neighbours had turned out, muffled up in warm clothing; sailors had wandered up from the Key, tankards in hand, and more than one whore was taking the opportunity to drum up some business. The man who sells buttered barley at the Cale Cross had come up in the well-justified hope of customers. And all of them speculating on the story the spirits would tell, relishing the thought of wild arguments, horrible fights and spurting blood . . .

At the back of the crowd, I saw a figure I recognized at once: Fowler, lounging in a doorway on his own. He saw me, curled his lip. I would have liked to speak, but that would only have drawn attention to him, which was decidedly not a good idea.

McLintoch was smoking a pipe in the shelter of the shop doorway; he greeted me with a grimace. 'Reckon we should go in, Mr Patterson, sir. That way we can speak to the spirits private. And it'll be warmer.'

He was wrong. There was the chill of a hundred winters in the house. McLintoch lit a branch of candles and set a couple of the delicate chairs upright; we perched in the oppressive darkness, made worse by McLintoch's acrid pipe smoke, listening to the hubbub of conversation outside. I wondered if there was any way of getting Fowler into the house without drawing suspicion down on him. Probably not.

'Can't properly get my mind round this,' McLintoch said after a long pause, adding conscientiously, 'sir. Don't seem right that a slip of a girl should kill four people. Daresay it comes of her having been in London.'

'There's no news of her?' I was startled by the sound of my own voice in the near darkness.

'We've had the spirits asking,' McLintoch said, 'but they've heard nothing. Not of the girl nor the money. She's left town, sir, I'm sure of it. It weren't too bad weather Sunday morning. She might have got out then.'

We fell silent again. Outside, it seemed to have gone quiet. 'Snowing hard, I warrant you,' McLintoch said imperturbably.

He had a flask of brandy which he generously shared. We sat for two hours, growing colder by the minute, glancing round every so often in case we'd missed the faint gleam of a new spirit. Towards the end of the time, McLintoch began to shiver almost uncontrollably. He was not a young man and occasions like this must try him sorely. A church bell distantly struck; we counted the chimes – two. Outside was only silence.

McLintoch dragged himself out of his chair and stumbled over to the door. He pulled it open and I saw the snow-spattered form of a watchman, looking miserable. Behind him, snow was falling almost as heavily as it had on Saturday night. McLintoch gestured the watchman in.

'Here.' He gave him the flask of brandy. 'Not much left, but you're welcome to what there is. Stay for the rest of the night. There's blankets in the press upstairs to keep you warm. But *don't fall asleep!* And if the spirits disembody, send word to me and Mr Patterson at once. *At once!*'

The watchman, beaming with delight, promised to do everything required; we left him clutching the brandy with a blissful smile.

McLintoch drew the door closed behind him and we stood on the doorstep in the driving snow. The crowd had entirely dissipated and the surrounding houses were dark. I looked about for Fowler; I couldn't see him but I was sure he'd still be there, taking shelter in the small chapel at the end of the bridge, perhaps.

'I'm off to my bed,' McLintoch said. 'Looks like we'll have to wait a while.' He glanced at me; something in my expression must have elicited his sympathy. 'Never you mind, sir,' he said soothingly. 'Spirits who've died a violent death often disembody late. They'll be here by tonight, I warrant you.'

'Yes,' I said. 'Yes, of course.'

It was an unpleasant journey home. Snow drove in my face all the way up Westgate; I put my head down and plodded against it, feeling its cold fingers on my exposed skin. The streets were deserted, and I imagined thieves and robbers in every alley and doorway. I was excessively glad to see the street that led to Caroline Square.

I'd taken a house key with me so I didn't need to disturb the servants, but there was one occupant of the house who never slept; it was waiting for me at the foot of the stairs.

'Master?' George whispered, a bright gleam clinging to the banister. 'It's cold.'

Compared to the weather outside, the house was delightful. 'Go into the kitchen,' I whispered back. 'That'll still be warm.'

'It smells of onions,' the spirit said peevishly. 'There's a note for you.'

The note sat on the hall table, a rectangle of greyish paper with my name neatly written on it, in large childish letters. I felt a sudden surge of excitement.

'Thank you, George.'

'Master . . .'

'Yes?'

There was a little silence; the spirit said in a very small voice, 'I don't mean to annoy you, Master.' The words came out in a rush. 'It's just— I don't like being dead.'

That brought me up short. Thinking of Fowler's Ned. I said, 'I'm sorry too, George. I should have taken greater care of you when you were alive. If I had . . .'

'It was my fault, Master,' he said, sounding as if he was about to cry. 'You told me what to do and what not to, and I didn't take any notice.'

That was true. 'Well,' I said. 'Perhaps we can get on better now.'

'I'd like that, Master,' he said, brightening with mercurial speed. 'You really don't mind me living here?'

'Not if you don't argue with the servants.'

'I'll try, Master!' the spirit said exuberantly and shot off in the direction of the kitchen. I wondered how long this display of contrition would last.

The note was sealed with black wax, of the type one finds in cheap inns. The ink was watery, the words written in that big childlike hand. There was only one sentence; it said:

I did not steal the money.

Fifteen

I forgot to advise you to go to every tea party you are invited to; the conversation will be dull, but the women are well worth looking at.

[Letter from Louis de Glabre to his friend Philippe Froidevaux, 20 January 1737]

Esther was asleep when I crawled into bed and still asleep when I dragged myself out again. I had almost a full day of lessons ahead of me and the disturbed night had left me with a headache and tired eyes. Worse, I found a note on the breakfast table, left there by Esther the previous night; she was visiting Mrs Blackett later that morning and, knowing I taught the Blackett children, wondered if I would be there. The note depressed me hugely. Married only five months and we were already communicating by notes.

It was still snowing, a steady silent fall of heavy flakes that piled up on windowsills and doorsteps, in street corners and hedge bottoms. The snow, almost untrodden in Caroline Square, was crunchy underfoot; flakes trickled through the gaps in my clothing and down my neck. A thick layer of it coated the front of my greatcoat before I was on Westgate.

I had a little time before my first lesson; I turned up the street towards the clockmakers. Carts had traced pale lines down the street but the snow was filling them in again; I slipped crossing to Hugh's rooms but managed not to fall. In the sheltered alley beside the clockmaker's, I stamped my feet clear of the snow and went up the stairs.

The door to the dancing school was shut so I continued up, past the rooms occupied by a widow and her three children, to Hugh's attic room above. The door was ajar; I pushed at it — and stopped in amazement. Bedding was all over the floor, Hugh's clothes were scattered everywhere, his one chair lay overturned. Pages torn from books of dance tunes were crumpled and trampled underfoot.

In the middle of the mess, Hugh stood, hands on hips, glaring.
'What the devil's happened?' I said.

'He's taken the buttons off my coats!' Hugh said outraged.

My gaze went instinctively to a pile of clothes on the floor. I could see at least two coats and a waistcoat, and not a single button on any of them. And I'd have noticed the buttons; Hugh's taste runs to the large and bright.

'Is anything else missing?'

Hugh set the chair upright, sat down on it and stared bleakly at the clothing. 'A little money, the ring I found— Oh God, Charles, my coats!'

He was clearly in mourning. Hugh adores his clothes; they're the only thing he spends his money on.

'I wonder why he didn't take the coats themselves.'

'Couldn't carry them probably,' Hugh said gloomily. There was indeed a large pile, but even one or two would have brought in a fair amount of money at one of the secondhand shops on the Key. 'Do you have any idea how much those buttons cost?'

'And your fiddle? Did he take that?'

'Had it with me.' Hugh sighed. 'I got back very late last night to find the room like this. I couldn't face dealing with it so I slept on a couple of chairs downstairs in the dancing school. Charles, what am I to do? I've a lesson to give in less than an hour and I'll have to wear the same clothes I was in yesterday!'

'You've time to get those coats to the tailor. He can have them mended by this evening.'

'The villain cut the cloth on some of them,' Hugh said, growing ever more morose. 'You'd have thought he'd have taken a bit of care!'

I went back to the door. Raw wood showed where it had been forced.

'It must have been done late,' Hugh said, glumly. 'I was here at eight, getting some music, and it was all right then.'

'Tell the Watch,' I recommended.

He crowed with derision. 'What can those ancient wrecks do?'

'They could keep a lookout for the buttons. The thief will sell them as quickly as possible.'

But he was deep in despair. 'Not worth it.'

There was no arguing with him in this mood; I said, 'Do you want me to help tidy up?'

'No, I'll do it.' But he didn't move.

I left; there was plainly no point in showing him the note from Alice Gregson as I'd planned. Hugh would come around soon; he was rarely low-spirited for long. But woe betide the thief if we ever found him!

Maybe someone had seen something suspicious. Hugh's house is unspirited, so there was no help there, but the widow downstairs might have information. I knocked on her door with some trepidation, knowing she'd not be pleased. She's never pleased to see me.

She made me wait before opening the door, and had an eyebrow raised and ready. Behind her, a boy of ten or so scowled.

'Mr Patterson,' she said coldly. 'I trust you enjoyed your carousing last night.'

How very interesting. 'In Mr Demsey's rooms?' I smiled sweetly, which seemed to infuriate her. 'I wasn't there. Did you see who was?'

'I do not spy on my neighbours, Mr Patterson,' she said. 'And if I *should* see someone disreputable leaving my landlord's rooms, then that is *his* business, not mine. Even if the man is plainly drunk.'

'He fell in the snow,' the boy said censoriously. 'Serves him right.'

'You would do well, Mr Patterson,' his mother said, 'to tell Mr Demsey to be more discerning in the company he keeps.'

I was tempted to tell him to raise her rent.

She shut the door on me before I could ask if she could describe the man.

It was a tedious morning. My mind was still running on the deaths and wondering if I'd get a message at any moment from McLintoch to say the spirits had disembodied, and I found it difficult to concentrate on correcting wrong notes and worse phrasing. At least the snow eased; by early afternoon, when I had time for something to eat, there were merely a few desultory flakes in the air.

I was in the upper reaches of Newgate Street by then, and it was a long walk down to the Sandhill and Nellie's coffee house, but I felt the need for air and exercise.

I strode out, concentrating on my footing to avoid disaster. From Newgate, I cut into the Bigg Market and thence into the Groat Market. And stopped in amazement. A group of workmen with spades and picks were just going down into the pit where the mercer's shop had been, ploughing unhappily through the deep snow. Presiding over them, directing them where to go and what to do, was Claudius Heron. He saw me and waited until I came up with him. He was immaculately dressed as ever; even in warm winter clothing he never looks less than gentlemanly. 'It is unfortunate there has been more snow,' he said, without greeting. 'It has covered up the place where we discovered the coins and pottery yesterday. However, I am hopeful of finding the place again.'

The workmen were hauling themselves over the fallen timbers with the air of men who know that the sooner they get the job started, the sooner they'll get it finished, and be able to go home.

'The ground must be rock solid,' I said. 'We had a week of hard frosts before the snow.'

Heron nodded. 'If necessary, we have the wherewithal to build a small fire. I have been meaning to talk to you. Do you think Demsey will be inclined to sell that ring if I increase my offer?'

I was taken aback. If Heron was willing to offer more than twenty guineas, the ring must be more valuable than I'd suspected. 'I'm afraid the situation doesn't arise. Hugh was burgled last night and the ring was amongst the items stolen.'

Heron looked annoyed. 'It should not have been left at risk. He should have taken more care of it! Nobody seems to understand how valuable these antiquities are. When I spoke to Jenison about digging on his property, he obviously had not the slightest idea of the value of the find – he told me to do as I liked without even wishing to see the coins!'

I left him to do as he liked, which was ordering the workmen around in the cold – to do him justice, he would certainly be paying them well – and repaired to Nellie's coffee house for a quick warming pie before setting off for my afternoon lessons. I didn't think it would do a great deal of good but I asked one of the spirits to take a message to McLintoch telling him about Hugh's burglary and asking him to keep an eye out for the stolen goods.

In mid-afternoon, I found Mrs Blackett entertaining what seemed like half the ladies of Newcastle. Six ladies in total, including Esther, and a spirit hovering on the handle of the tea-kettle; this was, I gathered, the spirit of Mrs Blackett's much-loved elder sister. Every one of them – even the spirit for all I knew – regarded Esther and myself with a dew-eyed romantic gaze. When we married, I was afraid the difference in wealth and status between myself and Esther would cause the ladies to throw up their hands in horror and ostracize us from polite society. Instead, they threw up their hands in delight and welcomed us as prime gossip material. Esther cast me an apologetic smile as I sat down beside her. She was nibbling on some sweetmeat Mrs Blackett had provided for her guests – this sudden taste for sugary things was persisting, it seemed.

There was one lady who did not greet me with enthusiasm, however: Mrs Fletcher. She sat sternly upright at Mrs Blackett's side, an odd contrast: Mrs Fletcher neat and drab and thin, Mrs Blackett comfortably plump and fashionable, and with suspiciously dark curls. Mrs Blackett patted her hand.

'You know Mrs Fletcher, do you not, Mr Patterson? I met her in the bookshop and said at once she must drop in on us any time she liked. Such a dreadful thing.'

'Mrs Blackett has been most gracious,' Mrs Fletcher said.

Mrs Blackett poured a dish of tea and leant across to bestow it on me. 'I knew Sophia Gregson well.'

'The mother,' Esther murmured in my ear.

'A *very* agreeable woman.'

There was a chorus of tales relating Mrs Gregson's generous behaviour. She was apparently close to being a saint.

'I didn't know them at all,' I said. 'Of course Gregson himself had a very good reputation.'

Mrs Fletcher gave me a contemptuous look.

'I met the youngest girl, Sarah,' Esther murmured, 'but not Alice.'

'I was in the shop one day last week when she was very rude to her father.' The lady who spoke was Mrs Cunningham, a thin spare woman with a down-turned mouth. 'Demanded money to buy some bag or other. Said she'd seen it in the mantua makers and was determined to have it. She said if she was going to have to stay in such an out-of-the-way place, she'd at least have the necessities of life to comfort her.'

'Out-of-the-way place!' Mrs Blackett said horrified. '*Newcastle?*' She looked extremely offended. 'This is not Scotland! We have every new thing here as soon as one could wish it.'

'I suppose,' Esther said, 'she must have been annoyed when her father refused her.'

'No such thing,' Mrs Cunningham said, the lines about her mouth deepening. 'He gave her a sovereign straight away and sent her off again. Just to be rid of her, I daresay.'

'But if he gave her the money she wanted,' Esther said, 'I can't understand why she killed him.'

'Children are ungrateful,' Mrs Cunningham said with calm hard certainty. 'There's nothing more certain in this world.'

'My sister was, certainly,' Mrs Fletcher agreed. 'But that doesn't make her a murderer.'

There was a flutter of excitement amongst the ladies. 'In any case—' Mrs Fletcher spoke more loudly to be heard over the hubbub. 'I thought we were agreed, Mr Patterson, that it was an accomplice who carried out the killings.'

There was a great deal of commotion; Mrs Fletcher overrode the ladies' excited exclamations. 'You may not be aware of it, but Mr Patterson was attacked yesterday in the street and the key to my father's house taken. Then the house was ransacked. The villain was plainly looking for anything that might incriminate him.'

The spirit on the tea-kettle shrieked in an attempt to be heard as the ladies asked a dozen questions all at once. Was I all right? Had I been injured? (Oddly enough, it was the hard and unpleasant Mrs Cunningham who asked after my health.) Was anything taken from the house? Had the villain left any clue as to his identity?

'But of course,' Mrs Blackett said, 'I *knew* the daughter couldn't have done it. No daughter could.' She trailed off into silence, and it was obvious she was thinking of her own two daughters.

'No,' Esther said, in an oddly curt tone. 'I don't believe any daughter could.'

'Surely,' Mrs Cunningham said, 'it should be a simple matter to see whether anything was taken from the house? If such things as candlesticks and other valuables have disappeared, then the man was probably a common thief, seizing his opportunity to raid a house he knew would be empty. If they're still there, however, then it would suggest this man was indeed the murderer, revisiting the scene of his dreadful crime.'

'Mrs Fletcher would know if anything was stolen!' Mrs Blackett cried.

The ladies took up the idea with enthusiasm. If they'd had their way, they'd have packed Mrs Fletcher and me off to the Gregson's shop immediately and made a picnic out of it. I remembered I'd meant to contact Armstrong and had not yet done so and said, mendaciously, to put them off, that I thought it was snowing heavily. Some of the ladies immediately got up, frightened they wouldn't be able to get home again. But a servant who came in response to calls for carriages said it wasn't snowing and in fact the sun had come out and it was very pleasant. The ladies subsided again.

'If the murderer was indeed an unknown man,' I said, 'that doesn't completely exonerate Alice. She may have plotted with him to rob her own family, she may have let him into the house. If she was entirely innocent, surely she'd have come forward by now.'

'I believe my sister is innocent of *any* wrongdoing,' Mrs Fletcher said directly. 'I think she's guilty of no more than being fleet-footed enough to escape. Let us consider another possibility.'

The ladies were breathlessly attentive. Esther cast me an uneasy glance.

'The apprentice and the key,' Mrs Fletcher said. 'In fact, the apprentice *is* the key. We all know what such youths are like.' A chorus of agreement; I was glad Fowler wasn't here to hear the contempt in their voices. 'This unknown man was intent on robbing the shop and he suborned the apprentice, persuading the boy to let him into the house. I'm told the key was in the lock inside the house, which is where it would be if the boy let him in. The villain found money but the apprentice was afraid he'd take it all and leave none for him. They argued, and the villain stabbed the boy. Meanwhile, the noise of their argument woke everyone else . . .'

'And he killed them all!' Mrs Blackett cried, in a kind of triumph.

'They tried to prevent his escape!' the sister's spirit squeaked. The ladies broke out in eager embroidery of the facts; in the hubbub, my insistence that the Gregsons were all asleep when they were killed, went unheard.

I glanced at Esther; she was looking very tired. I stood up. 'I believe we must go.'

The ladies protested, but I insisted and Esther rose with a grateful sigh that fortunately went as unheard as my previous protests. But, as we were on the verge of leaving the room, Mrs Fletcher said, 'I have some time spare tonight, Mr Patterson. I would be happy to look over the house with you.'

With the ladies all eagerly supporting the idea, I thought it politic to acquiesce. 'Very well,' I said. 'Tonight.' And we agreed a time.

In the hall, the servant gave us our outdoor clothes and we paused on the doorstep. The sun had indeed come out, sparkling off the drifts of snow.

'I'll call for a chair to carry you home,' I said, looking at Esther's pale face.

She shook her head. 'I need some air, Charles. That room was stuffy.'

I wished I thought that was all it was. 'Let me call the apothecary. Or Gale.'

'I do not need a surgeon!' she snapped. 'Or an apothecary!' She stopped, bit her lip, then laid a hand on my arm. 'Forgive me, Charles. I am merely feeling low. I loathe this dreadful weather.'

She'd seemed to delight in it on Saturday night. 'You're too tired to walk.'

She drew her cloak up over her head. 'I will be all right, Charles, I promise you. I will walk up Westgate so that if I feel tired I can call in on Mr Demsey for a rest.'

I had to let her go – it was plain she'd settle for nothing less. But I was worried as I watched her walk away. She'd seemed all right when I arrived in the drawing room. Something had distressed her, something that had been said – but I couldn't for the life of me think what.

Sixteen

The public buildings, I must say, are generally very attractive,
but they have their slums, just as we do.
[Letter from Louis de Glabre to his friend Philippe
Froidevaux, 20 January 1737]

I found a spirit to take a request to Armstrong and was about to
walk off to my next lesson when it called me back hurriedly.
The spirit had plainly been a young man in life, rough but good-
natured. 'Message for you from Mr McLintoch. Could he have
the honour of your company on the bridge, he says.' The spirit
positively twinkled. 'Polite man, Mr McLintoch. Always mindful
of his manners!' And with a flourish, it shot off.

I altered direction and was with McLintoch on the bridge in
five minutes. He was wearing an ancient greatcoat that looked
held together with goodwill, and saluted me as if I was a naval
commander. 'Mr Patterson, sir!'

'The spirits have disembodied?'

'No, sir.' He must have seen my disappointment; he made an
obvious attempt to try and cheer me up. 'We've found where
the girl hid, when she fled from the house.' He gestured along the
Key. 'Out to the west. Did you want to look, sir?'

Even this was a disappointment, I thought wryly: they'd found
the place but not the girl herself.

I fell into step beside him as he led the way along the riverside,
following the route I'd taken the night of the murders in pursuit of
the girl. We passed the snowy ruins of the town wall and came
to the alley where the woman's spirit had brought me to a halt with
her cries of *rape*. There was no spirit in evidence this time. McLintoch
led me into the alley, bore left then right. We walked into a court,
narrow and evil-smelling, with undisturbed snow on the cobbles.
Three houses faced on to the court and all looked derelict – windows
broken or boarded-up, doors hanging askew on twisted hinges.

'No one's lived here since we cleared out a nest of thieves

last year,' McLintoch said. 'We've a spirit who keeps an eye on it for us.' He raised his voice. 'I wants a word with you, young lady!'

There was a pause, then a spirit slid down to a window pane at eye level.

'Now, young lady,' McLintoch said, winking at me. 'Tell the gentleman here what happened last Saturday night.'

'Don't know why I should,' the spirit said sullenly. I stared at the dull gleam; it was the spirit I'd spoken to on the night of the murders.

'We're trying to find who killed Mr Gregson and his family,' McLintoch said. 'That's a good thing, don't you think?'

Apparently the spirit didn't agree. It was silent.

'You see, Mr Patterson,' McLintoch said, conversationally. 'We have a network of spirits throughout the town. Good law-abiding folks who let us know if any malefactors are working their wicked ways. Couldn't manage without them.'

This blatant flattery had its effect; the spirit said, a trifle coyly, 'If *you* would like it, Mr McLintoch, I dare say I don't mind saying something.'

'The night the Gregsons died,' he said. 'Tell us what happened.'

'Came running in here like the devil was after her, she did,' the spirit said. 'Hair about her shoulders and wearing only her nightgown under her shawl!'

'Young female, was it?' McLintoch said. 'Pretty?'

The spirit sniffed. 'If you like them fair.'

'Anyone with her?'

'No, Mr McLintoch.'

'What did she do?'

'She found herself a corner and stayed there the rest of the night.'

'When did she leave?' I asked.

'Didn't see,' the spirit snapped.

'Sunday, was it?' McLintoch said.

'Might have been.'

'What time Sunday?'

'Didn't see.'

I glanced at McLintoch but he apparently thought that was as far as he could persuade the spirit to go. 'Let's have a look at the place then,' he said.

The spirit glided off its windowpane, and made its way towards the end house, disappearing through a gap in the broken-down door. McLintoch had come prepared; he dragged a couple of candle stubs and a tinder box out of his pocket.

I held the stubs while he lit them, wondering why the spirit was lying. I'd seen the girl when she fled the house and she'd been wearing not a shawl but a cloak. Nor had she been wearing a nightgown. Nightgowns are flimsy and white in colour; the girl had been wearing something dark and substantial. And, now I came to consider, her hair had been up, neatly arranged. More evidence against her – a woman fleeing in panic doesn't have time to put her hair up.

I must have been very close to catching the girl that night and the spirit's intervention looked more suspicious with every moment.

We came into a damp, dank, stinking darkness. I paused to let my eyes adjust to the gloom. The room was bare except for dirt and dust, and a pile of rags in the corner furthest from the window. A stick was propped against the wall; I used it to prod the rags. A stench of decay rose.

'She slept here?'

The spirit didn't answer. McLintoch asked the question again.

'Yes, sir,' the spirit agreed.

'Did the girl bring anything with her? A box or bag or blanket?' McLintoch dutifully repeated the question.

'Nothing at all, Mr McLintoch.'

'Did she say why she was here?'

With a little encouragement from McLintoch, the spirit said she'd thought it an elopement.

'But you must have heard about the murders,' I said, trying not to sound confrontational. 'I know how quick and clever you spirits are when it comes to passing messages.'

'I was otherwise occupied,' she said with great dignity, and apparently could not resist adding, 'There are always some *gentlemen* who like to pester spirits. You'd think they'd have some respect for the dead, but no, they come blundering in and bother good, god-fearing folks . . .'

'Now don't you get yourself in a fash,' McLintoch said soothingly.

'I don't shelter murderers,' the spirit said indignantly. 'I don't have nothing to do with people of that sort. I always was on the right side of the law. *You* know that, Mr McLintoch.'

McLintoch gave me a speaking look.

'I never knew nothing about the girl being the one from the bridge until the Watch came and told me.'

I couldn't understand why she thought I'd believe this. Every spirit in town would have had the news of the murders within minutes of the child screaming.

'You've not found anyone else who saw her here?' I asked McLintoch.

He shook his head.

'And there's no word of her after she left here?'

'Nay. Nothing.'

McLintoch went through a great charade of wishing the spirit well, and flattering her, leaving her giggling. We threaded our way through the narrow alleys; as we came out on to the Key again, McLintoch said, 'I've been hearing of a fellow from Kent who might have come north. Robs big houses. He woos the maids and gets them to let him in. After he's had his way with them, he robs the house and is off, leaving them to face the music next morning.'

I shook my head. 'The Gregsons had no maid – the women did all the work themselves.'

'Aye,' McLintoch said with a grimace. 'Saves money that way. I wasn't so much thinking he might have robbed the Gregsons. Unless he persuaded the apprentice to give him the keys.'

So that story was already halfway round town was it? I remembered the spirit sitting on Mrs Blackett's tea-kettle and suspected she'd found the idea too good to miss passing on.

'If this fellow's in town,' McLintoch pursued, 'he's no doubt looking at all the rich houses. You'd do well to have a word with your maids, sir, just to put them on their guard. You know the womenfolk can never resist a smooth tongue.'

He'd just proved his point, with the spirit, but I defy anyone to cross swords with either of the maids in our house. They're young and attractive, but have minds of their own, and clever minds at that. It gave me an odd feeling, however, to be the recipient of advice like this; five months ago I was a jobbing musician living on around sixty pounds a year, now I'm a gentleman with a smart house, servants and an income too large to think about without getting indigestion. And, apparently, robbers are queuing up to plunder me.

'Oh, and will you tell Mr Demsey we've found his buttons,' McLintoch added. 'Some lads picked them up in the Lort Burn. Looks like the thief dropped them off the Low Bridge.'

I stared at him. 'He threw them away?'

'Probably thought they weren't worth keeping.'

I wasn't going to tell Hugh that – it would only add insult to injury. 'What about the money, and the ring?'

'Not found those,' McLintoch said cheerfully. 'Stands to reason the money won't turn up and the ring's probably on the finger of some whore at the Old Man Inn by now.'

I was going to be very late for my next lesson; I thanked him and hurried off. He was wrong about the ring. When I had glimpsed it the night I was attacked, it had been cleaned up but was still very tarnished. I doubted any whore would think it worth having.

I spent a tedious couple of hours listening to more young ladies cultivating the arts in the hope of attracting good husbands. It was difficult not to be distracted by thoughts of Alice Gregson and her unknown lover. I kept thinking of Esther too; I hated parting from her on bad terms. Surely she could see I had a right to be concerned about her health. Was there time to get back home? Would she not just be *more* irritated if I dashed back to check up on her? Damn it, what was I supposed to do?

I had a message from Armstrong after my third lesson, agreeing to my allowing Mrs Fletcher in the Gregsons' house on condition I took 'great care to ensure she touched nothing and took nothing out of the house'. A suspicious man, Armstrong – he's seen too much. By this time, I was ravenous. My next pupil lived on Butcher Bank and that put me in mind of the seller of buttered barley at the Cale Cross, which stands at the foot of the bank.

The sun was lowering rapidly in the sky and gleamed in my eyes all the way down the street to the Cross, dazzling me. A cart loomed out of the glare as I started to cross the road; I jerked back to safety, and bumped into someone who had come up on me from behind. I turned to apologize – and saw Joseph Kane.

He stood looking at me, his handsome face torn between a leer and a smile. 'Charlie Patterson,' he said, in what was plainly a deliberate attempt to bring me down to size. His southern accent was very pronounced. 'You've gone up in the world.' His gaze played over my clothes. 'I remember the fellow who didn't have a shilling to pay for me taking care of him on board ship.'

Kane's taking care of me had consisted largely in leaving me alone. I said carelessly, 'Would you care for it now?'

He flushed. His own clothes suggested he was not particularly poor, but not particularly well-off either, and he certainly didn't like me playing the wealthy gentleman with him. I didn't particularly like myself at that moment either.

'I heard you'd married money,' he said, not troubling himself to hide his contempt. 'And that you fancy yourself a fine upholder of law and justice.'

I didn't see why I should occupy my time trading insults with a man I disliked and who plainly despised me. I said, 'I'm sorry, I have a lesson to give,' and turned away.

'I need your help,' he said angrily.

I turned back and looked at him. He was stony-faced.

'You want to find a murderer,' he said, 'and so do I. And I think we're looking for the same fellow.'

Seventeen

Find yourself one of the young men about town, Philippe – he will show you where all the best entertainment is – the cock-fighting, bear-baiting, &c.
[Letter from Louis de Glabre to his friend Philippe Froidevaux, 20 January 1737]

I abandoned the thought of buttered barley and took Kane to the coffee house where I could find a spirit to send a message warning my next pupil I'd be delayed. Trying to juggle lessons and this investigation was beginning to be well-nigh impossible. Luckily, tomorrow should be easier; I usually teach in the country on Thursdays and in this weather I'd not be able to get out of town. The town was virtually snow-bound, which at least meant the murderer couldn't leave either.

Kane looked around the coffee house contemptuously. 'Fine lot of gentlemen in here.' He threw himself down into a seat by the window, pre-empting an elderly man who was making his slow way towards it. The gentleman stopped dead, with a look of baffled fury.

I told the girl to bring coffee and game pie; Kane declined the pie and asked for beer. 'I'm a plain man,' he said, sneering. 'I like plain food.'

There was no point in getting angry with him; that was what he wanted. I sat down opposite. 'Who's this fellow you are looking for?'

'A fellow from Rochester in Kent, by the name of Thomas Hitchings.' Kane gave a direct and insulting stare to a merchant who was talking too loudly about his latest deal. 'Does he think the whole world wants to know how clever he is?'

I thought that very probable. 'What's this man done?'

'Made himself plenty of money. Poses as an exciseman and makes up to the maids in the big houses. Then they let him in for a roll in the hay and when they're sleeping he helps himself to the candlesticks and jewellery.'

This began to sound familiar; I said, 'You've talked to the Watch about this.'

'Spoke to a Scotch fellow – ex sailor, *he says*.' Those last words were dripping with disbelief, which was unfair to McLintoch, who'd sailed on the coal boats more years than I'd been alive. Kane ignored the serving girl who brought our food and drink. 'He said to see you. He says you're the one *as knows about these things*.'

'I'm taking an interest in the Gregson murders, certainly. It doesn't sound like your man was involved. The Gregsons had no maid and not much was taken. The inquest decided the daughter killed them.'

Kane downed beer in a long draught. He snorted derisively. 'A girl? Stabbing a grown man? Never! My man's killed before. Twice. Householders who had the audacity to try and stop him.'

'Newcastle's a long way from Kent. What makes you think he's here?'

'The last killing made the county too hot – everyone was looking out for him. He went up to London, got on a coal boat. That was two, three, weeks back. I found traces of him in Whitby – he hired a horse there, rode north. He's here all right.'

'If I were him, I'd be trying to get a boat out to the Colonies,' I said. 'Start again where no one knows him.'

'Hitchings is too sure of himself to do that.' Kane poured more beer. 'Taunt the law and get away with it, that's the game he's playing. But no one gets the better of me.'

I cradled the coffee dish in my hands, watching him. I'd forgotten quite how obnoxious he was. 'What's your interest in finding him?'

'Money.' He sneered. 'The man he shot has a brother who wants a rope round his neck and he's paying me to put it there.' So Kane had left the sea and turned to thief-taking. He put the tankard down with a snap. 'And I ain't having no interference from gentlemen like you, Patterson. You're doing this for the fun of it. I'm doing it to keep food in my stomach and a roof over my head. No interference!'

If he went on this way, he'd get no cooperation either. I said, 'What does this man look like?'

'The sort of fellow who appeals to the ladies.' I presumed he meant the man was young and handsome, and was startled when he went on. 'Rough-looking, big, strong. Not the prettiest of fellows but he's full of charm, sweet words and big talk.'

'His age?'

'Middling. There's a groom who saw him clearly. Taller than you, much taller, dark hair and eyes.'

'He doesn't sound the sort that could pass as an excise man. They're usually more gentlemanly.'

'He can put on an educated voice when he chooses.'

'But he's definitely not a gentleman himself?'

'Born in the gutter. Mother a whore. He's here, Patterson, I *know* he is, and the way this snow's come down, he won't be able to get out. I have him and I'm not letting him slip through my fingers!'

I said placatingly, 'I've no wish to stand in your way. But

I'm far from certain your man was involved in the Gregsons' deaths.'

He leant forward. 'It bears all his hallmarks!'

I shook my head. 'I do suspect there were two people involved but your man doesn't sound the sort to appeal to a young delicately reared society miss.' Or perhaps he might have; he'd be well out of Alice's experience. He might have attracted her by his air of danger. Roughness has a power of its own.

'That Watch fellow says there've been suspicious characters hanging around, and they say you was robbed and the murder house ransacked last night.'

'Monday night.'

'That was my man! Out for the valuables he left behind. Come on, Patterson!' he said impatiently. 'He took the key from you – that's the way he does it. So he can lock himself in and no one outside the wiser.'

He had a point. I was not convinced, but it could do no harm to keep an open mind. I wondered if Fowler might know something of this Kentish fellow – he has contacts in the rougher parts of town. I was not about to give his name to Kane, however; I said, 'I can recommend places where men like him might go . . .'

'I've tried the taverns,' Kane said. 'I haven't been wasting my time, you know, waiting on your lordship's favour.'

He really was abominable. 'Including the Old Man Inn on the Key? And the chares behind the inn are a hotbed of crime – if he's hiding anywhere, he'll be in there.'

'I want to know everything as happens,' Kane said, without troubling himself to thank me for my advice. 'As soon as you know, *I* want to know.' He drained his beer and stood up, knocking the chair back into that of the gentleman behind him and taking no notice of his protests. 'And once we've got our hands on him, I'm taking him back to Kent. He'll hang there.'

He walked out, treading on someone's foot on his way.

More lessons. More pupils who hadn't practised since the last time I saw them, but swore they'd assiduously sat at the harpsichord for hours; malicious fate guaranteed I had none of my good pupils that day. I wondered how reliable Kane's story was, whether a flighty young girl would have fallen for an older, tougher man, whether Esther was feeling better. If only I could get home.

But I'd promised to meet Mrs Fletcher and in the gloom of the early winter evening, I walked along the Key, shivering in the piercing cold despite my greatcoat. No one was lingering for long in the open; even the whores were indoors. On the bridge, the snow had been worn down, the cobbles showing through; a frost was settling and making the cobbles treacherously slippery. Mrs Fletcher, wrapped up in a thick cloak, was pacing about the road; she said with a lift of her chin, 'You're late, sir.'

I wasn't going to argue with her. 'Business.'

The watchman at the door of the shop was yawning. 'No sign of them spirits yet, sir. Reckon they'll come tonight. When they're killed violent, they always come at night.'

I unlocked the shop, and lit the candles on the shelf beside the door. They were very short now, one of them little more than a stub; I hunted behind the counter and found a box of new candles, lit them from the old.

Mrs Fletcher had followed me in; I looked up to see her very still in the middle of the room. She shivered. 'It's cold.' She didn't sound her usual self; she was subdued and obviously unnerved. 'I can feel the dead,' she said. 'Like a heavy weight.'

I hadn't expected anything of that kind from her; she seemed too prosaic a woman for such fancyings. She walked round the counter to stare at the stained mattress that still lay there, and the dark marks on the floorboards. 'We all do things we later regret, do we not? Do you think the killer is regretting this even now?'

'I don't have the least idea.'

'Or perhaps,' she said, more lightly, 'he's even now delighting in getting away without anyone suspecting him.'

I let the pronoun pass without comment. 'The spirits may know something.' Despite myself, I shuddered. 'It feels almost as if there's a thunderstorm in the offing.'

She strolled about the room, fingering pictures on the wall, setting an overturned chair upright. 'I can't tell if anything is missing from the shop but I suppose my father must have kept records of everything here. Of course, the apprentice may have altered them.'

Past time to dispose of that theory. 'I don't think the apprentice had anything to do with the killings,' I said bluntly. 'He was an innocent victim.'

'Oh, no, Mr Patterson.' She bestowed a mocking smile on me. 'We're none of us innocent.'

We climbed the stairs to the drawing room, the candles casting dancing shadows before us. The child's bloody footprints could still be seen on the steps. Mrs Fletcher went to the mantelshelf above the fire, lifted down another branch of candles and lit them from mine. I watched her intent face as she went about the task; I said, 'The apprentice didn't let the killer in. He was asleep, and died in his sleep. *All* the family were asleep – they were no threat. Whoever killed them – Alice, her lover or an unknown third party – it was an unnecessary act. There's only one conclusion to be drawn: the killer *wanted* to kill them. Which means that any robbery was purely incidental.'

Mrs Fletcher set the extra branch of candles on a table so she could look about the room more easily. She said, almost indifferently, 'I disagree. It doesn't matter what the true state of affairs was, Mr Patterson – the family may have been no threat, but the murderer may have *thought* them one.'

'I don't see how he, or she, could have.'

She worked her way methodically around the room, looking at pictures, fingering ornaments. 'I hear from the spirits,' she said, 'that you've found the place Alice was hiding.'

I nodded. 'A derelict house not far off the Key. She doesn't seem to have stayed there long, and where she went after that I've no idea.'

'She's frightened, I suppose,' she said. 'I can see nothing missing here. Shall we go up to the bedrooms?'

We did so. Mrs Fletcher hesitated on the landing then went into the girls' room first. 'Do you sleep in a room like this, Mr Patterson?'

I was startled.

'No,' she said, 'I thought not. Something rather bigger and more comfortable, I should think. That's what Alice was used to in London. Is it any surprise she hated coming back here?'

She picked up the scattered clothes from the floor, started to fold them, brushing off the clinging feathers. 'I've always had mixed feelings about Alice,' she said. 'She's a winning little thing that can charm you to her side in moments, but underneath that charm is a selfish, calculating girl.' She glanced up at me. 'That's a warning, Mr Patterson. Nevertheless, I don't believe I should condemn her for a crime she didn't commit.'

She laid a shawl on the ruined mattress, opened a chest and looked down at the contents. 'I'm sure Sarah had a necklace – nothing very valuable – but it was given to her by an aunt. A chain, blue stones in a star shape. I thought she kept it in here.' She turned over a few clothes.

'She certainly wasn't wearing it.'

She closed the chest, walked past me back on to the landing and into her parents' room. Here she stared at the bloodstained bed; I saw her mouth twist slightly. 'They didn't suffer,' she said.

'They would have known nothing,' I agreed.

Her mouth twitched; remembering what she had said about her father previously, I wondered whether she thought that necessarily a good thing. Surely she could not be as unforgiving as that? She went about her search of the room in a businesslike fashion, going through her mother's clothes, her father's shirts, shifting the coins and the medicinal powders on the bedside table, and even shaking the Bible that lay beside the coins, as if she thought something might be hidden inside. 'There's certainly some jewellery missing. Some pieces left to my mother by my grandmother.'

'Can you describe them? We could see if anyone in the town has been offered them for sale.'

She nodded. 'By all means. I'll write them down for you. Upstairs again, Mr Patterson?'

We turned for the stairs to the attics. 'Did you know about the money boxes in the cellar?'

She did not answer until we stood in the attic. 'I knew Father kept his takings down there.' She paused at the foot of the child's abandoned bed. 'Judith was lucky to escape.'

I nodded. 'There must have been a reason for that.'

'Surely she was merely forgotten?'

'I don't think so.'

'But what other reason could there be?'

'I don't know.'

She studied me for a moment then walked through into the storage area, bent to finger the fine fabrics of her sister's London clothes, spilling from the open trunk. 'I don't know what Alice brought with her from London so obviously I can't say if anything has been taken.' Her gaze met mine. 'You're a clever man, Mr Patterson.'

I was embarrassed. 'I hardly think—'

'I've no doubt at all that you will solve this matter.'

'Thank you.' I wished I had her confidence.

'And when you do,' she said, sweeping past me towards the stairs, 'you will see I'm right. The apprentice had a hand in it. Look for the killer amongst *his* friends.'

Eighteen

Never trust servants in inns. They will smile at you but in their hearts they hate you.
[Letter from Louis de Glabre to his friend Philippe
Froidevaux, 20 January 1737]

Ned's friends. *Fowler.* No, the idea wasn't worth considering. I'd seen his reaction to Ned's death – he couldn't have killed him. I couldn't understand why Mrs Fletcher was so adamant Ned had had a part in the robbery. But people do get worked up about apprentices, always believing the worst of them.

I started home with a great deal of relief. It had been a long day and promised to be even longer: I had to turn out again later, to see if the spirits disembodied. I wasn't looking forward to another wait in a freezing house. I wanted to be at home. With Esther. To make up that coldness between us. To make sure she was well.

I was halfway up the Side when a spirit slid down a window-pane calling my name; the spirit had a sickly yellowish hue and flickered as if it was shivering.

'Message for you, sir. From a Mr Balfour. Could you go to his rooms urgent. In the George. Nice inn, that,' the spirit said wistfully. 'Warm.'

'My thanks for the message,' I said. 'I think you should get back indoors.'

'Thank you for your concern, sir,' the spirit said courteously and shot through a tiny gap between window frame and wall.

Sighing, I turned for St Nicholas's church and the George, fighting the temptation to ignore the message. If Balfour merely wanted to discuss some detail of the new Rooms I'd give him very short shrift. At least it wasn't far out of my way.

The George's yard was curiously quiet; a maid in the passageway just inside the inn directed me to a parlour and I walked in to find Balfour sitting morosely over a beer. He leapt up at once, seizing a branch of candles. 'Patterson! Thank God! Come and see.'

He hustled me up a flight of stairs, and into the warren above. The George was built centuries ago and has had wings added, and taken away again, and something else added instead, and rooms subdivided and amalgamated until it's a bewildering labyrinth. Balfour clearly knew his way but if he abandoned me, I doubted my ability to find my way out again.

We came at last to a dark corner and Balfour flung open a door. 'Look!'

Inside was a surprisingly large square room, with long windows looking out over the Clothmarket; the curtains were at the moment drawn back and I saw the glimmer of lanterns in the street. Balfour's candles cast a bright light over the furniture – the bed, a cane chair, a small table, a wash-stand of an antique variety. And a chaos of belongings. Clothes were scattered about the floor; one boot lay on its side under the window, another stood upright on the washstand. A travelling trunk had been flung open, and letters and books flung about.

'I've been robbed!' Balfour cried melodramatically.

I advanced cautiously. It bore a close resemblance to the scene in Hugh's room. As far as I could see, nothing belonging to the George had been damaged – the bedclothes were straight and the curtains undamaged – but Balfour's personal possessions had been treated very badly. He grabbed up a coat that had a long rip. 'Look what they've done to my clothes!'

It was an expensive coat of fine cloth, and well made. The buttons were still there but then they weren't as showy and expensive as Hugh's – which reminded me I hadn't yet told Hugh his buttons had been found.

'What's been stolen?'

'Money. Neckerchiefs, stockings . . .'

I pottered around the room. The plans for the Assembly Rooms poked out from under the bed, close to the chamber pot, crumpled, but not torn. Balfour was keeping something from me; I said, 'What else?'

He said nothing; I looked at him. He reddened. 'There was a coin.'

What an odd way to put it. 'Money?'

He looked even more embarrassed. 'One of the Roman coins.'

'The ones Heron found?'

'I thought he wouldn't miss one,' he said defensively. 'It was such a beautiful thing. Can you imagine something surviving that long? For century upon century?' He trailed off, looking self-conscious. I remembered how disappointed he'd been at not persuading Hugh to part with the ring; it seemed he had obtained an antiquity of his own by other, more dubious, means. 'There was a whole pot of them – I thought it wouldn't hurt if I took one. I put it on the mantelshelf.' He nodded at the fireplace where a couple of china shepherds stood. 'Do you think the thief was one of the servants?'

'Not at the George,' I said instantly. 'Believe me, they're very careful with the people they hire. They're all very respectable.'

I turned on my heels, surveying the room. Both Hugh and Balfour had been burgled and lost the usual portable trifles that thieves take. But the buttons taken from Hugh had been thrown away almost immediately – something no common thief would do. Was this simply a coincidence or something more?

I was suddenly weary; all these puzzles were beyond me. I needed sleep. 'Tell the Watch. They'll keep an eye out for the coin.'

That was a long shot and we both knew it. Balfour said mournfully, 'I was hoping *you* might look for it . . .'

Which was even more of a long shot. The Watch knew the places where stolen property was sold or pawned; I did not. 'I'll keep it in mind,' I said.

And I made my escape and hurried home as fast as I could.

I was exhausted by the time I arrived. I stripped off my greatcoat and hat in the hall and gave them into Tom's capable hands; I was just sitting down to let him pull off my boots when the drawing room door opened. I glanced round, and saw Esther, dressed in one of her loveliest gowns, cut low, white petticoats dotted with little green leaves, the sleeves frothing with lace. The candlelight gleamed on her pale hair, on the long curve of her neck. She was smiling at me, rather ruefully. My heart turned over.

'Brandy, Tom,' I said as soon as the boots were off, and went stocking-footed to Esther. I shut the drawing room door behind us and she fell into my arms, laughing.

'Oh Charles, I have been such an ill-tempered shrew, have I not?'

'I was worried,' I admitted. Esther is tall for a woman, and her hair tickled my cheek. Her lavender scent, as always, tempted me wickedly.

'I was so annoyed at Mrs Fletcher,' she said, sighing.

We heard footsteps in the hall and hurriedly separated; when Tom came in with the brandy and glasses, Esther was straightening ornaments on a table and I was strolling across to poke the fire into further life, as dignified as one can be without shoes. We didn't fool Tom; he was clearly trying to repress a smirk as he withdrew. He'd brought some macaroons too, and Esther bit into them immediately.

'How could Mrs Fletcher accuse that boy?' she resumed, through an inelegant mouthful. 'There is no suggestion at all that he was involved. He was killed while he slept! And then of course all the ladies start telling old tales of rowdy apprentices. As if that was anything to the purpose!' She stopped for breath. I said nothing, suspecting there was more to come but she merely sighed again. 'I have been feeling so low – this constant feeling of lethargy . . .'

I resisted, just, the temptation to mention Gale.

'However,' she said brightly, 'the fresh air and the walk did me a great deal of good and I have been sitting here all afternoon, feeling dreadfully guilty over snapping at you!' She bent to pour brandy and held a glass out to me. 'Tell me everything. No, no, Charles, do not protest – I know when something has happened. You always have an air of repressed excitement.'

'Frankly,' I said, 'my only *air* is exhaustion.'

She pulled me down on to the sofa. 'Then you will simply want to go to sleep, I suppose?'

I looked at her, and she raised a mischievous eyebrow. Perhaps I wasn't so tired after all. In fact, I definitely wasn't.

'Tell me everything first,' she said, reaching for her own brandy.

I gathered my thoughts and related my visit to the derelict house with McLintoch, the encounter with the unpleasant Kane, and the search of the house with Mrs Fletcher. When I described Balfour's burglary, she looked thoughtful.

'Hugh loses the ring, Mr Balfour the coin,' she mused. 'And don't forget, Charles, that there was a third theft of an ancient artefact. You have assumed that the aim of the attack on yourself was to get the keys for the Gregsons' shop, but *you* lost an ancient coin too. Can the antiquities be the real object of these thefts?'

'But then presumably he was looking for antiquities at the Gregsons' too.' I stopped, struck by a thought. 'The box from which the money was taken on the night of the murder – could that have had ancient coins in it? The coin I found in the street, the one Alice dropped, looked very like those Heron found. She might have had it from the box. Although there was a receipt there . . .'

'Who was it made out to?' Esther asked practically.

'A man called Threlkeld – William Threlkeld.'

She sighed. 'Charles, when will you learn to tell me *everything*? You must know who William Threlkeld was!'

'*Was*?' I said, blankly.

'The man who lived in the house where those coins were found,' she said. 'The mercer.'

Nineteen

You must be prepared to rely on your own resources because you will get little assistance should anything go wrong. As it will.

[Letter from Louis de Glabre to his friend Philippe
Froidevaux, 20 January 1737]

I set my head back against the sofa. 'Then it's much more complicated than I thought.' I tried to adjust my thoughts. 'I talked to a spirit in the tavern next door to the mercer's shop. He said Threlkeld had had his shop and house redecorated just before the fire. Perhaps Gregson did the work and the receipt refers to the payment?'

'Check in Gregson's ledgers,' Esther recommended. 'There should be a record of the work there.'

'But the existence of the receipt suggests that there was modern coinage in the box – the money Threlkeld paid Gregson.'

'Not necessarily,' Esther said. 'Gregson's habit was to invest income as soon as possible. Any money Threlkeld paid him would have left the premises long ago. Suppose Gregson's workmen came across the coins in the course of their work.'

I leapt up and started pacing about the room. 'They can't have. The coins could only have been found during work on the cellar and Gregson's men wouldn't go down there – no one decorates their cellars! That sounds much more like *building* work. I wonder if Threlkeld had any repairs done first.'

'But if that box did contain ancient coins found in the course of building work,' Esther mused, 'how did Gregson get his hands on them? Did Threlkeld offer them in lieu of payment? He surely would not have simply given them away.'

I stared at her, beginning to feel very uneasy. 'A spirit in the tavern next door told me there was something unnatural about the fire. Everyone assumed the mercer was bankrupt and trying to do a midnight flit. But suppose—' I took a deep breath. 'Mrs Fletcher told me her father was a violent man.'

Esther's eyes widened. 'You are suggesting that Samuel Gregson attacked the mercer, stole the coins, then set the fire to hide the fact? And then he took the coins home and simply left them in open view in the cellar?'

'In a money box which he knew, or believed, his family wouldn't touch.' I threw back my brandy. 'It looks like he could have been a murderer too.'

Esther contemplated her glass. 'That's a wild theory, Charles.'

It was, but now I'd thought of it, I couldn't let it go. 'I wish I could talk to the apprentice's spirit. He might know more about the box and what was in it. I can't understand why the spirits are taking so long to disembody.'

'That doesn't usually bode well,' Esther agreed. The brandy was bringing colour back to her cheeks; she looked at the macaroons consideringly as if wondering whether to take another. I went off on another tack.

'If the antiquities *are* the object of the thefts,' I said, 'What does the thief plan to do with them? Such things can't be spent.'

'The thief could be a collector.'

I thought fleetingly of Heron – no, I couldn't see him sneaking into Balfour's room at the George and ransacking the place. Actually, that theft had been particularly foolish; if the thief had taken only the ancient coin, Balfour might not have missed it for some time. Ransacking the room simply drew attention to the theft. But then our murderer didn't seem a careful thinker.

I went back to the main point. 'The thief might *know* a collector. Or might simply plan to melt the coins down.'

Esther reached for another macaroon.

'Alice must have found the coins when she came back to the town,' I mused. 'She told her accomplice – her lover – when he followed her.'

Esther nibbled genteelly on the macaroon. 'That coin you found in the snow – perhaps that was a sample she took to show him?'

That sounded very possible. I paced again. 'The thief might have found the coin in my pocket by chance when he went for the keys to Gregson's shop. As for Hugh's ring, he was showing it to anyone who asked. And any servant in the George could have seen the coin on Balfour's mantelpiece and mentioned it casually to someone else, or in the thief's hearing.'

'If the thief, or thieves, want to melt them down,' Esther said, 'the Watch will know the likeliest places they would be taken.'

I nodded. 'Unfortunately, I don't think that's what they're doing. If they wanted to melt them down, one or two stray coins would be neither here nor there. But a collector would want every coin he could lay his hands on. And it's unlikely you'd melt down a ring.'

I pounded my fist against the mantelshelf. 'Nothing, but *nothing*, alters the fact that the victims were all asleep when they were killed. *They were no threat.* Why should they be killed?'

I straightened the ornaments on the mantelshelf, then unstraightened them again.

'Charles,' Esther said patiently. 'There is no point in repeatedly going over the same ground. You are tired. Let us think of something else.'

I looked at her. At her fair hair shimmering in the candlelight, the curve of neck and shoulder. The amused look in her eyes.

'It's late,' I said.

She giggled. 'Charles, it's only eight o'clock.' As if to emphasize her point, the clock on the mantelshelf struck the hour.

'Very late,' I said and took her hand.

I came down to breakfast the following morning feeling much refreshed, if a trifle guilty about not having gone out to attend the disembodiment. Nothing could have happened, however, or McLintoch would have sent a message. There was indeed a note resting on the salver at the bottom of the stairs, but I knew at once who *that* was from.

This time, it said: *I didn't kill them.*

I turned the note over in my fingers. Why was Alice sending me these messages? If she meant to be helpful, there were better ways. These notes came over as merely taunting. I remembered the girl who'd tempted me into the other world, her insolent mischievous look. I felt I was being manipulated.

I was hardly in the breakfast room before George came rushing in. 'Message for you, Master. From Mr McLintoch. He just says *no news yet.*'

'Thank you, George. Could you send a message to Mr Heron's house? To his manservant, Fowler. Ask if I could speak to him sometime today.'

'Yes, Master!'

The spirit rushed out of the room again; its cooperative mood clearly lingered. I poured myself coffee and took some eggs. Esther was still asleep so I presumed I'd be alone for breakfast. She seemed worse in the mornings, so it was good she was sleeping so well for once. I cast a glance at the window. The clouds were low and grey; the garden was blanketed in thick snow. Nothing had changed; it was plainly impossible to get out into the country. I had a whole day to dedicate to this affair.

George was back before I'd had a chance to work my way through my first dish of coffee. The spirit looked very bright; it said nervously, 'Master – do you want me to repeat the *exact* words Mr Fowler used?'

'The general gist will do.'

The spirit was plainly relieved. 'He says he does have a job to do and do you think he can jump to it the minute you ask? He says he'll see you at noon.'

'Did he say where?'

'In the Old Man Inn, Master.'

Trust Fowler to pick the most disreputable tavern in town.

Esther was not awake before I left; I scribbled a note saying I'd try to get home in the early afternoon, and went off to fit as much as I could into the day.

The part of the town to the west of the Sandhill, close upon the ruins of the town wall, is relatively little frequented, although there were some footprints to be seen in the snow: a tribe of children had run through recently, and a dog, besides the ever present spider-like tracks of small birds. But no one had gone into the alley that led to the derelict court. The spirit let me get well into the alley before sliding down a drainpipe to flicker, evilly green, in front of my nose.

'Get out!' she said stridently. 'I won't have you in here!'

Shivering, the cold biting at my nose and ears, I lounged against the wall. 'What are you going to do? Cry *rape* again? What's the point? No one came last time.'

'No one ever comes,' the spirit said contemptuously. 'They hear a woman scream and they just laugh.'

'Is that why you're protecting Alice Gregson?'

'I ain't protecting her. She ain't here.'

'Not now,' I agreed. 'But she was last Saturday night. And you *knew* she was here. More than that, you knew she was *going* to be here.'

The spirit said nothing, clinging to a broken length of guttering.

'She never stayed an entire night, in a derelict house, with no fire, in the middle of the coldest part of the winter, in heavily falling snow, without some sort of protection,' I pointed out. 'She probably didn't expect the snow, but she'd certainly have known it was going to be an extremely cold night. At the very least, she must have had blankets.'

Still nothing from the spirit. I huddled in my greatcoat, and wondered why Alice should have stayed here at all when she could simply have stepped through to safety in the other world.

'She would have brought those blankets here earlier,' I said, 'perhaps some food too. You must have seen her while she was making her preparations, and *she* must have been confident you wouldn't give her away. You only told the Watch about her when someone directly questioned you, when she was long gone and it no longer mattered. Why are you protecting her?'

'Why not!' the spirit burst out, the guttering creaking. 'Do you know what Samuel Gregson was like?'

'No,' I said. 'How do *you* know?'

But the spirit had recovered its composure. 'I don't have to tell you nothing,' it said, sulkily. 'Anyhow, it wouldn't count if I did. Judges don't take no notice of spirits.'

That was unfortunately true; spirits can't give evidence in a court of law, perhaps because there's no means to penalize them if they lie.

I leant back against the wall feeling, unexpectedly, pity. Spirits like company as much as living men, and this spirit patently had none in this derelict place. There was talk of tearing these streets down – what would happen to the spirit then? Spirits evicted from their place of death have a hard time of it. Some have been known to make the transition to a new building on the site without any problem; others disappear without trace. Old spirits and new have the most trouble: spirits on the verge of final dissolution, or spirits not well established.

'Four people have died,' I said, at last. 'Not only Samuel Gregson but his wife and daughter and an apprentice as well. Innocents who deserved a chance at life. Whatever you thought of Gregson himself, surely you can have pity on them.'

The spirit shrieked with bitter laughter. 'Pity! When did they ever have pity on me! Samuel Gregson was the foulest, nastiest, unkindest, most filthy-minded, miserly, miserable man that ever lived. And his wife wasn't much better. I'm glad they're dead!'

It shifted, rapidly. I heard a loud creak, then a snap. I had a moment's warning, enough to step back smartly out of the way. Then a portion of the rotten gutter came rocketing down, four or five huge slates with it. They smashed against the wall on the way down and shattered; a fragment flew off and stung my cheek.

I shouted up into the derelict eaves. 'I know she had a lover! Did *he* kill them?'

There was no reply. The spirit had gone.

It was unwise to linger. I left the alley, hurrying past the debris in case any more slates came crashing down on my head.

At least I'd learned one thing – or had my suspicions confirmed, at any rate. Samuel Gregson was not an innocent victim; his dealings began to seem murky in the extreme. His misdeeds could not justify his murder but they might explain it.

I needed to know more.

Twenty

There are few things more enjoyable than a disaster – you will find the English react very little differently from us in this regard.

[Letter from Louis de Glabre to his friend Philippe Froidevaux, 21 January 1737]

The small room at the back of the tavern stank overwhelmingly of beer. And pickles – two shelves were laden with home preserves. The landlord looked up from his contemplation of an array of barrels, a spare man with thin dark hair receding from his unlined forehead, and straggling over his shoulders. He wore a stained apron over an old shirt with rolled-up sleeves, and looked relieved to be interrupted.

'She's away for the day,' he said.

'Wife?'

'Sister.' He gave me a rueful smile. 'Runs my life. Mind you, I let her. Easier that way. You're Mr Patterson, aren't you? Saw you yesterday looking at the ruins next door.'

'I'm helping with the plans for the Assembly Rooms.'

'Reckon I'll get more custom if that goes ahead,' he said.

'You must have been worried when the fire broke out.'

He nodded. 'Middle of the night. And the maid comes

screeching in to say we're all going to be burned in our beds.' He grinned. 'Must have given her a shock, given what she was doing. She thought we didn't know she had a young man in, silly girl.'

'So the maid was – er – *entertaining* her young man, and they smelt the fire?'

'Give the lad credit,' he said, sitting down on top of one of the barrels. 'He put his clothes back on and stayed to put out the fire. The whole street turned out, of course. Lucky there was a bit of a wind and it was blowing away from us.'

'You couldn't save the mercer?'

He sighed. 'Reckon the smoke got him in his sleep. At least he'd have known nothing about it.' He gave me a shrewd look. 'Think there's something odd about it, do you?' Perhaps my expression gave me away; he added, 'There aren't many who don't know your name, Mr Patterson, and haven't heard you've found out a few villains this past year.'

I wasn't entirely sure I appreciated that kind of notoriety. 'Do you know how the fire started?'

'William Threlkeld,' he said, 'was just about the most annoying neighbour a man could have. Always coming in to tell you your lantern was out, or a roof tile about to fall off, or the gutter was loose, or you weren't supposed to put barrels out in the street. Lived on his own all his life, and got fussier as the years went by.'

'Not the sort of man to leave a candle burning carelessly?'

He shook his head. 'He was particular about everything. Checked the windows and doors were locked three or four times every night.'

'So what do you think happened?'

'Oh no,' he said, wryly. 'You'll not get me guessing. I'm just telling you what I know of the fellow. Make your own mind up from that.'

I perched on a barrel under the shelf of pickles. 'Did he have many visitors, other than customers?'

'Not much of a man for friends, poor soul. Went out to the Literary Club every Thursday night but I never saw anyone come here. Spent most of his time beautifying his shop and house. He liked his home comforts.'

'I heard he'd just had the place redecorated before the fire.'

The landlord nodded. 'Had some work done on the roof, and other bits and pieces. Then had the place painted and papered to within an inch of its life.'

'People say he bankrupted himself over it.'

He pursed up his lips. 'Maybe. I've heard say he was planning to run from his creditors and set the fire to cover it up. Doesn't seem logical to me.'

Nor to me, I reflected. 'Who did the work?'

'Gregson,' he said promptly. 'I was thinking of having some work done myself and kept an eye on the workmen. They were good, but from what Threlkeld told me, Gregson charged for everything three times over.'

'Did Threlkeld argue with anyone?'

'He tried,' he said, with a wry grin. 'But we all knew it wasn't worth arguing back. We let him say his piece and just said, *yes, William, no, William.* He had a go at everyone in the street one time or another. We none of us held it against him – now and again, he did us a favour by pointing something out. You can live with a man who grumbles a little.' He gave me that rueful smile again. 'I'm used to it.'

I took it he was referring to his sister. 'Did he have any servants?'

He shook his head. 'He nagged so much none would stay. A woman came in during the day to clean and cook, but she was a soldier's wife and went off some time back. Probably fighting the Frenchies by now.'

A pity. I would have liked to talk to her. 'Can I have a word with your maid?'

He laughed. 'You can if you can find her. Took herself off to find somewhere better. Said she didn't like the stink of beer.'

'What about her young man? Did he go with her?'

'Oh, he's still about,' the landlord said. 'Knew better than to lose a good place. He's an apprentice at the deal yard. That's what she liked about him,' he added with a chuckle. 'All those muscles from sawing up wood! Lemuel Atkinson, he's called.' He got up. 'And talking of work, I'd better get back to it.'

I left him counting up his barrels.

The other neighbours were less reticent in their speculations about the fire. The woman who ran the lodging house on one corner of the street insisted six men had leapt out of the mercer's windows in bursts of flame, carrying unimaginable treasure. The cheesemonger on the opposite corner enjoyed himself expiating at length on the faults of the mercer before piously saying, 'Well, mustn't talk ill of the dead.' A hairdresser above the cheese-mongers said he was away the night of the fire but had heard *exactly* what had happened, but his story didn't match the landlord's, whom I rather trusted. And the wig maker who shared the hairdresser's premises said she'd slept through it all but knew for a fact the mercer had kept a branch of six candles which he'd knocked over, setting his bed on fire.

I went in search of the apprentice.

Mr Usher's deal yard is a large place, employing a considerable number of men. In the middle is a large warehouse which is sometimes used as a makeshift theatre; I performed in it myself this past June, in Race Week. In hot weather, the smell of freshly-sawn wood is almost overpowering; in winter, only the faintest whiff of it came to me on the icy air. The yard had been swept clear of snow, which lay in grimy piles around the walls of the buildings; men were stacking and turning wood, manning the saw pits, loading seasoned timber on to carts. Many of them wore only thin shirts and breeches, and were still sweating with effort.

I accosted a man and asked him if Lemuel Atkinson was at work. He directed me to a small hut in one corner of the yard; inside, I found a young man totting up figures in an account book. The landlord was right – Atkinson was a fine figure of a young man, not particularly tall but strongly built, and with bright chestnut hair falling about his shoulders.

I introduced myself. 'I'm told you were one of those who tried to put the fire out at the mercer's last year.'

He sat up, a little defiant. 'I don't hide the fact.'

'I was wondering if you would tell me about it.'

'Is there any problem?'

'No.'

'No one's ever said I did anything wrong.'

I wondered if he was always so defensive. 'I'm involved with the plans for the new Assembly Rooms on the site and I'm merely making sure nothing's been overlooked. Some of the neighbours are convinced there was something untoward about the fire.'

He seemed to relax, laughed. 'Their kind always look for excitement!'

I smiled back. 'Six men leaping out of the windows, brandishing swords . . .'

'I was there,' he said scornfully. 'The *first* one there. There was no one inside but the mercer.'

'I suppose you were warned when you saw the flames?'

He shook his head. 'Heard the glass break.' He reddened, said awkwardly, 'I was – *visiting* someone at the tavern next door. When I heard glass, I thought someone was trying to get in. So I looked out of the window and that's when I saw the flames.'

'The glass shattered with the heat of the fire, I suppose.'

'It was well alight.' He shrugged. 'Nothing anyone could do, except keep it from spreading.'

'That must have been hard work. Did you know the mercer?'

'If anyone says I set fire to the place, he's lying!'

I considered him for a moment; he dropped his gaze and fidgeted with his quill. 'I presume the mercer had said something sharp to you about visiting the maid.'

He went a fiery red. 'Stupid old man. I don't suppose a woman ever looked at him once in his life!'

'Then all the more credit to you for fighting the fire,' I said, 'when you didn't have very charitable feelings towards him.'

His face was still flaming; he said, 'He was a interfering old idiot.' At that moment, he looked absurdly young; he added, almost resentfully, 'Not a nice way to die.'

He was right.

I walked back out into the yard, musing on what Atkinson had told me, and almost walked into Mr Usher himself; he was dressed in his best and had his psalm book in his hand. 'Just off to my sister's wedding,' he said, with a sly grin. 'Never thought we'd get her off our hands.' Mr Usher's in his early sixties and his sister's not much younger. 'Were you looking for me? I'm willing to talk if you'll walk with me.'

I fell into step beside him; we turned out of the yard, on to the snowy cobbles of the street. 'I wanted to ask about Threlkeld, the mercer. He had work done on his house last year and I was wondering if you did it.'

Usher chuckled. 'I did. That was a very profitable job. A houseproud man, William Threlkeld. Had a passion about draughts, I recall – had us running all over the house filling up mouseholes. As if you can ever get rid of draughts!'

'Was there anything more substantial wrong?'

'Foundations,' Usher said. 'Subsidence. Half of the house was sinking into the ground. A crack as long as my arm in the shop wall. When we dug it out, there was a hole down there. Some previous building on the site.'

That wasn't in itself unusual; in Newcastle, as in most towns, every site is built on again and again. But given the coins, I wondered if occupation on the site had been long-lived indeed.

'Was Threlkeld easy to work for? According to the neighbours, he seemed always to have his own ideas.'

Usher made a so-so gesture, as we turned on to Westgate. 'He was sensible enough to know he didn't know anything about building.' He laughed. 'He did have one fit of madness. We got there one morning to find he'd torn down part of a brick wall in the cellar. We'd just put it up, but he had the audacity to say it had fallen down of its own accord. My men,' he said vehemently, 'do not do shoddy work.'

'Why should he tear down a wall?'

'Wanted to see what was behind it. We'd found a lot of old pottery and when he saw it on the carts, he wanted to know if there was anything valuable. We kept telling him there wasn't, but he didn't believe us, insisted we left it all behind for him to look at. Just bits and pieces and a coin or two. Nothing special.'

Usher was patently not a collector of antiquities. 'When was this?'

'April sometime.' We came to St John's church and he paused at the porch. Three or four people were gathering there in fine clothes, looking miserably cold in the icy weather. 'I can check for you in my books.'

I shook my head. It was enough to know Threlkeld must have discovered the coins about two months before the fire, perhaps when he tore that wall down. He must have put them aside, only for Gregson to discover them while the redecoration was being done. And then? Had Gregson bought them from Threlkeld or taken them in lieu of his bill? Or had there been something more sinister?

'And two months later he was dead,' Usher said reflectively. 'The Lord has his own ways and we can only guess at them. Doesn't do to get above ourselves. Shouldn't give ourselves airs and graces – we could be dead tomorrow.'

And on that cheerful note, he walked into the church.

Twenty-One

The conversation of gentlemen is rather more to my taste – providing you can get them talking about horseracing and gambling. Avoid politics, unless you particularly want to tease them.

[Letter from Louis de Glabre to his friend Philippe Froidevaux, 21 January 1737]

The Key was busy with sailors and the passing of feet had worn most of the snow into muddy slush; Fowler was already waiting for me outside the Old Man Inn, a savage sneer on his face. 'I can't just jump to your commands, you know,' he said. 'Don't want to get myself fired, do I?'

I stamped snow from my boots. 'I'd wager you can sneak out of the house any time you like without Heron knowing.'

'He's working his way through those old coins,' Fowler said, tacitly acknowledging the point. He pushed open the door of the inn. 'Cleaning 'em, cataloguing 'em, writing 'em up. Keeps him quiet.'

A cloud of smoke billowed out of the inn. Through the fog, I saw it was crowded with the rougher sort of man – sailors, labourers, ruffians of all sorts. Two or three greeted Fowler cordially; one of the serving girls clung on his arm with obvious affection.

He ordered beer and worked his way through the crowd to a bench in a corner; men playing with dice shifted to make space for us. The girl brought the beer and hung over Fowler with the neckline of her dress deliberately loosened. He gave her a lascivious grin. 'Later, Meg, later. Got to talk to the fine gent first.'

She withdrew, pouting. I watched her go and turned to see Fowler watching me in turn, with that malicious sneer. 'Got to look after my reputation, haven't I?' He took a great gulp of his beer. 'Wouldn't want people thinking I didn't like the ladies. A little *activity* now and then, and no one suspects a thing.'

I couldn't believe his recklessness, talking so openly. I glanced around. 'For God's sake!'

He ignored me. 'You know what they're saying, don't you? They're saying Ned let a robber in. They're saying they planned to rob the house together. They're saying Ned killed all the family before the fellow arrived and then got killed himself in a quarrel. They're saying *well, he was an apprentice, wasn't he? We all know what apprentices are like!*'

'Be quiet,' I said. Several men were looking in our direction. Fowler started again; I said sharply, 'Damn you, be quiet!'

His face twisted; he stared down into the beer.

'The inquest said Alice Gregson killed her family,' I said. 'That's the official verdict. And you know how the Watch and the Constable and the Coroner and the Justices of the Peace will defend official decisions to the death. No one thinks your Ned had anything to do with it!'

He glowered down into the tankard. 'That's not what they're saying.'

'It doesn't matter what *they're* saying.'

'The devil it does!' He flared up again. 'It's Ned's reputation and he can't defend himself. I won't have it! It's her fault – that witch! When I get my hands on her—'

It took some minutes to calm him down. He cosseted the fury as if it was all that was left to him; he didn't want to let it go. He'd settled on Alice as the villain and wouldn't hear anything else. I poured more beer and let him talk himself out.

He wound to a halt eventually, breathing heavily, his face flushed. After a long silence, he said, 'You know me, Patterson. Never thought anyone in this world but Heron worth putting myself out for – and only Heron because he rescued me from a sure death at the noose's end, because he doesn't *judge*. But Ned

– he was different somehow.' He glanced round, for the first time checking if anyone was listening, a sign of returning sense I noted with some relief. 'A little innocent he was – devil take it, he was only seventeen! But he had a sense of fun, a real joy in being alive.'

He fell into a brooding silence, obviously lost in the past. 'I'll have her, Patterson,' he said at last. 'I don't care, I'll have her.'

'I need your help,' I said, hoping to distract him.

He looked at me sharply. 'To catch her?'

'Possibly. It's about the money that was stolen from Gregson. I think at least some of it may have been made up of ancient coins.'

'Like Heron's?'

I nodded. 'From the same source, as far as I can tell. Those ancient coins can't be spent, so the chances are the murderer will be looking to sell them – probably for melting down.'

'Melting down? That'd break Heron's heart,' Fowler said sarcastically. He leant forward to pour himself more beer and drained the last of the jug into my tankard.

'I need to know if anyone has been approached about the coins.'

Fowler bared his teeth at me. 'You think I'm likely to know that sort of low life?'

I glanced pointedly round the rowdy clientele of the Old Man. 'I thought you might. Alternatively, of course, the thief might try to sell them to a collector.'

'Heron'd buy them, no questions asked.'

'And you're in a good position to know if he's offered them, aren't you?'

Fowler gave me a malicious grin. 'I'd be the one he'd get to do the dirty work of buying them.'

I thought – sincerely hoped – that Heron wouldn't be so tempted by the thought of the coins that he'd forget to take steps to apprehend the villain who offered them. 'And you'd tell me of the offer straight away, of course.'

'I might,' Fowler said mockingly.

'You wouldn't know if he was approached about something similar last June or July?'

He shook his head. 'Not that I heard.'

I digested this, conscious of a little disappointment. However Gregson had obtained the coins, he must have had some reason for wanting them; financial gain – selling the coins to some collector – was the most obvious. As an upholsterer, he'd have known what value some people place on genuine antiquities; he'd certainly have known, or been able to discover, those gentlemen who were interested in such things and had money enough to acquire them. He might, of course, have decided to allow some time to elapse before selling, to make sure the coins weren't connected with the mercer's shop.

Fowler signalled for more beer; the girl came with a seductive flounce in her step. She didn't give me a second glance, which was unflattering.

'You should tell Heron to be careful,' I said, when she was gone. 'It looks very much as if someone's stealing all the antiquities he can find; he – or she – may may attempt to get hold of Heron's coins.'

Fowler laughed. 'Steal from Heron? Have you any idea how locked up tight that house is?'

'*I* realize that. A thief may not.'

'You reckon this thief might be the girl?'

'Or her lover.'

'Maybe we ought to encourage them to try,' Fowler said, only half-joking. 'We could lay a trap.'

I've set the odd trap in my time. Too much can go wrong. 'There's one other thing.'

'There always is with you,' Fowler said. He swore at a man who knocked against him as he barged past.

'There's a thief-taker in town, looking for a man who's robbed houses in Kent.' I hesitated, reluctant to give Kane's robber more importance than he warranted. 'There's a possibility – no more than that – that the Kent fellow could be Alice's lover. He poses as an exciseman, apparently.' I gave him Kane's description of the man: burly, middle-aged, strong and charming.

Fowler shrugged. 'Sounds like a dozen men.'

'He'll be new to town and have a Kentish accent. You're a southerner yourself, you'll recognize that kind of accent faster than most. But don't go near him if you spot him. He's apparently killed twice already – he could be dangerous.'

'And you think *I'm* not, do you?' Fowler said with soft mockery. He contemplated me for a long moment. 'Does this really have something to do with the killings or are you just trying to give me something to do, to distract me from what happened to Ned?'

'Both,' I said.

He laughed sourly.

Outside it was snowing heavily again, softly, silently. Merchants trudged, heads down, along the Key; whores huddled in doorways. Ice edged the keels of the boats; across the river, the trees on Gateshead bank were dark behind a curtain of white.

I hurried for the protection of the coffee-house, to wash away the taste of the Old Man's thin beer. The cobbles were slippery; the previous snow, worn to slush, had frozen during the night and the fresh snow, falling on top, hid the icy patches. I was watching my feet when I heard my name and glanced up to see Joseph Kane hailing me. He broke away from a group of sailors and strode across, slipping and sliding.

'Any luck?' I asked.

He was exuberant, bullish. 'Maybe, maybe! A couple of fellows who might be my man. One made off yesterday to Shields for a boat.'

'He won't have got far.'

'Nonsense!' His lip curled; it was clearly my day for being sneered at. 'It was a fine sunny day yesterday! I'm off following him. If you get any news—' his expression said he thought my chances of finding anything were pretty small— 'leave a message at the Fleece.'

I watched him stride away, his dignity marred by a slip on the cobbles. Perhaps someone who knew the area might have got through to the coast yesterday – though I doubted it – but only a fool would try it today in the thickening snow.

Nellie's coffee house was surprisingly quiet, perhaps the weather was keeping everyone at home. But sitting in the far corner, scribbling away on a scrap of paper, was Hugh.

He glanced up as I settled into the chair opposite him. 'I can't get this damn advertisement right. Here, you have a look.'

He pushed the paper at me; I read:

NEWCASTLE: JANUARY 21st 1737

Mr HUGH DEMSEY, Dancing-master, begs the honour of
informing the Ladies and Gentlemen of this Town, as well
as the Public, that his Ball, originally intended to be held
on the 29th Inst., is now postponed until—

I glanced up at him. 'I don't see a problem. This seems very
wise – the weather's much too bad to risk any public
entertainments.'

'It's not the postponement that's the problem,' Hugh said irritably. 'It's the wording. You know how touchy the ladies and
gentlemen are. I've got to make it clear I'm putting this off for
their convenience, not mine.'

I'd ordered coffee and a hot pie on my way in; the serving
girl laid them in front of me and I tucked in with relish. My
toes were warming up again.

Hugh threw down his pen, and swore as ink splashed over his
draft. 'All this running around about the Rooms is tiring me out.
Balfour is meeting with the Directors right now. The meeting
started late because Heron didn't turn up on time, and when he
did turn up, he just wanted to interrogate me on how the ring
was stolen! Thought he'd never stop. The other directors were
not best pleased – started to get very fractious. So I pleaded other
business and made a quick escape.'

'And left poor Balfour to deal with it?'

Hugh was unrepentant. 'He's in a good mood today – very
chirpy. I thought he was a nice quiet, restrained fellow, Charles,
but let me tell you, now he's got over his sea-sickness, he's working
his way through every whore in town!'

I cradled the hot coffee dish in my hands. 'Damn it, I knew
I'd forgotten something. McLintoch said to tell you they've found
your buttons.'

Hugh sat bolt upright. 'They've caught the thief?'

'Not exactly. He tossed the buttons off the Low Bridge into
the Lort Burn.'

Hugh's mouth dropped open. I resigned myself to an indignant
tirade and sat through it patiently. Or more or less patiently, until
he started repeating himself.

'Hugh,' I said, businesslike. 'I want to talk to you.'

'You *are* talking to me,' he said irritably. 'My buttons! Tossed away as if they didn't matter!'

'That,' I said, 'is proof our thief was after the antiquities. Hugh – I think I know how the murders were done.'

Twenty-Two

The English gentleman has as many *affairs d'amour* as you do, my friend – he merely does not brag about it as much.
[Letter from Louis de Glabre to his friend Philippe Froidevaux, 21 January 1737]

I drew circles in the condensation on the table. 'Alice Gregson has been brought up in London and doesn't want to come back to the "barbaric" north. She especially doesn't want to leave her lover, whom we have to presume no one knows about.'

Hugh's brows drew together in disapproval. 'I still don't entirely believe in the existence of this unknown man.'

'Of course he exists! He's robbed three of us now and I've seen a letter from him. And your widow saw him run from your rooms. *And* neighbours say Alice was constantly looking out for someone.' I went back to my theory. 'Newcastle is conveniently close to Scotland, ideal if you're planning to run away and be married. They make their plans. Alice will come back home and search her father's house – he's wealthy so they think there's bound to be some money about. Even a small amount might be sufficient to enable them to run off. After they've eloped, they reckon the family will have to be reconciled to them, to save Alice's good name. And Sarah's name too – her rich merchant won't want a girl from a disgraced family.'

Hugh looked begrudging. 'Go on.'

'Alice comes home, searches the house and finds two boxes of coins in the cellar.'

I explained about the coins, and the mercer, and my suspicions about Samuel Gregson; Hugh whistled. An elderly gentleman gave him a disapproving look from behind his paper.

'Alice took at least one of those boxes of coins, probably both. At some point she took a single specimen from the old coins, possibly to show her lover – she dropped it in the snow after the murders and I picked it up.'

I sipped at the coffee, to give myself a little time to sort out details.

'Alice then knotted a rope made of sheets and hid it. She may have done this on Friday afternoon. She may have met her lover then too – she absented herself from the shop and no one knew where she went. On the night of the murders, she crept down-stairs to meet her lover, opening the front door with the key which was easily accessible to anyone in the house. She was going to walk out of there with him and head for Scotland. Only something happened.'

'Wait!' Hugh held up a hand. 'If they were going to walk out the front door, why the rope?'

'To make people *think* she'd escaped that way.'

He wrinkled up his nose. 'Doesn't sound convincing to me.'

'Maybe it was a contingency measure, an alternative means of escape if they were caught.' He made a sceptical face; I doggedly went on. 'There was an argument. Alice fled upstairs and . . .'

I ground to a halt. Hugh was shaking his head.

'Yes, I know,' I said wearily. 'If there'd been an argument, the family would have woken up.'

'And,' Hugh pointed out. 'If they'd argued in the shop, the apprentice would have been the first to wake and therefore the first to die. But the murder weapon was with his body, so he was presumably the *last* to die. Unless there were *two* murder weapons.'

I grimaced. 'I don't need more complications, Hugh!'

He had a bright gleam in his eye. 'I know what happened! She double-crossed him in some way, he chased her upstairs. She escaped down the rope and he killed the rest of them in a raging fury . . .'

'The timing won't work,' I said, gloomily. 'We heard the child screaming very shortly after Alice had climbed off the end of the rope. There wouldn't have been time for the accomplice to kill everyone before she raised the alarm. And if I'd been him, I'd have raced downstairs and tried to cut Alice off as she came ashore. There was simply no need for the killings.'

We contemplated the problem in silence. The gentleman with the paper expounded loudly, and at length, on the iniquities of the government.

'I'd just have cut her rope,' Hugh said. 'Let her get out of that!'

'Some of it's right,' I said obstinately. 'I know the events leading up to the murders – I'm sure of that. But what exactly happened on the night . . .'

'What I don't understand,' Hugh mused, 'is where she's hiding now. If there *is* an accomplice, well, by the sound of it, he's a rough fellow and the town's full of rough fellows. No one would notice one extra. But a gently reared girl who's a stranger here – where the devil could *she* hide?'

I sighed, and told him about my encounter with Alice in the other world. He scowled; he loathes the very idea of the other world. His one experience of it was not happy. 'Don't look at me like that,' I said. 'I didn't invite this ability to *step through* – it just happened.'

'You're going to get yourself in serious trouble one day, Charles,' he said, and refused to talk about it any further.

I left him rewording his advertisement yet again, and went to find Abraham McLintoch in his cosy room behind the Printing Office. In the Watch office, two men were enjoying the huge fire, smoking long pipes with the contented air of men who intend to spend the rest of the day there. A jug of ale stood on McLintoch's table, beside a platter that held a few crumbs. He was writing an advertisement too, though both he and Hugh were far too late for this week's *Courant*.

'Good day, Mr Patterson, sir.' The smoke got in the back of my throat; McLintoch paused to let me cough. 'I was just writing a notice for the paper. Mr Philips sent to tell me to put one in.' He handed me a sheet of paper, rather grimy. 'Would you do me the honour, sir, of giving me your opinion on the wording.'

The note was written in large unformed childish letters, but impeccably spelt and punctuated.

Wanted [it read]. Alice Gregson, 23 years old, five feet four inches high, pale Complexion, fair Hair, blue Eyes, small Hands and Feet. Speaks in a London Accent. Last seen wearing a white Dress with blue Flowers, a flowered Shawl and white Slippers. Wanted for the Murder of Joseph Gregson, Alice Gregson his Wife, Sarah Gregson their Daughter and Edward Hills, Apprentice, on Saturday 16 January 1737 at their Shop on the Tyne Bridge. Anyone having Information on the Whereabouts of the said Alice Gregson should deliver it to Abraham McLintoch at the Watch office, or at the House of Charles Patterson, Esq. A Reward of one Guinea will be paid if the Suspect is apprehended. N.B. No more will be offered at any time.

'Well?' McLintoch asked anxiously.

Oddly, the thing that most impressed itself on me was that I'd never seen my name with 'Esq' after it before; it made me feel quite a different person. I stifled another cough. 'Where did you get the description of her?'

'Mr Fleming, the stationer.'

'Then it will be accurate,' I said. 'I presume that's what she was wearing when he last saw her?' McLintoch nodded. 'A pity I didn't see her more clearly when she fled. She was certainly wearing something dark then.'

McLintoch handed the notice to one of the other watchmen. 'Here, Sam – take this to the Printing Office.'

The watchman departed, grumbling at having to leave the fire. 'Do you think it will do any good?' I asked.

McLintoch picked up his pipe again. 'It does, sometimes. But it depends.'

'On?'

He lit the pipe. Damp logs on the fire spat and crackled. 'On whether it'll pay her associates better to hide her or betray her.'

'A guinea's a lot of money.'

'It is to a working man,' he agreed.

I interpreted that easily enough. 'You think she's being sheltered by someone more respectable?'

'Stands to reason,' he said. 'This is nothing personal, sir, you understand, but no working man's going to shelter a girl like that. He'd want her to work for her living. He'd pimp her, use her to attract men and then help to rob them, mebbe. But there're plenty of girls he could use that way – why should he take the risk on a girl the whole town's looking for? He wouldn't do it. Any working man would have turned her in days ago. It would get him some credit with the Watch and the constable – always useful.'

'And a respectable man?'

'Now that's a different matter,' he said. 'She's his own kind. You don't give away your own kind.'

'I wouldn't have her in my house.'

He nodded. 'But *you* don't know her, Mr Patterson. Suppose there's someone as does, someone she manages to convince she didn't do it? And she's got money, Mr Patterson, remember, the money she stole from her father – that'd help.'

'It would appeal to a working man too.'

'True, but all that means is he'd take the money first, *then* turn her in.'

'You've a very jaundiced view of human nature.'

He nodded, almost proudly. 'You would too, if you did my job, Mr Patterson.'

I'd no doubt of that. I thought of the letters Alice had sent me: *I didn't steal the money; I didn't kill them.* Was I the respectable man she was working on? She certainly knew I was the person to appeal to – that I was investigating the matter. But *how* did she know? Someone must be keeping her informed.

'The thief-taker from London – Kane – thinks the man he's looking for had something to do with this matter.'

'Aye,' McLintoch said. 'Sounds a nasty sort.'

'Kane thinks he might have wanted to rob the house, wooed the girl—'

The watchman threw another log on the fire; I shifted my chair away from the blaze. McLintoch looked in annoyance at his pipe, which had apparently gone out again. 'Mebbe he did, mebbe he didn't. But I knows who killed the Gregsons, and it wasn't no fellow from Kent.'

I didn't pursue the matter; McLintoch was an efficient, hard-working man, but he believed what was in front of his eyes and went after it with dogged determination. Very like Fowler, in fact.

'Anyhow,' he said. 'This Kentish fellow's probably on a ship and long gone. If he's any sense, that is.'

I rather agreed with him. Weather permitting, of course. 'There was something else,' I said. 'The spirit in the court. I've my suspicions about her. She didn't trouble herself to tell us about the girl hiding there until it was too late to do anything. Do you know who she was?'

'Lydia Letitia Mountfort,' McLintoch said with some relish.

'She was never from this town!' I said. 'Not with a name like that.'

McLintoch chortled. 'Born in Amen Corner, right under the spire of St Nicholas's church. Her mother was a bit fanciful.'

'And her father?'

'Wouldn't know. I'd be surprised if her mother did either. *She* was plain Smith – Letty was the one who called herself Mountfort, years later.'

'Her mother was a whore?'

He nodded. 'I reckon her father was a sailor, mebbe a foreigner – little Letty was pretty but in a dark sort of way, if you get my meaning. When her mama died, she was put out to a woman who kept a flock of hens, out by St Ann's chapel, and wanted someone to help. Don't reckon Letty liked it much, judging by the number of times she ran off. You can guess what happened.'

'A child?'

McLintoch nodded. 'The baby died, I remember, and the midwife said she'd never have another. I don't know much what happened to her after that. I went off to sea, and by the time I got back, she was dead. I heard a man she was living with took offence at something she said, there was a fight and she fell and hit her head.'

'When was that?'

He mused, obviously working out dates. 'Twenty years back, maybe.'

So Alice Gregson might have known Letty Mountfort. But surely she wouldn't remember a woman she'd last seen at the age of three or four? 'Why is this spirit so intent on protecting Alice? Did she know the Gregsons?'

McLintoch winked at me. 'Course she did. Samuel Gregson liked the ladies – spent more money on them that he did on his own wife. Why d'you think Mrs G never had anything nice in the jewellery line? Mind you, she *was* a sour individual.'

'Maybe she was a sour individual *because* he spent his money on whores,' I said dryly. 'And Letty Mountfort was one of them?'

'Word is he was the father of Letty's baby.'

This put quite a different complexion on things. The spirit in the court had once been Samuel Gregson's whore – she'd borne his child. Had his treatment of her made her sympathetic to anyone who hated him?

McLintoch took his pipe from his mouth. 'The spirits ought to disembody tonight, Mr Patterson.'

'We've been saying that for the last three days.'

He shook his head. 'Never known it take longer than five days. They'll be here tonight at the latest.'

He seemed confident; I said, with resignation, 'I'll be there.'

We glanced round as the door opened, blowing in a gust of cold air and a flurry of snow. Mrs Fletcher stood looking at us with obvious distaste.

'Well,' she said with thinly veiled sarcasm, 'all the great minds thinking together. Have you come to any conclusions?'

We'd both risen, of course, when we saw the newcomer was female. McLintoch bowed and dipped, said, 'Madam, madam, my lady,' as if to make sure he was being polite enough. I knew by Mrs Fletcher's tone, and by her malicious smile, that she was enjoying the effect her rudeness was having.

'No? Well, I've been doing your job for you. I,' she said, 'have identified the man who killed my parents.'

Twenty-Three

Honesty is prized here, but not taken to extremes.
[Letter from Louis de Glabre to his friend Philippe
Froidevaux, 21 January 1737]

She gave us a contemptuous look, waved her hand across her face to make a point about the smoke. McLintoch hurriedly put down his pipe and launched into a flurry of apologies. Mrs Fletcher looked both pleased and annoyed with his urgent droppings of *Madam, my lady* and *not used to having ladies here*.

She said, '*I* am not used to sitting doing nothing, gentlemen.

If you cannot find the man who killed my family, then I will.'

McLintoch glanced at me. 'Your sister, madam . . .'

'My sister is a silly fool taken in by a plausible rogue. And there's a man in this town who can tell you exactly who that plausible rogue is.'

'Joseph Kane,' I said.

That took her aback. If she'd spoken to Kane, he'd not told her he'd already talked with me. I wasn't surprised; from the moment I'd met him on the boat north, Kane had struck me as a man who'd do anything to achieve his own ends. He'd tried to enlist my help and not succeeded to his own satisfaction, and had therefore tried elsewhere.

'The man Kane's searching for,' I said, 'seems hardly the sort to appeal to your sister. A burly, middle-aged man, with the sort of charm that attracts country servant girls? I'd have thought your sister would prefer someone younger, more handsome, more cultured.'

She gave me a long hard look. 'At the very least, you should be investigating the matter!'

'The fellow's long gone by now, madam,' McLintoch said. 'Hopped on the first boat to the Colonies, madam, I shouldn't wonder, madam.'

'There have been no such boats,' Mrs Fletcher said. 'I've enquired. It's hardly the weather to be sailing across the oceans, is it?'

McLintoch changed tack masterfully, with not a blink. 'I've yet to see any proof he was in the town at all, madam. And as for this Kane fellow, who says he knows anything of the matter, madam?'

I can spot a conversation that's going nowhere at six paces. 'I beg your pardon,' I said. 'But I've an appointment I mustn't miss.'

Outside, the snow had eased to a drifting flake or two but the pewter-coloured sky promised more. New snow lay thickly on top of the cobbles on the Key, and a smartly dressed young man tottered towards me, obviously with no confidence he was going to stay upright; he gave me a nervous look as he passed. Outside one of the chandlers' shops, a group of sailors looked morosely at the icy river. Even the Old Man Inn was quiet, the door shut tight.

I turned for home. For a quiet hour or two with Esther, something to eat and time to get myself ready to go out for the disembodiment. Surely it must take place tonight; it was already astonishingly late. I turned into the Sandhill, and saw two men on the other side, apparently having just come out of the coffee house. I knew one of those men too well to mistake. 'Hugh!'

He glanced round and stopped, waiting as I negotiated the treacherous slippery road. It was Balfour with him; as I came up, Hugh raised his eyebrows in exasperation. 'Anything new?' he said, with a look of pleading.

'No,' I said regretfully. I glanced at Balfour; he looked sullen and resentful, not *chirpy* as Hugh had described him. 'Is there a problem?'

'Apparently,' Balfour said moodily.

Hugh was shaking his head. I said, 'The Directors were not pleased with the design?'

'The design,' Balfour said with heavy sarcasm, 'is too elaborate, too fancy – too *fashionable*.'

'Too London,' Hugh said.

'Ah,' I said, understanding. 'Too expensive.'

'They were kind enough,' Balfour said bitingly, 'to suggest ways in which economies might be made.'

'Of course, they are businessmen,' Hugh said placatingly, slapping at his arms to keep warm. 'It's natural they should want to bargain.'

'I told them the truth,' Balfour said obstinately. 'I know my business and they don't.'

Hugh and I exchanged glances. *Never* tell a gentleman the truth. Unless, that is, you wrap it up in six compliments, three assurances of your undying belief in his infallibility, and at least three different ways of interpreting what you say, so he may choose which one he prefers.

'I told them plainly,' Balfour said. 'Any economies will result in a building that won't be worth having and that will probably fall down around their ears!'

What he should have done, of course, was to praise their discernment and their taste, and assure them that someone in London had paid twice as much for a building half the size. All the while giving the impression that he deferred to their judgement totally. Anyone who deals with gentlemen on a regular basis soon learns useful little tricks; I could only presume that, as an assistant on previous projects, Balfour had been accustomed to someone else dealing with the clients.

'And what did they decide in the end?'

'They want new plans drawn up,' Hugh said.

'Won't that cost more?' I asked. Which also should have been pointed out to the gentlemen.

Hugh nodded, brushed a few errant snowflakes off the shoulders of his greatcoat. 'Time, effort, more materials for the new plans – ink, quills, all the rest of it. And the cost of staying at the George.'

'First the burglary, then this,' Balfour said sullenly. 'Devil take it, who'd want to stay in a dirty, miserable town like this a moment longer than necessary!'

This was hardly tactful; Hugh pretended nonchalance, I curbed my irritation. Balfour had liked the town well enough last night. 'He should just wait a few days,' Hugh said, 'then take the same plans back and tell them he's done what they asked.'

I winced at this; there were certainly one or two gentlemen who wouldn't notice, but others were extremely acute. Heron, for instance. I said, 'Gentlemen like to exert their authority over these matters – I generally find it best to humour them.'

Balfour scowled; I hurriedly changed the topic of conversation. 'I've been talking to Abraham McLintoch. We're hoping the spirits will disembody tonight. It can hardly be delayed much longer.'

I saw Hugh shudder. Last time we saw a disembodiment, it was a young girl we knew and it had been an unpleasant experience. 'Well, I shan't be there,' he said. 'I'm for an early night. I've lessons to give tomorrow morning.'

We walked up the Side together, towards St Nicholas's church. The snow started to come down again, as if it was gathering itself up for something severe. It was an uneasy walk; Balfour could talk of nothing but the insult he'd been given; I thought of changing the subject, but the more Balfour talked, the less I was able to think of something to say. Hugh had apparently exhausted all his resources long ago. At the top of the Side, he said brightly,

'I'm off home. Do let me know if the spirits disembody, Charles!' Behind Balfour's back, he gave me a grin and a wink of mock sympathy, and was off before either of us could object.

Balfour and I walked past St Nicholas's church, up into the Clothmarket. At least it wasn't far to the George and I wasn't prepared to go even one step into the inn yard. 'They don't understand,' Balfour said morosely. 'You can't draw up plans like this in an hour or two! The whole idea will have to be thrown out of the window, and started again!'

It was obvious he'd no intention of redoing the plans and was looking for an excuse to avoid the exercise. If he wasn't prepared to give way to the wishes of his clients, I predicted his career as an architect would be short. He began to dissect the characters of the gentlemen. 'That fellow Ord was dead set against everything I said, but there was an elderly man who looked approachable. He might take my part. Do you think it would be worth approaching him privately, see if he can use his influence to convince the others?'

I didn't have the least idea who he was talking about; there are three or four elderly men amongst the Directors. 'Why the devil wasn't Heron there!' Balfour burst out. '*He* was happy with the plans!'

'Heron wasn't there?'

'People always let me down,' Balfour muttered, in unattractive self-pity.

It was too cold to be standing in the street. I made an excuse about wanting to see if my wife was better and took my leave. I wasn't sure Balfour knew I'd gone; he was still muttering and grumbling as he went into the alley that led to the inn.

I detoured briefly to the Cloth Market and the proposed site of the new Rooms. Heron's workmen were still there, although they weren't doing much work; one picked at the earth bank on the far side of the site with the corner of a spade, but the rest were enjoying beer from the tavern next door. There was no sign of Heron himself.

As soon as I entered the house, I could hear the harpsichord being played in the music room at the back of the house. If Esther was playing, and a lively piece at that, she must be feeling a great deal better. I was right; she looked up with a smile as I paused in the doorway. There was more colour in her cheeks; she'd done her hair in a particularly fashionable style, and was wearing one of her newest gowns.

'Oh dear,' she said. 'No sign of the girl yet? Or any accomplice?'

'Nothing at all.' I slid on to the harpsichord stool beside her, and she pulled in the voluminous petticoats of her pale gown to allow me more space. 'Mrs Fletcher is increasingly frustrated at the lack of progress, McLintoch is enjoying himself, Heron can think of nothing but the coins he unearthed, and Balfour has been told to totally redraw the plans for the Assembly Rooms.'

Esther laughed. 'Well, at least he knows he has work for some weeks to come!'

'I think that's exactly what he *doesn't* want. And now I must go out again. The disembodiment must surely happen tonight. I've never known one put off so long.'

'I wonder if it is because there are four of them,' Esther mused. 'Or the violent manner of their deaths. You know, Charles, I think I will come with you. I am *so* tired of sitting in the house, counting the pots and pans, and adding up the rents from Norfolk, and wondering whether you need more shirts.'

'It'll be very cold,' I warned, worrying at once that it would make her feel worse again. 'And there'll be a crowd – you'll have to wear a gown or risk scandalizing the entire town.'

She leant to brush a kiss against my cheek. 'I scandalized the town when I married you, Charles. But I will endeavour to be respectable for once. I've asked cook to provide an early dinner so there is plenty of time to eat before going out.'

I hesitated. 'I have such a sense of impending disaster. There was the oddest atmosphere in the shop.'

Esther tucked her arm through mine. 'They will not be happy – how can they be? The last thing they will remember is going to bed, perfectly normally, as if it was an ordinary day. And to suddenly come to themselves and realize the truth, that they have been cruelly deprived of life— How can that be anything but distressing?'

I nodded. 'I don't see how anyone can ever live in that house again. Four spirits, and dead under such circumstances!'

'Now, Charles,' she said, lovingly. 'Do not take all the cares of the world on your shoulders. It will be an unpleasant experience, no doubt, but if they can give you even a little information that helps you find Alice, or that accomplice – if he does indeed exist – it will be a very profitable night.'

She was right, but I could not shake off my anxiety.

Twenty-Four

They all – ladies and gentlemen both – enjoy making a fuss.
About anything at all. The more trivial the cause the better.
I confess I'm of the same inclination myself.
[Letter from Louis de Glabre to his friend Philippe
Froidevaux, 21 January 1737]

The snow fell, in huge flakes that settled on the cobbles and piled up in corners. There was a bone-deep chill in the night air. Lanterns burning outside the shops flared redly on the white snow; patches of slush froze over.

Esther pulled her cloak about her and nodded at the butcher who supplied us with meat. He was not the only tradesman who'd turned out to see if the spirits disembodied. The bridge was crowded. Neighbours were standing about or hanging out of their windows; four young gentlemen, slightly the worse for wear, joked noisily with two whores. I spotted one pickpocket being apprehended by the Watch, who were there in force.

Mrs Fletcher was there too, standing at the back of the crowd, looking at the sightseers with considerable contempt. She came directly to me, saying peremptorily, 'Mr Patterson! I trust you don't intend to let this rabble stay here!'

I looked over the noisy crowd. A chestnut seller had set up a brazier, and a local publican had loaded a cask on to a cart and was offering beer to the sightseers with considerable success. 'They're not causing trouble,' I pointed out, 'And if they were, it's up to the Watch to deal with it.'

'This is not a fair,' Mrs Fletcher ground out. 'It's undignified.'

I had to agree with that. 'But the spirits will disembody *inside* the house. The crowd will see nothing and hear very little. Shall we go in?'

Abraham McLintoch was standing at the door of the shop, stamping his feet and rubbing his hands together; a lantern on the end of a pole was cradled in the crook of his arm. His gaze settled on Esther then on Mrs Fletcher and I fancied I saw a little exasperation in his expression. But he *sir*ed and *madam*ed us in his best manner and told the watchmen to keep the crowd off, while I unlocked the door. I stood back to allow Esther and Mrs Fletcher to go first – and felt a hard grip on my arm.

Fowler. His dark lean face glowered into mine. 'I'm coming in.'

'Now, now,' McLintoch said, not wasting a *sir* on someone who was plainly a servant. 'We can't have everybody in the house!'

'It's all right,' I said quickly. 'Mr Fowler knows – *knew* the apprentice well. It would be a good idea to have a friend of the lad's here.'

'Knew him well?' McLintoch said suspiciously. 'How's that?'

'We went whoring together,' Fowler said, baring his teeth.

McLintoch, to my relief, accepted this.

When we were all five in the shop, it seemed cramped and crowded. It was almost as cold inside as it was out; three days without fires had made the house almost uninhabitable. With the door closed, we were left in a darkness relieved only by McLintoch's bright lantern, swinging at the top of its pole and casting erratic dancing shadows across the room. Esther, beside me, shivered; she said lightly, 'Perhaps it would have been more sensible to stay at home!'

'That's where I'd like to be, madam,' McLintoch said.

I called, 'Hello? Anyone here?'

No reply.

I looked around. 'Most of the victims died upstairs, so I think that's where we had better be. Mr Fowler, will you stay downstairs to talk with the boy?'

He had the sense to moderate his language and his behaviour; he ducked his head, said in his most deferential manner, 'Yes, sir.' His dark eyes gleamed in the lantern light.

As we turned for the stairs, he lit a candle from the lantern and fixed the candle in its own wax on the counter. It gave me a fine view of his lean figure draped in a drab serviceable great-coat; I saw the light glint on something protruding from his pocket. A pistol. Perhaps he subscribed to the idea that a killer liked to return to the scene of the foul deed. We needed to talk.

The killer was going to the Assizes; I didn't want to see Fowler there instead, charged with his, or her, murder.

A spirit may disembody anywhere in the house where the living person died, but it is most likely it will appear in the room where death occurred, so we went straight up to the bedrooms. On the landing, Mrs Fletcher withdrew into shadows; Esther hesitated in the doorway to the girls' room, looking at the blood-stained bed, its sheets tumbled on the floor where the intruder on Monday had left them.

'I think I will stay here,' she said. 'The girl – Sarah – might be glad of a woman's consolation.'

McLintoch, with his bright lantern, planted himself in the doorway of the larger room where the parents had slept. There was a nervous energy in the air, a tingling; it set my teeth on edge. McLintoch said, 'It's going to be bad.'

The air seemed to shimmer then settled. We waited. Long minutes. Perhaps tonight was not going to be the night after all. Perhaps they were never going to disembody. It happens, occasionally. But to four people in one house? In such circumstances?

We heard a noise from the darkness downstairs. Fowler's voice, speaking very quietly. 'The boy,' Esther said. Mrs Fletcher walked impatiently into her parents' room, looked about at the debris of her parents' lives: coins, jewellery, books. She sat down on the mattress with a heavy sigh of annoyance. In the dark shadows cast by the lantern, I imagined I saw figures, shapes, the scurry of rats or mice. Something squeaked.

And still Fowler's voice downstairs. Then a cry of distress – unmistakeably a boy's voice. I thought about going down, changed my mind. Better let Fowler deal with the lad. There were things they'd want to say that no one else should hear.

And still nothing up here. McLintoch said, 'Never liked the waiting.' Something seemed to scrape across my skin; I jumped. There was a scream of fury, a shout. The washstand in the larger bedroom toppled over. Candlesticks clattered on to the floor. Mrs Fletcher instinctively started up from the mattress. Light flashed; I closed my eyes against the brightness.

'God almighty,' McLintoch said hoarsely. I opened my eyes again. The books and coins on the bedside table shot into the air then clattered to the floor. The curtains danced across the window, whipped up. One ripped across with a great screech.

A great roar – a male voice.

'He's gone mad!' McLintoch took a step back. I turned to tell Esther to go downstairs, but she was moving into the daughter's bedroom. Through the open doorway I could see a feeble gleam of pale light on the bedstead.

Fowler called up. 'What's happening?'

I wished I knew – this wasn't normal at all. 'Stay down there,' I called back. 'We'll deal with it.'

He was sensible enough not to argue; I heard his footsteps retreat. McLintoch said, 'Don't reckon we ought to interfere.' He was poised with his weight on his back foot, ready to flee. The curtains flew up again and the tumbled bedding stirred. Mrs Fletcher took three swift steps to the door, on to the landing.

I tried to stop her. 'Someone has to bring him to his senses.'

'He never had any,' she said.

I didn't want to talk to Gregson, but it looked like I had no choice. I edged into the room. There ought to be a gleam where the spirit was – pale because new spirits are always weak.

The remains of the curtains swung. One of the books had fallen spine down and the pages riffled violently.

'Samuel Gregson?' I called. 'My name's Patterson—'

A gale swept through the room. The bedding at my feet leapt into the air. I was standing on a corner of it, realized too late and was already falling before I could take evasive action. I stumbled back against the door. The door jerked forward, catching me painfully in the back. It crashed back against the wall with a force that nearly took it off its hinges. I fell back with it, hit my head. The door bounced forward, and I leapt out on to the landing. The door swung, slammed shut, then crashed open again.

The entire house was shaking. The spirit must be mad! Fowler yelled up from below. The door to the girls' room opened and Esther hurried out.

There was no reason the spirit should confine its havoc to one room. It had to be pacified. I gritted my teeth, called, 'Mr Gregson? I want to talk. I know who killed you.'

There was a sudden overwhelming silence. The door had come off one of its hinges and was hanging oddly. From the girls' room came the sound of soft, inconsolable weeping.

'I think your daughter Alice was involved,' I said. 'And a man who was her lover. But I'm not sure *why* they did it. I was wondering if you knew anything.'

Silence still. I had to get the spirit thinking rationally, divert him from this wild fury. I edged nearer the door, hoping to see the spirit. Even *two* spirits – if Mrs Gregson had disembodied, she might be a calming influence on her husband.

I could see nothing.

A tingling crawled across my skin again. McLintoch said, 'I don't like this.'

I didn't want Esther in this house any longer. This was too strange, too unpredictable. 'Esther, Mrs Fletcher, leave the house. Now. And tell Mr Fowler to go too.'

Mrs Fletcher began to protest but Esther took her arm and turned her to the stairs. She glanced back, said, 'Be careful.' McLintoch looked as if he would like to follow them.

I turned back to the room. 'Mr Gregson . . .'

The bed jumped.

It was a big wide bed, good solid oak, and it jumped at least a foot off the floor at the head end. I felt the vibration as it thudded back down on to the floorboards. One of the boards broke and the end snapped up. I stood my ground, fighting the temptation to dash for the stairs. Surely even a spirit as out of control as this one couldn't move anything as heavy as that oak bed more than a few inches.

Footsteps. I glanced round. Fowler hesitated behind me, his pistol in his hand. McLintoch barely waited for him to step off the stairs before he was on them himself, clattering down.

'What's going on?' Fowler said.

'The spirit isn't happy,' I said dryly. I nodded at the pistol. 'That's not going to do much good.'

'It's got me out of worse situations than this.' Fowler raised his voice. 'Gregson! Stop fooling around, man, and talk to us!'

The bed jumped again; Fowler swore. 'Don't worry,' I said, 'that thing's far too heavy . . .'

The head of the bed rose up, lifting until it was standing vertically. Books and candles and water jug and all the bits and pieces of jewellery and coins spun up into the air, came flying across the room towards us. I ducked, but was struck on the cheek by a coin; the sharp corner of a book caught the back of my hand.

The bed started across the floor, the legs on which it stood screeching and screaming.

Fowler raised his pistol and fired at the far wall. Picture glass shattered.

In the sudden deafening silence, the air seemed to thicken. I gasped for breath. Fowler put a hand in my back, pushed me towards the stairs. We hurtled down into the dark shop below. A feeble spirit gleamed on the counter; a young voice quavered, 'Fowler?'

'Get on to the door!' Fowler roared. 'The outside of it!'

We toppled out on to the bridge, slipping and sliding on the snow and ice. I stumbled, and Fowler hauled me up and dragged me across the bridge. The crowd scattered in alarm, screaming and shouting. McLintoch yelled for everyone to run.

We crashed into the parapet of the bridge opposite the shop. Twisting to look back, I saw a faint gleam on the door of the shop – the boy. The spirit was slipping and sliding in that odd way that new spirits do when they can't quite control themselves; I could hear him crying out.

Fowler started back towards him. I tried to grab his arm but he was too quick. Devil take it, if he wasn't careful, he'd let something slip, someone would guess . . .

And then there was a rumbling, and a huge noise, like a clap of thunder directly overhead.

Every window in the house exploded outwards.

Twenty-Five

The best thing of all about England is that everyone is very sociable, liking nothing better than a good gossip. Time passes very pleasantly, even on long journeys.
[Letter from Louis de Glabre to his friend Philippe
Froidevaux, 22 January 1737]

Fowler flung up his arms, ducked his head, then slipped on an icy patch and fell. Glass rained down, and the rumble and roar seemed to go on for ever. I dragged the skirts of my greatcoat up over my head and dodged forward to grab Fowler. Still glass danced in the air amongst the snowflakes; one fragment whipped an inch past my nose. On the door of the house, the boy's spirit was screaming.

I seized Fowler's arm, dragged him to the far side of the bridge. The glass clattered to the ground.

We stood in silence. Snow drifted. The crowd had scattered. Mrs Fletcher was nowhere to be seen but I spotted Balfour sheltering in the doorway of Fleming's shop. Esther had turned her back to the fall of glass and was just looking cautiously over her shoulder to see if the worst was over.

The backs of Fowler's hands were covered in a myriad tiny cuts, dripping blood, where he'd flung them up to protect his face. The boy's spirit had disappeared from the door.

Balfour emerged from his doorway, incredulous. 'How can a spirit do that?'

'I saw something like that once,' McLintoch said. 'In London. A Levant sailor who died raving mad. They had to pull the house down in the end to get rid of him. No one could go near the place.'

'Very cheering,' Esther said dryly. 'Charles, what do we do?'

Fowler seemed to come to his wits, started towards the house. I took McLintoch's arm. 'You'd better send all these people home. Set up a guard on the house overnight. Then tomorrow someone can board up the windows.'

He nodded, plainly relieved; this was more his style of thing; keeping order was something he could do in his sleep. 'Should I get Mr Bell, the vicar? Mebbe he could calm Gregson down.'

'It can't do any harm,' I agreed. 'And in the morning you'd better let Mr Philips know what's happened.'

He grimaced. 'He'll not like it.'

Balfour wanted to talk to me, but Fowler was at the door of the shop, calling the boy's name; we'd left the door open in our flight and he was venturing inside again even now. I hurried after him. The shop wavered in the light of the candle Fowler had stuck to the counter. 'There's nothing you can do.' I glanced back to make sure no one could hear. 'The lad knows you were here – he's not going to think you've abandoned him.'

'I can't leave him on his own.'

There was an ominous creaking and rumbling overhead. I said uneasily, 'That sounds like the stairs.' Lime plaster drifted down from the ceiling; I took Fowler's arm. 'You won't help Ned by getting yourself killed!'

A bang and a clatter; something seemed to snap. 'I'll be back,' Fowler yelled and, yet again, we ran for it.

The minute we were out of the shop, the noise and the rumbling stopped. 'Well, that message is clear enough,' I said. 'He wants everyone out of the house.'

It was a difficult night and it got worse. Esther wanted Fowler to see the surgeon about the cuts on his hands – we could see fragments of glass in the wounds. Fowler was adamant he didn't want to be fussed over. He was going home, he said, before Heron missed him. I didn't believe him – he was probably going to lurk in an alley until he could get back to the bridge unseen. Esther solved the problem by putting her arm through his and turning him along the street towards Gale's house. Fowler might know exactly how to handle women like the whores at the Old Man Inn, but he didn't know how to deal with a lady. It doesn't come within his experience, Heron being a widower.

Balfour insisted on accompanying us, asking questions all the while. Had Gregson done all that damage? Why? Had he said anything? What would happen now? I put up with him as long as I could, even stood on the street with him outside the surgeon's house, in the hope that the cold would drive him away. It didn't.

'It's late,' I said eventually. 'There's nothing more to be done tonight. Why don't you go home?'

He thrust his hands into his pockets, hunched against the cold. 'You're right, I suppose.' He still didn't seem inclined to move. 'My father was killed in the house,' he said, 'and his spirit was so bitterly angry he couldn't say anything that wasn't an insult. He made our lives a misery and we couldn't move.' He shrugged. 'I suppose I'm looking for understanding – wanting to know how such things happen.'

'You'll find no understanding in the Gregson house,' I said bluntly. 'Because Samuel Gregson has no understanding himself. And his family will have a worse time than you did. As spirits they're trapped with him for the next eighty or hundred years.'

He sighed and gave me an apologetic smile. 'I'm afraid I've had a dreadfully trying day. I suppose this is all of a piece with it.'

I didn't see how he could equate having to redraw architectural plans with what had happened to Ned or Sarah.

He went off at last, glancing back several times through the thickening snow. He was heading in the wrong direction for the George; I suspected he'd probably duck into the first tavern he saw.

Fowler was uncharacteristically quiet when he came out of the barber-surgeon's house, and went home with only a token protest. I didn't think he had given in; I thought that he'd abandoned his first impulsive thoughts and was hatching some other, more carefully considered plan.

I slept badly, dreaming of being caught in blizzards of glass and snow. And in the morning, there was another note sitting on the table at the foot of the stairs, a folded piece of rough paper, of the sort one gets in inns. George hung on the edge of the table and said disapprovingly, 'It must be from a ruffian, Master. Why are you mixing with ruffians so much now?'

So much for his good intentions. I bit my lip in an attempt to say nothing but it was useless. 'George. Mind your manners!'

The spirit flared green for a moment, then faded, 'Yes, Master,' it said, subdued.

Esther was already in the breakfast room, reading a newspaper over her coffee and toast. She smiled up at me, then saw what I held. 'Is that another note from Alice Gregson?'

'It looks very like it.' I eased up the blob of sealing wax on the back of the folded note. The neat childish hand was very familiar by now, but this time Alice had gone beyond a mere protestation of innocence. I read aloud:

> You have not heeded me. I told you I did not steal the money. Now I tell you plainly – I did not kill my parents, nor my sister, nor the boy. I suppose you will take no notice of this either. You are a fool like all the rest.

Esther grimaced wryly. 'She knows how to win people to her side, does she not?'

I waved the note. 'Does she expect me to act on this? Does she think it will enlist my goodwill on her behalf?'

Esther poured me coffee. 'I suspect she doesn't think very much at all. She is a silly girl, though dangerous.'

I sipped the coffee and tried to be more calm. 'I suppose I ought to go down to the shop and see if there have been any developments overnight.'

'Do you not have lessons today?'

I sighed. 'I'll have to cut some short, and be late for others. No way to recommend myself to pupils.'

'Cancel them,' Esther recommended. 'If you were ill, you would not hesitate to do so.'

Last time I was ill, before my marriage, I worked through all my lessons as usual. Esther was brought up in a household that was never short of money; I was brought up in one that knew you should earn as much as you can today in case disaster strikes tomorrow.

'If Alice does have an accomplice,' Esther said, 'he must surely have followed her up from London.'

I nodded.

'And of course,' Esther said, 'we do know someone who came up from London recently.'

'Do we?'

'The thief-catcher,' she said, 'Joseph Kane.'

'*Kane*?' I echoed incredulously.

'Think about it,' she recommended. 'You only have his word for it that he *is* a thief-catcher. Or that he was hired by someone in Kent. Or has followed someone north. You only have *his* description of this exciseman he says he's looking for – this Hitchings might be entirely fictional.'

'It can't be Kane,' I protested. 'Hugh and I saw him arrive in town on Monday evening, nearly two days after the murders.'

'But who is to say he was not here before that? Perhaps he was staying out of town – Gateshead, perhaps – and crept into town on Saturday night to meet Alice. If everything had gone to plan, no one would ever have known he was in the area. But things went wrong and he invented the tale of a thief-catcher to divert suspicion.'

'Why did he not simply flee?'

She considered, sipping her coffee. 'Because he wants to know how the investigation is proceeding. He wants to be aware if any danger threatens him.'

'He'd be in no danger if he hadn't stayed in town!'

Esther was not discouraged. 'Then perhaps he is looking for Alice. Suppose she was the one who killed the family and tried to blame it on him, and he is trying to get his revenge. And,' she added, 'he is personable, in a rough sort of way – he might have charmed Alice.'

I didn't entirely agree with her, but I couldn't afford to ignore the idea. I sighed. 'I suppose I'd better go and talk to him again.' If I could find him, I thought uncomfortably. Yesterday he'd been talking of following someone to Shields; what if that had been simply an excuse to flee? 'I want to go up to Heron's too, and check on Fowler.'

Esther played with her toast. 'I saw Claudius Heron yesterday.'

'He wasn't in the vicinity of the Groat Market, was he?'

'Only a street or two away. He ignored me.'

I stared at her in outrage. 'He snubbed you!'

'No, no.' She smiled in amusement. 'I do not think he even registered who I was – he was very preoccupied.'

'It's these damn antiquities. He seems to think of nothing else. He didn't attend the meeting Balfour had with the Directors of the Rooms yesterday.'

Esther looked thoughtful. 'I admit that my acquaintance with Mr Balfour is slight, but I probably would happily have missed a meeting with him too. He was full of his own woes last night.'

I laughed. 'I'll go up to Heron's house now and challenge him to give me satisfaction for ignoring you.'

'Do so,' she said cordially. 'Would you care to invite him to dinner too? Now I am better, I feel like being sociable again.'

I promised I would, but doubted I could persuade Heron to it.

The day was overcast and cold but at least it wasn't snowing. I went to the house on the bridge and found a watchman super-vising the fastening of boards over the shattered windows. The watchman was a big man, and cheerful despite the cold.

'All quiet, sir. Hardly seen sight nor sound of any of the spirits.'

'Not even the apprentice?'

He shook his head. 'Heard weeping upstairs once, or thought I did, but it stopped pretty quick.'

'That would be the daughter.' I glanced around; a few sightseers lingered but mainly in passing rather than coming specifically to watch. 'And no one's tried to get in the house?'

'Don't you worry, sir,' he said, almost in happy anticipation of an attempt, 'no one'll get past me.'

I believed him. I also believed Fowler wouldn't sit passively at home. And just at the moment, keeping Fowler from running his head into a noose was more important to me even than finding Alice Gregson, and this mysterious accomplice of hers.

But I was going to do both.

I went off to talk to Joseph Kane.

Twenty-Six

There is no point in trying to disabuse a gentleman of any idea he has formed; once he has conceived it, he'll never give it up.

[Letter from Louis de Glabre to his friend Philippe Froidevaux, 22 January 1737]

Kane was in one of the Golden Fleece's parlours, eating his way through a breakfast of cold meats, pies, bread and cheese, and copious amounts of beer. He sat back with his habitual insolence.

'Didn't know you paid social calls on the likes of me.' He sneered. 'Didn't leave your card.'

I refused to rise to the bait, relieved to see him; surely his return from his trip meant he wasn't our man. I leant my hands on the back of a chair. 'Did you have any success in finding your man yesterday?'

'Wouldn't be here if I had,' he said. 'Never was in this town before and I can tell you I never will be again. What's with you Scotch? Suspicious lot, all of you.'

I bit my tongue on the 'Scotch' insult. Kane was doing his best to annoy me, and I wasn't going to show him he was succeeding. 'No one cooperating?'

'So,' he drawled, spearing a piece of beef on his knife, 'have *you* found your girl yet?' A malicious grin blossomed on his face. 'A slip of a lass, they tell me. A flighty, flirty sort, with nothing on her mind but pretty little ribbons and shoes.'

I sat down on the chair, crossed my legs and cultivated a nonchalant air. He hadn't told me what had happened in Shields; I suspected he'd not got through the snow and was refusing to admit it. 'I thought you were of the opinion *your* man was behind the murders. That he'd seduced the girl with sweet nothings and got the keys from her to rob the house.'

He was chewing hard on the beef, knife in hand. 'Devil take it, say what you came to say, instead of all this dancing around the subject. If you've got it in mind to accuse me of something, do it.'

This was rather more confrontational than I liked, but I was committed to it now. 'I want proof of this fellow you're after.' I saw his face darken. 'I've only your word he exists.'

He roared with fury. 'Damn you! You're still the same insolent know-it-all you were on the boat! Smirking and preening at your own cleverness! Accusing honest men!' He jabbed his knife in my direction. 'Get out of here before I do something I don't regret! Get out!'

With a flick of his wrist, he threw the knife.

I sat rigidly still, felt the draught as it skimmed past my cheek, heard it thud into the door behind me. And saw Kane's face twist in fury, because I didn't react as he wanted me to.

'Well,' I said, getting up. 'I'll leave you to your breakfast.' I turned my back on him. The knife was still quivering in the door jamb; I took hold of it. It resisted for a moment, then jerked out. I leant across the table and held the handle out to Kane. 'Your knife.'

Then I made a quick exit while he was still gawping.

That went well.

In the freezing cold, I walked up the Side to St Nicholas's church, cut across the High Bridge and came out on to Pilgrim Street, brooding on Kane. He'd seemed genuinely outraged, but if he'd had the audacity to commit such murders and stay in town, he'd certainly be capable of lying convincingly. On the whole, I was inclined to believe in his innocence.

At the top of Pilgrim Street, I came on to Northumberland Street where the houses of the wealthy lie in extensive gardens. Fresh snow lay at the edges of the street, against the walls, but in the centre of the road, the snow had been worn to slush by the passing of carts and pedestrians and was uncomfortably slippery.

Heron's house is in the upper part of the street behind a high wall, one of the oldest houses in town, its old-style architecture forbidding. The carriage drive to the door had been cleared, as had a path round to the stables at the back, but the wide lawns on either side were snow-covered. Heron's butler bowed me in and asked me to wait, disappearing towards the back of the house. I waited, looking round the hall, faintly intimidated, as always, by its expensive floor-to-ceiling mirrors, fashionable wallpaper and elegant Chinese statuettes. A niche was filled with three ancient figures: athletes poised forever in the act of throwing javelins, their skin polished to a fine smoothness, marred only by a chip or two that time had taken out of them.

The butler came back and bowed me into Heron's study, a room heavy with old wainscoting and tall bookcases. To my astonishment, the curtains were still drawn and the room lit by dozens of candles. Heron himself was standing behind a large table, draining a wineglass. He looked tired; his coat was wrinkled as if he'd been wearing it too long. I was astonished – I've never seen Heron less than immaculate.

He told the butler to bring coffee and startled me further by asking, 'Is it morning?' Maps and plans were spread on the table, a few ancient coins placed carefully on a bed of cloth in a small box. Heron pushed them towards me.

'These are the best preserved coins from the hoard. I have tentatively dated them to the first arrival of the Romans in this part of the country, but they could be a little later – it is difficult to be certain. I have been correlating what is already known . . .'

I watched as he shifted papers. *Horrified* was perhaps too strong a word for my feelings on seeing him, but only by a trifle. Heron is always rational and cool; this seemed to be bordering on obsession. He'd not greeted me, or asked me if I'd come for any particular reason, or asked after Esther, which he was usually punctilious in doing.

The butler came back bearing a salver with coffee and two dishes; he gave me a long steady look, as if trying to convey some meaning without disturbing the impassive demeanour expected of a man in his position. Heron pushed a map across the table. 'As you can see, the present Tyne Bridge is built almost exactly over the original Roman construction. Here is the line of the main road cutting through the town. The Romans tended to build in straight lines, so it is easy enough to trace.' He pointed out numbers he'd marked on the map. 'These indicate the finds discovered in the vicinity of the mercer's shop: a skeleton found last century, the coins, and Demsey's ring.' He glanced up at me. 'I take it the ring has still not been recovered.'

I poured two dishes of coffee. The butler had also brought a few wedges of bread and cheese but Heron shook his head when I offered them to him.

'There's no sign of the ring.' There was plainly no point in talking to Heron about anything but the antiquities; I said, 'Were you approached last year — about June or July — with the offer of coins like these?'

He raised an eyebrow. 'No. Do you mean to say there are more?'

'I believe similar coins were in one of the boxes in Gregson's cellar.' I explained my reasoning. 'It's not clear whether Gregson acquired the coins legitimately, or stole them, but his intention was probably to sell the coins on to a collector like yourself.'

Heron shifted the papers, sipped at his coffee, put the dish down, shifted the papers again. 'Do you know where these coins are now?'

I decided against mentioning Fowler directly. 'I've asked someone to check whether they've been offered for melting down.'

'Melting down!' Heron gripped my arm. 'You must find them! If they have fallen into criminal hands, I will buy them back. No questions asked, no charges brought. We must move quickly. They must not be destroyed!'

This was beginning to seem like madness. 'I'll find them,' I said rashly, merely intent on calming him. 'I've no reason to believe they've yet been offered to anyone. I suspect the murderer is waiting for the fuss to die down before trying to dispose of them.'

Heron paused, let go of my arm, reached for the coffee again. 'Of course. I was worrying unnecessarily. Of course.'

'The reason I came,' I said, 'was that I was worried an attempt might be made to steal *your* artefacts.' I indicated the coins in their box.

He frowned. Heavens, but he was thinking slowly today!

'When I was attacked in the street,' I explained, 'I thought the villain was after the keys to Gregson's shop. That may be true, but he also took the coin I'd picked up in the street. Demsey's ring was stolen. Balfour's rooms were also ransacked and a Roman coin was taken. It's beginning to look like this villain is specifically after the antiquities.'

'You think he is a collector too?'

'Or he knows one who'll pay handsomely for them.' I nodded at the coins. 'If our villain knows about Hugh's ring, he'll certainly know about your coins – he only needs to buy beer for one of your workmen and he'll have the whole story. He may decide to burgle this house to try and obtain them.'

Heron laughed without humour. 'There is not the slightest chance anyone could break into this house.' He looked uncomfortable, however, and bent to ring the bell for the butler.

I persisted. 'The villain may be a man from Kent – he's broken into a number of houses there. His usual method is to woo one of the maids and get the keys from her.'

'My maids know better than to listen to any plausible rogues.' Heron sounded totally confident of that fact; perhaps there was a little threat in his voice too. The butler returned. Heron said, 'You were telling me about some untoward occurrence last night. Repeat what you said for Mr Patterson.'

The butler glanced at me. 'It was a small incident, sir. Someone tried to force the garden gate.'

'I take it he was unsuccessful.'

'Of course, sir.'

Heron poured himself more coffee. 'I want a watch kept. Someone sitting at the scullery door all night. And let the dogs loose in the garden.' He dismissed the butler. 'Who is this man from Kent?'

Was Kane's story true? Best to work on that assumption for the moment. 'A man called Hitchings. But that's probably not the name he's going under at the moment.'

'And you think he seduced the Gregson girl to get into the house?'

'It's possible.'

Heron nodded. He fingered the coins. Not quite circular, tarnished, and a little worn, that strange, almost barbaric monarch's head slightly raised from the surface. 'So old and so enduring. I never cease to be amazed at the beauty of such things.'

'Yes,' I said. 'I mean, no. Of course.'

He drained the coffee. 'I must sleep. Don't worry, Patterson, no one is going to get into this house. You will keep me apprised if you find the coins stolen from Gregson?'

'Of course.'

He nodded.

I left the house more worried than when I'd come. I'd never seen Heron in this state before. To dismiss the attempt to gain access to the house so easily when the villain had already got into the Gregsons' shop and murdered the entire family!

I didn't want to see another death added to the list.

Twenty-Seven

It has to be said that no one particularly gives themselves up to philosophizing. They would all much rather drink.
[Letter from Louis de Glabre to his friend Philippe Froidevaux, 22 January 1737]

I was hardly out of the house when Fowler stepped out from behind a clump of bushes. He jerked his head for me to follow and led the way along the cleared path that led to the stables. Just under an arch, he drew me back into a corner by an old pump. He glanced round but the stable yard was silent except for the snuffling of a horse and a brief clatter of hooves. He had taken the surgeon's bandages off his right hand, I saw, presumably so he could use the hand more easily, and the skin was red with cross-crossing scratches. One or two had bled again recently.

'Seen his Lordship?' he said sourly.

'He looked appalling! I take it he hasn't been to bed?'

'Can't get his mind off those bits and pieces of rubbish.' Fowler bared his teeth. 'Told me not to worry him. So I went off and had another word with Ned.'

'There's supposed to be a watchman on the shop at all times,' I said dryly.

'Watchmen drink, don't they?' Fowler sneered. 'A word or two and a coin, and they fancy a few minutes in the warm tavern.'

'What did Ned say?'

Fowler's face was white; I'd never seen him so angry. 'Gregson's spirit is terrorizing the household. Told the women he'll make every minute of the day and night a misery if they don't do as he says. And doing as he says means keeping quiet. He's got them in the girls' room and won't let them out. Has the other room to himself. But he doesn't much care about Ned.' His voice was bitter. 'Never cared much about him when he was alive, not going to change now.'

A vicious breeze drifted around the stable yard. 'Does Ned remember what happened on Saturday night?'

'Not a thing, thank God. Everything as usual. Except everyone was in a bad mood because Alice was gone when she was wanted. Gregson was in a devil of a state, evidently. When Ned got back after seeing me, he was telling his wife they should pack Alice off to London. But the moment the girl said she'd go gladly, he refused her! Couldn't bear not to have his own way.' He added grudgingly, 'Ned says he knows about the coins in the cellar. I told him he should talk to you about them.'

I recognized this for a peace offering. 'I'd very much like to talk to him.'

Fowler gave me a long hard stare. 'He's worried about what might happen if Gregson gets wind of it.'

The lad was dead; there wasn't much more that could happen. But I suspected he wasn't thinking about himself.

'Didn't want me to go back,' Fowler said, his mind apparently running on the same track. 'Said people would start asking questions about why I'm there.'

'Say you're helping me look into the murders.'

He nodded slowly. 'Maybe that would ease his mind. But once you've got the girl, there's no excuse left, is there?'

I didn't think he'd find it a consolation if I said I didn't antici-pate catching Alice soon. 'We'll deal with that situation when we get to it. When can we speak to him?'

He contemplated me long and hard, said finally, 'This afternoon.'

'In daylight?'

'If people can see you,' he said, 'they always reckon you can't be doing anything wrong. Besides, if we're seen, it'll convince people we're working together, won't it?'

I thought of what his life must be like, always hiding his true self, always thinking of what people might see, or do. 'I'll mention it to one or two people, to add credence to the tale.'

He nodded. 'Sometimes I wonder why we're any of us here at all.' He gave me a sour look. 'We're all just getting through our days somehow, making the time pass. His Lordship has his coins, and you've got your music, and I press clothes and fold 'em and store 'em, and kill a bit of time with a handsome lad with a keen sense of fun and a way of making you forget yourself. But it's all pretty nothings to distract us from the truth. It comes down to one thing – we're all looking for some way to get ourselves from the cradle to the grave in the least painful way we can think of.' He leered at me. 'And you know, I can't see the point.'

I hesitated to speak, alarmed. I didn't want to patronize Fowler, but I certainly wanted to discourage this kind of thinking. 'I don't know what the point is,' I said at last. 'But whatever *you* think, Sarah Gregson no doubt thought differently, *and* your lad – they wanted to go on living and weren't allowed to. You don't have to believe in some higher purpose to life to know that killing them's wrong.'

He laughed harshly. 'That's what I like about you, Patterson. You see things so clearly.' And he walked off, back to the house.

I had to rush to my first lesson of the day and found my pupil impatiently pacing up and down the drawing room floor as if *she*'d never been late. She tossed the music on to the music stand with a great display of hauteur and started playing a jig at top speed with a good many wrong notes. I sat down and reconciled myself to being ignored for half an hour while the young lady played the pieces exactly as she chose. My next two pupils were more cooperative but neither had much interest in music for its own sake; one preferred to tell me, at length, about the young man she had in mind for a husband. I didn't think her parents would be happy to know she'd set her eye on a mere clerk from the Printing Office.

And all the while, this business was running in my head. Alice Gregson, surely now in that other world. An unknown lover or accomplice, perhaps the man from Kent, perhaps Kane himself. Fowler – devil take it, did all that talk mean anything? He'd certainly do nothing until Alice was caught, then the problem would be to stop him killing her. Heron, obsessed with those coins; I'd never seen him so heedless of everyday niceties. And there was something else – some*one* else I'd forgotten. Who?

I escaped at last and made my way home, anxious to have a bite to eat and some of Esther's soothing presence before hurrying on to my next lesson. Esther was at the harpsichord in the music room again, going over a phrase she always plays wrongly. The winter afternoon was so gloomy she'd lit a branch of candles; I stood for a moment in the doorway, admiring her slender figure in the pale gown, the graceful curves of arms and neck. Looking at the pale eyelashes lying on her cheeks as she glanced down at the keys of the harpsichord, the way she pursed her lips in concentration . . .

She said irritably, 'Yes, I know it is bad, Charles. There is no need to grin like that!'

'I wasn't grinning at your playing, but at you.' I kissed those lips which is exactly what I'd been thinking of. If I hadn't had to go out again, I would have lingered a lot longer on that kiss. I leant on the harpsichord. 'You're trying to put too many ornaments in the piece, too many grace notes.'

'Too many?' She raised an eyebrow. 'Really, Charles, the length of time I have practised those trills and now you tell me they are unnecessary!'

'You're distracting attention from the melody. It's the air itself that's important – the graces are merely an additional pleasure.'

She sighed. 'I would not mind so much if it was not such a

dull piece of music.' She took my hand lovingly. 'Write me something of your own, Charles.'

'Mr Scarlatti,' I said severely, sitting down beside her on the harpsichord stool and putting an arm round her waist, 'is considered the best composer of harpsichord music now living. And *I* am decidedly not a great composer.'

'But your music is fun to play,' she protested. 'Always full of delightfully unexpected Scotch tunes. Surely music should be entertaining?'

'Don't start on that topic again!' Last time we had dinner with Claudius Heron, we spent three hours discussing whether music should be mere entertainment, whether it had an educational purpose or, as Heron insisted, a moral imperative. It had been a stimulating discussion, but at one point Heron had become so heated, I thought we'd come to blows. Which reminded me . . .

'I forgot to ask Heron to dinner,' I confessed. She sighed. I protested and told her the tale of my encounter with the gentleman.

'It is not like him to be so preoccupied with trifles,' she said, frowning.

I laughed. 'He'd be horrified to hear you call them that!'

She made a dismissive gesture and the lace on her sleeve tickled my hand. 'There's nothing important about ancient coins or half-broken statuettes with neither grace nor beauty, whose only virtue is that they are old.'

I'd have loved to see Heron's reaction to such heresy. I kissed her again. She emerged a little ruffled. 'I take it you have been teaching all morning. Have you heard what is going on at the shop?'

'Gregson's not causing trouble again?'

'You have to remember I have not ventured out of the house yet,' she said, 'and the tales have been brought to me by George, which means they will have been slightly embellished—'

'Only slightly?'

She gave me a mischievous grin. 'Apparently Mr Bell the vicar went down to talk to Gregson and the spirit threw the tiles off the roof at him.' She leant close to my ear and whispered, 'I am afraid all this is setting George a very bad example – he has been trying to lift the candlesticks on the mantelpiece!'

The prospect of George's spirit tossing household furniture around appalled me. 'He didn't succeed?'

'Thankfully, no. Charles—'

I heard a certain note in her voice and knew we were coming to what she really wanted to say. She said carefully, 'You surely do not need to go back to that house?'

I remembered my appointment with Fowler and winced.

'Charles!' She drew back, exasperated.

'I want to talk to the apprentice,' I said apologetically. 'But there's nothing to worry about. I don't intend to disturb Gregson's spirit.'

'I know you don't *intend* to.'

She spoke lightly enough but I saw real anxiety in her eyes. That decided me. This affair was going on much too long; it was time I put an end to it, before anyone else got hurt. 'George!' I called, and the spirit slid between the door and the jamb. 'I need you to take some messages. I'm cancelling all my lessons this afternoon.'

Whoever had murdered the Gregsons, I was going to catch them. And very soon.

Twenty-Eight

Have I already said? I adore the women!
[Letter from Louis de Glabre to his friend Philippe
Froidevaux, 22 January 1737]

My first visit was to Balfour. The servants told me he was in his room, and gave me the sort of useless instructions – *up the stairs, turn left and it's straight in front of you* – that people who are used to a house think are sufficient for strangers to find their way. I insisted on one of the maids taking me up and paid her a penny for doing so. Following her through the twists and turns and odd corners, I thought wryly that the thief had been lucky to find his way. Which, of course, suggested he was familiar with the inn.

'I suppose you're happy working here?' I asked.

The maid dimpled at me. 'Mustn't complain, sir!'

'No awkward souls amongst the other servants?'

'Not here!' she said, shocked. 'It's a good place, this.'

'I can tell you know your business,' I said admiringly. 'Have you worked here long?'

'Five years last Monday,' she said promptly.

'You'll know everyone here then, I daresay. You wouldn't have noticed any strangers hanging around?'

'Look,' she said, stopping dead in the middle of a passageway. 'If you're going to suggest I robbed the gent, then just say it! And I'll tell you what I told the gent himself. I wouldn't risk my job for his silly little trinkets, and neither would anyone else here!'

And she flounced off, leaving me stranded which, I supposed, was what I deserved.

I looked for Balfour's room by scratching on every door I thought might be his, disturbing in the process a middle-aged couple reading their Bible aloud, and a whore who turned on me with a winning look until she saw I wasn't the person she was expecting. 'And tell him to hurry up!' she yelled after me.

I eventually scratched on the right door. Balfour called entry and I found him sitting over the plans for the Assembly Rooms, which lay unrolled on the table with tankards and dirty plates weighing down the corners; he'd apparently been scrawling notes for changes on a scrap of paper. He looked tired, as if he hadn't slept, but was cheerful.

He tossed down his pen. 'Patterson!' he said with open-faced pleasure. 'I'm glad to see you! Or anyone,' he added, which was less than complimentary. 'I'm beyond caring about all these alterations!'

'You look as if you've been up half the night with them.'

'Working till the small hours.' He pushed the scrap of paper on to the plans, released the weights and let the plans roll up. 'And nothing to show for it but a headache and sore eyes.' He leapt up. 'Come for a bite to eat.'

'I've just eaten. To be honest, I wanted to ask about that burglary you had.'

'Oh, that's not worth spending time on! Nothing but a minor irritation.' He tucked his arm through mine and turned me to the door. 'At the very least, have a drink with me and tell me what's been going on. They're saying the spirit tried to kill the vicar!'

He led the way through the maze of corridors as I detailed what I knew of the vicar's adventures.

'Gregson's behaving abominably,' Balfour said, laughing. 'But then *I'd* be furious if my daughter had killed me and stolen all my wealth.' He sobered. 'I don't mean to treat the business lightly. Do you still have no idea where Alice Gregson is?'

'I was wondering,' I said, determined to get out the question I'd come to ask, 'whether you saw anyone suspicious hanging around the George in the day or so before you were burgled.'

We'd come to the head of the stairs down to the yard; Balfour stared at me in some perplexity. 'Why?'

'I think your burglary may be connected to the murders.'

'But how?'

Reluctantly, I explained. 'It's possible someone is collecting antiquities and it was the coin he really wanted from you.'

Balfour silently assimilated this.

'Who knew you had the coin?' I said. 'Did anyone see you take it from the ruins?'

He shook his head.

'And you put it on the mantelpiece?'

'The servants knew it was there,' he said. 'It must have been one of them.'

'Not necessarily. *Did* you see anyone acting suspiciously?'

'Well . . .' He hesitated. 'Yes. And no. For heaven's sake, there are always odd people around inns! You never know whether they should be there or not. Most of them are drunk.'

I described Kane's exciseman to him. 'Did you see anyone of that description?'

He shook his head dubiously. 'Is he significant?'

'He's committed some burglaries in Kent. A thief-taker's looking for him.'

He looked shocked. 'Do you mean— Did he kill in Kent too?'

'Apparently.'

For a moment he plainly didn't know what to say. He paced up and down, his face bright red, his fists clenched. 'Everything's wrong!' he burst out. 'The whole world! Just like my father! Everyone at each other's throats . . .'

'Not at all . . .'

But he was clattering down the stairs ahead of me; I heard an ostler call to him to take care on the slippery cobbles. By the time I reached the yard, he was out of sight.

I dawdled around the ostlers, and the stable boy, and the maids, asking if they'd seen anyone suspicious. As far as the ostler was concerned, anyone who wasn't a horse was suspicious; to the stable boy, all *women* were suspicious – and he loved the idea of finding out more. The maids were mostly too busy to spare me much time; I suspected they'd been warned off by the one who'd escorted me upstairs.

I abandoned Balfour's burglar and tackled Hugh's. There was plainly no prospect of getting any more useful information out of the widow, but I wandered into the clockmakers on the ground floor of the building and found two talkative apprentices. One lived off the premises, but the other slept in the shop and had heard Hugh's burglar leaving. He'd even peered out through the shutters to see who it was. But there wasn't a lantern burning nearby – all he'd seen was a man wearing a greatcoat. Tallish, thinnish and darkish, he said. That description didn't sound like Kane's exciseman.

I went back to the inn next to the mercer's house and found the landlord enjoying new prosperity, serving the workmen who were digging up every part of the mercer's shopsite with enormous enthusiasm. They were apparently getting paid by the day and were determined to make the job last as long as possible.

The landlord had seen no one hanging around but one of the workman had. 'Very nice she was too,' he said grinning. 'Tall lady, in a cloak and hood. Stood watching for an age. I thought she might like to come back home with me but she declined.' He said the last word with an elaborately cultured accent, in gentle mockery.

'Fair-haired?' I asked.

'Dark,' he said regretfully. 'But a handsome figure for all that.'

A dark-haired woman in a hood and cloak. There was something I'd heard, or seen, but I couldn't quite remember what. Half-distracted by the fugitive memory, I asked, 'Did she say anything?'

'*Have you found anything?*' He mimicked her voice again, giving his fellow workmen the chance for a hearty laugh.

'And you said?'

'I said, '*It's more than my job's worth to tell you what we've found in here.*'

'Buried treasure,' someone called from the back of the crowd of workmen.

'Spanish doubloons!'

'Nay,' said the workman. 'It were the Holy Grail!'

I walked to the end of the street along the alley behind the inn and back along to the other side of the site, still mulling over that annoying half-memory. Here the snow still lay more thickly, almost undisturbed. Beyond the site, I found the place where Alice Gregson had tempted me into the other world and stood contemplating the snow. Why should she have betrayed her ability to *step through*? It seemed ridiculously foolish.

Only one explanation occurred to me: it had been a test to see if I had that ability too, and to what extent.

Behind me, the workmen laughed and joked over their digging. How could Alice have known there was even a possibility I could *step through*?

Now I remembered what had been eluding me! Sunday. In Gregson's shop with Balfour, looking for a hint as to why Alice Gregson should have killed her entire family. I'd seen someone on the bridge while I was trying to fix the broken shutter, and found myself briefly in that other world, facing a cloaked and hooded woman who'd hurried away from me. *A dark-haired woman.* Like the woman the workman had seen.

She'd known I could step through. Had she passed that information on to Alice?

I'd suspected Alice had an accomplice, but had been looking for a man. What if it had been a woman?

Twenty-Nine

They love nothing better than love, which is a delight for someone of my tastes.

[Letter from Louis de Glabre to his friend Philippe Froidevaux, 22 January 1737]

And as if I'd conjured her up out of the air, Alice Gregson was watching me. She leant against the wall of the alley, her cloak pulled tight against the cold; I glimpsed demure white petticoats beneath. She was toying with improbably golden curls hung with ribbons, and gave me a coy look. 'Mr Patterson? I'm charmed to meet you again, sir.' She bobbed a little curtsey, mockingly. 'I've been watching and thought you might appreciate a little conversation.'

'And in our own world too,' I said. 'Aren't you afraid of being captured?'

She grinned. 'There's no holding me, Mr Patterson.' She gave me a flirtatious look. 'If I was captured, I could simply walk out of my prison cell into that other world.'

That was, I had to admit, a problem.

'You gave me a test to see whether I could step through too,' I said. 'The first time we met, you tempted me to follow you into that other world.'

She giggled. 'Alice said you might be dangerous. I was just seeing if she was right.'

'*Alice?*' I echoed blankly, not comprehending.

She opened her eyes wide, innocently. 'But surely you know about her, Mr Patterson – you saw her outside the shop on the bridge in the other world. She was just out for a walk and there you were!' Her impish grin widened. 'Why, Mr Patterson, don't say you hadn't guessed.'

Dear God, there were *two* Alices? Almost everyone has a counterpart in the other world, and sometimes, as in Hugh's case, those counterparts are not identical to us. There was no reason the Alice of our own world should not be fair-haired and slight, and the Alice of the other world, taller and darker. But how had they met?

She was watching me with a demure smile. 'You *have* guessed! So delightful, isn't it? To meet one's own self in another world? Have you ever met yourself, Mr Patterson?'

I had, briefly, and had run away almost at once. And in all my visits to the other world, I had carefully avoided him, and tried my best to do nothing to damage his reputation. And Alice Gregson had plainly danced straight into conversation with her counterpart and apparently found a kindred soul.

Two of them trying to run rings round us! Which had sent me the notes? More importantly, which had done the murders? Both? Or neither?

'You're not very alike,' I said, to gain time to absorb this shock.

'We're not in the least alike!' she said gaily. She leant forward to confide. 'She'd be horrified if she knew I was here!'

That was interesting. Were they not acting entirely in unison? 'So why are you?'

'I thought I might persuade you to forget about us.' She danced forward, took hold of my coat, stood very close, looking up at me winningly from under her eyelashes.

'Forget about four murdered people?'

'Oh, who cares about them!' She ran her finger over my chest. 'You've no notion how irritating my father could be!'

'And that was reason enough to kill him, was it?'

'You should have met *Alice's* father,' she said. 'He was even nastier than mine!'

'And did she kill *him*?'

'She didn't get the chance.' She sighed. 'He fell under a cart!'

'Very disobliging of him,' I said. The shock was turning to anger. 'So which of you killed *your* family?'

That wheedling look again; her eyes were remarkably blue and sparkling. 'We didn't do it.' She smoothed her fingers across my shoulder. Her scent was thick and heavy; the curls on the top of her head tickled my chin. 'Didn't you get our notes?'

'Indeed I did. Very melodramatic.'

She giggled. 'I went to a play in London where they used that trick. *True Lovers' Tales*! Alice said it was too ridiculous for words, but I thought it would tease you.'

Tease was not the word I would have used; I felt an unexpected pang of sympathy with the absent other Alice. 'What happened last Saturday night?'

She stared at me a moment, then sighed. 'You really aren't going to forget about this, are you?'

'No.'

'But it's so silly!' She looked up at me, blue eyes brimming with tears. '*Please,*' she said brokenly.

She was very pretty, and had all the fashionable winning ways of a society Miss, but I encounter such wiles every day when my female pupils want to persuade me they really *have* practised. They have no effect on me any more. And especially not when I am so angry I can hardly speak. How dared she believe she could pass all this off with a few pouts and pretty glances! How dared she think me such a fool as to fall for a such tricks!

'And was your mother irritating too?' I snapped. 'And your sister?'

'Sarah was going to be married,' she said viciously, all hint of tears gone. 'And I was going to be stuck at home, cleaning and cooking and serving in that foul shop.'

'And Ned?'

She stared at me blankly. 'Who?'

'The apprentice.'

She wrinkled up her nose. 'He was *horrible.*'

'He didn't respond to your overtures, I suppose?'

Obviously an accurate guess; she flung herself away from me sulkily. The voices of the workmen carried in the thin cold air; a dog barked. I worked to keep control of my anger. I had to learn all I could, think of some way to outwit her, to counteract her ability to *step through.*

'I met someone in London,' Alice said, gesturing grandiloquently. 'Someone *beautiful.* We fell in love. We wanted to marry. We *could* have married – I'm of full age, I didn't need my father's permission.' She didn't seem of full age; she seemed like a particularly capricious miss in her teens.

'But we'd no money.' She pouted. 'I had my allowance of course, but that was *ridiculously* small and *he* had nothing at all. And then my uncle died and I had to come back here.'

'So you thought your father might have some money.'

'He did – lots and lots of it!' She danced back to me, fluttered her eyelashes. 'I did *try* to persuade him to give me some, you know, but he wouldn't let me have a penny.'

I knew that to be a lie, according to Mrs Cunningham's first-hand account. 'So you decided to take it anyway. And did you honestly intend to ride to Scotland with this young man of yours? Does he have a name, by the way?'

'Richard,' she said dreamily. 'He's *so* handsome!' Another coy look. 'We were almost married anyway. In Scotland, we would have been – all you have to do to be married there is to live together as man and wife.'

I was hazy on Scotch wedding customs, having myself done the traditional thing and married in church. I wasn't going to argue with her, or show her how shocked I was at what she'd just admitted. I wanted her to stay and tell me the rest of the tale about *Richard*.

'He's a naval officer,' she said dreamily. 'He looks so dashing in his uniform!'

'A naval officer,' I said, heavily. Kane was a sailor – he could easily have posed as an officer.

Alice giggled. 'I'm not silly, you know. I know he wants the money more than he wants me. But that's all right. I want my freedom and I don't care how I get it. I don't have to share the money, do I?'

So the trip to Scotland would never have taken place. 'But you'd share it with the other Alice?'

She nodded. 'It was *his* idea, you know,' she said. 'Robbing the house, I mean. He's done this sort of thing before.'

'In Kent?'

A huge smile transformed her face. She looked childlike, mischievous. 'You found that out? So you *are* as clever as Alice said. He robbed *dozens* of houses.'

'Did you also know he'd killed some of the people he robbed?'

'I read the papers,' she said. I remembered the cuttings I'd found in her trunk; I reminded myself to look at those more closely. 'But *he* don't know *I* know. He thinks I believe every word he told me. He said he inherited lots of money but had to spend most of it since he'd left the navy. He *says* he was injured in battle.' She smiled fondly. 'He has such a nice little limp.'

God, but he'd tried every trick on her, and it looked as if she'd believed none of them. 'So you came north,' I said, going back to the essential part of the story. '*You* were to look around the house and find out where the money was.'

'It was foreign money,' she complained. 'Richard wouldn't believe me, so I took him a coin to show him. And he was excited – he said they were really valuable!'

'So on the night you got the key and let him into the house . . .'

She nodded, wandering about the alley, pressing a toe of her fashionable shoe into the remains of the snow under the wall. 'He went down into the cellar for the box of coins, because it was really heavy and *I* couldn't lift it. I waited for him in the shop. That idiot boy was snoring – I was scared he was going to wake up. Then Richard came back up from the cellar and he was angry.'

'About what?'

She shrugged and gave me an innocent look. 'I don't know.'

'Found out about the other money box, did he?' I suggested. 'The one you'd already taken?'

She pouted. 'There wasn't much in it.'

'Yes, there was. If there wasn't much, you wouldn't have had to take the entire box – you could just have slipped the coins into your pocket.'

She giggled, not at all disconcerted by being found out. 'There was fifty-two pounds!'

That had been almost a year's income for me before I was married. Gregson had been bluffing when he said he kept no money in the house.

Alice was watching me closely; when she saw me looking at her, she dropped her eyes. But I'd seen the calculating expression there.

'He went wild!' She waved her hands to try and convey how angry this Richard had been. 'He started killing people and I had to flee for my life!'

'He went wild – with a heavy box of coins in his hands?'

'He put them down!' she said indignantly.

'Where?'

Now she was annoyed. 'I don't know. I didn't look. I was running to escape having a knife in my back!'

'So you ran upstairs?'

'And flung myself out of the window!' She pranced across the alley, waving her hands dramatically. 'I slid down into the river, on to the ice and the mud, and scrambled out on to the Key. Then I ran and ran and ran until I was certain no one was following me!'

She hadn't done *that* very well – after all, she hadn't noticed me.

I contemplated her in silence for a moment. Some of this was probably true, as far as it went; there was too much detail to be entirely imaginary. But at the point when Richard came up from the cellar, it became much too vague. And that rope of sheets had been prepared in advance, not on impulse under a murderous threat. She was manipulating me, telling me just enough of the truth to convince, while hoping I wouldn't notice the inconsistencies. But she wasn't a good liar.

'Why did he kill everyone?' I asked.

She looked surprised I should ask. 'He was angry. Furious!'

'At *you*, not them.'

'He has a *dreadful* temper,' she protested. 'In London, I saw him nearly throttle a man who tried to rob him!'

Attacking a man who's just tried to rob you might be considered self-defence. Not in the least like killing four innocent, sleeping people because you've just argued with someone else entirely. Alice was hiding a great deal and I wanted to know all of it.

'What's Richard's surname?'

But I had asked one question too many. For a moment I thought she wasn't going to answer at all. She kicked at the snow, bit her lip. 'Alice says we mustn't tell you about him. Not until we've got what we want.'

'Which is?'

She started to sound shrill. 'I want my inheritance. Father had lots of money, and stocks and shares, and property – he owned several cottages in the country, and a forge too. I want my share.'

'You'll have to prove your innocence first,' I pointed out. Which was going to be rather difficult; even if this Richard had indeed done the actual killings, Alice would be in court beside him as an accomplice. Not that I intended to point that out right now. 'Give me Richard's real name, and tell me where he is.'

'Not until you give me the money!' she said furiously. 'Then I'll tell you who he is.' She pulled her cloak more tightly round her. The freezing cold seemed suddenly to intensify, became almost unendurable.

I realized what was happening, jumped forward, tried to grab her arm. Darkness swept over me. Then daylight flooded in again, and Alice Gregson was running away from me across frosty cobbles. I started after her . . .

Something hot and musty and rough came down over my head, stifling me. I couldn't see, could hardly hear, and the stink of the thing over my head made me sneeze. I felt a push in my back, staggered into a wall, and slid to the ground. Somewhere close, a horse snorted.

A moment of panic as I grappled with the unyielding folds of the material. Then I disentangled myself, breathed in fresh cold air with relief.

I was in a stables. A grey horse was looking at me over a low partition, blowing out clouds of breath in the cold air. And the material was a horse blanket.

It didn't take a great deal of effort to guess who'd thrown the blanket over my head. I scrambled up, ran out to the street. No one in sight.

I'd lost them.

Thirty

It is perfectly true that England is full of shops and tradesmen, and – much though it pains me to admit it – they are far more enterprising than our own.

[Letter from Louis de Glabre to his friend Philippe Froidevaux, 22 January 1737]

I went back to my own world, cursing my inability to lay hands on Alice. She was a mere flighty girl but she tricked me every time!

As the alley behind the site formed around me again, I calmed down, started to think more rationally. I believed some of what Alice said. I believed in the existence of *Richard*, although I was certain that wasn't his true name; the letter he'd sent to Alice had been signed with something like a T or an F. I believed he'd been a sailor and I felt a niggling suspicion of Joseph Kane; there was no evidence against him, yet . . .

But I wanted to know what Alice hadn't told me. Why had Richard run amok? Where did he get the knife? Why was the apprentice the last one killed? What had Alice been planning when she made that rope of sheets, in advance of the robbery?

What part, if any, had the other Alice played? Which of the three of them had killed the family? I believed Kane was capable of killing. But four people? In their sleep? No one had yet explained to me *why* that was necessary.

And, crucially, why was Alice telling me all this – and why *now*?

Snow drifted down. The workmen were still laughing at their work; the light seemed much the same as it had before. Had I lost any time in stepping from one world to the other? I ducked into the tavern next door to the site and looked at the big clock standing in one corner; not much more than an hour had passed.

I went after Joseph Kane, slipping and sliding down the steep Side to the Sandhill. In the busy centre of town, the snow had been worn away almost entirely; carts rattled across the cobbles, a cluster of fisherwomen stood gossiping. I glanced in the coffee house window as I passed and spotted Hugh leafing through a newspaper, but went on to the Golden Fleece.

A coach was standing in the yard, an elderly man arguing over it with the landlord. 'Devil take it! If I want to leave, I *will* leave!'

'But it's late,' the landlord protested, 'and they say the snow on Gateshead Fell is impassable.'

'Then I'll go north,' the old man said obstinately. 'Or east or west!'

One of the ostlers was lounging against the wall of the yard; he nodded at the elderly man. 'He expects me to let him take horses out in this weather! They'll break their legs!'

'I'm looking for Joseph Kane,' I said impatiently. 'The thief-taker.'

'He ain't here. Went off to Shields again this morning.'

'Shields,' I repeated, with a feeling of dread.

'Something about catching a ship.'

I was too late.

Hugh looked over the top of his newspaper, as I sank into the chair opposite him, thankful for the warmth of the coffee house's fire. 'Heard about the uproar last night,' he said. 'I should have come after all. Entertaining, was it?'

'Not in the least.'

'Gregson always was a sour individual.' He folded the newspaper. 'Wouldn't like to be trapped in there with him. Did any of them know anything?'

'Never got the chance to ask.' A trio of gentlemen hurried in and went straight across to the fire to toast their backs. 'Esther had a word with the daughter, but the girl burst into tears and there wasn't time to calm her down. I'm going to talk to the apprentice.' I glanced at the coffee house's clock. 'Very soon. Hugh, I think I know who the accomplice was.'

He sat up. 'Who?'

'Joseph Kane. I went to the Fleece to ask him a few questions and found he's gone off to Shields. Left this morning. He said he'd be back but there's nothing left in his room.'

He whistled. 'Devil take it, I should have expected that. Handsome fellow, just the rough sort to appeal to the ladies. And the only proof we have that he's following a thief is what he himself says. How do you know it's him?'

I told him about my encounter with Alice. 'She's certainly not telling me the *whole* truth,' I said, 'and it's obviously in her interest to convince me the accomplice is the murderer. She wants me to leave her alone and she's holding on to this fellow's name as a bargaining tool. But she gave me enough information to guess the truth.'

'You've got to follow him!' Hugh urged. 'He's not going to get a ship in this weather. He'll still be at Shields.'

'It's getting late, Hugh!' I protested. 'I'll never get to Shields before dark. And it's starting to snow again.' I got up. 'I must go. I've a meeting with Fowler on the bridge. To talk to the apprentice.'

Hugh raised an eyebrow. 'Fowler knew the apprentice, did he?'

'Yes,' I said, and resisted the temptation to add *in the biblical sense.*

Snow danced in the wind; the cold seemed even more intense as I crossed the Sandhill and climbed the slope on to the bridge. A woman with the hem of her petticoats muddied with snow trudged towards me; a man and a dog drove a pig into town. The shops were open, and I saw through Fleming's window a young girl looking intently at a book.

Fowler was leaning against the wall of Gregson's shop, as if merely idling. He said, 'Keep your voice low,' and jerked his head at the upper windows.

'Any sign of them?'

'He's gone quiet,' someone else whispered. The faint gleam of a new spirit hovered on the door jamb, just below Fowler's eyeline. 'Hasn't said a word since the house was boarded up. Hasn't come down either – stays up in his room.'

'Ned? I'm Charles Patterson. I'm grateful to you for talking to me.'

The spirit was startled, as if it hadn't expected this civility. 'Oh. Yes.' He sounded shyly pleased.

'What about his wife and daughter?'

'He's put them in the room at the back. Won't let them out.'

I glanced at Fowler but he was stony-faced. 'Has he said anything to *you?*'

The spirit sounded rueful. 'He don't care about me, long as I don't make too much noise. I've been having a word with the neighbours.'

I tried to be tactful. 'Saturday night – you don't remember —' I cursed my own ineptness.

The spirit said with a wavering voice, 'Not a thing, sir. I was asleep.'

He sounded on the verge of tears; I hurried on. 'Did you ever think Alice Gregson might do something like this?'

'No, sir.' The spirit glowed a little brighter; I thought that, young as he'd been, he was resilient. 'Thought she would run off. Went on about London until we was all sick with it.'

'Did she have any particular friends here?'

The spirit thought about this. Snow drifted across the bridge; I shivered. Fowler shifted into the shelter of the doorway. 'Said she knew a spirit or two. But she didn't sound like she thought much of them. I think she might have been expecting someone, mind. Kept looking out the window.'

I started to speak and barely managed to prevent myself mentioning Gregson by name, glanced uneasily up at the dark, boarded, upper windows. There was nothing to prevent Gregson sliding on to the outside of the building and eavesdropping. 'Did *your master* have any trouble? Anyone threatening him?'

'Never heard of nothing like that.'

'What about money? Did he have any in the house?'

'In the cellar, sir. Usually kept about ten or fifteen pounds there but I reckon there might have been more. Couple of gents had just paid their bills on the Saturday morning.'

Fifty-two pounds, Alice had said. And Gregson had not had time to get it out of harm's way.

'I've been down to the cellar,' the spirit said. 'There were two boxes and the one with the takings in it is gone, and the other's empty.'

'Do you know what was in the other box?'

'More money, I suppose.' The spirit laughed. 'Never knew a man with more money and less inclination to spend it. Took weeks to get my wages out of him.'

Fowler muttered something I didn't ask him to repeat.

'Do you know where he got the second box from? Or when?'

The spirit hummed and haahed. 'Middle of the year, it was.'

'June?'

'Maybe. I can't remember. No, wait! It was the day we went to the fair!' The spirit appealed to Fowler. 'Do you remember that?' Its voice trembled; it said, 'I was so happy . . .'

'Don't sniffle, Ned!' Fowler said, roughly.

I held my breath but the sharpness seemed to work wonders on the spirit; it continued, more strongly, 'We was coming back and I said I had to hurry or Master would have me in chains! And we saw flames above the houses – a big fire. I wanted to go and have a look but didn't dare. And I came back, and lay down on my mattress and couldn't sleep, I'd had such a good time. That's why I was awake when Master came in. Well gone midnight, it was.'

I chose my words carefully, not wishing to influence the spirit.

'The mercer William Threlkeld was one of your master's customers, wasn't he?'

'Lord, yes, sir. We did out his entire shop and house. Last April or May, I reckon. He'd had a lot of building work done and had to redecorate. It was his house burnt down that day of the fair.'

There was a noise behind those boarded upper windows; the spirit said waveringly, 'He's moving around, sir.' I held my breath, looking up. The evening was starting to draw in now, the twilight straining my eyes. Fowler muttered; snow settled on his dark uncovered head and the shoulders of his greatcoat.

No more sounds. I said, 'If anything happens, Ned, you are to go at once. Look after yourself – there's no point in antagonizing him.'

'Yes, sir,' the spirit said gratefully.

I lowered my voice still further. 'Did Alice ever do anything suspicious?'

'I knew she was up to something as soon as she arrived,' the spirit said scornfully. 'Poking her head into every corner, saying she just wanted to find her way around. She looked at all the business books – the letter books especially. She said she wanted to know what her father had written about her to the lawyers in London.'

'Did she go into the cellar?'

'Didn't she!' Ned said a little too loudly, with the indignation of youth. He lowered his voice again. 'I saw her taking the key off the wall.'

'The key to the cellar?'

'To the *box*,' the spirit said. 'I said, *that's the money box key, you shouldn't be touching that.* And she said, *mind your own business.* I said, *the master won't be pleased.* And she said, *You can't tell* me *what to do.* Real annoyed, she was.'

I stared at the faint gleam. Was that argument the cause of the lad's death? Had Alice taken offence at his interference? Was that all there was to it?

'There's a man you might have seen her talking to. A dark man, in his forties, handsome in a rough sort of way. A London man. Speaking with an accent not much different from Fowler's.'

'Don't remember anyone like that,' the spirit said doubtfully.

'No one of that description ever came in the shop?'

'Never saw no one.'

More noise upstairs. Prolonged this time. Fowler took hold of my arm. 'Come away.'

'Don't leave me,' the spirit wavered. 'I don't want to be left alone. Please . . .'

'I'll be back in a minute,' Fowler said in that rough tone. 'Let him quieten down again first.'

'But—'

'You calling me a liar? I say I'll be back, I'll be back.'

Fowler drew me off to the other side of the bridge, turned his shoulder to the snow-laden wind. 'I've done your asking around,' he said, in a voice almost as rough as the one he'd used to the lad. 'No one's heard of this exciseman from London. And no one's been offering old coins for scrap, either.' He hunched in his thick coat. 'The thief'll be taking the coins off to London, soon as the snow clears.'

Or, I thought gloomily, on to a ship at Shields. Possibly at this very moment. 'Thank you for asking.'

He thrust his hands into his pockets; he was shivering almost as much as I was. 'His Lordship wants to see you.'

'I was up there only this morning.'

'You should have watched your mouth. Something you said set him thinking.'

I began to feel more hopeful. Heron's no fool – perhaps he'd heard something, or come up with some useful idea. 'Did he say *when* he wanted to see me?'

'At once.' Fowler mimicked Heron's patrician tones with cruel accuracy. 'You know how he is. Wants everything straight away.'

I nodded. 'Well, he'll have to wait. I haven't seen my wife all day and I'm cold and hungry and thirsty, and I'm going home. I'll go up in an hour or two. Are you going back now?'

'In an hour or two,' Fowler said mockingly, and walked back to Gregson's shop.

Thirty-One

Everyone loves a good intrigue.
[Letter from Louis de Glabre to his friend Philippe
Froidevaux, 22 January 1737]

Esther was in the estate room at the back of the house, sighing over account books; she looked pale, but a plate scattered with crumbs was at her elbow, next to a wineglass, so she'd evidently been eating, which was reassuring. She looked up and said at once, 'Tell me everything.'

I perched on the edge of her table, shifting the candles back for safety's sake. The curtains were undrawn and the white garden beyond the windows glowed eerily in the twilight. 'There's not a lot to tell. Except that you were right. It's looking very much as if the accomplice *is* Joseph Kane.'

She listened intently as I told her of my encounter with Alice Gregson and did not look happy.

'I do not see how you can be sure of anything she says. She is simply trying to blame everything on the accomplice.'

'And he'll blame everything on her.' I nodded. 'And I admit Alice became ridiculously vague when it came to the point of the killings. There's a great deal she's not telling me, but some of it I think is reliable.'

Esther reached for her wine glass and was plainly annoyed when she found it empty. I rang the bell for Tom. 'It *is* much more likely that a man carried out the killings,' she mused.

Tom came, and I asked for more wine and something to eat. While he was away fetching it, Esther toyed with her ledger and mused over what I'd told her, questioning me closely on some details. After Tom had returned with the wine, she said, '*Two* Alices — that is not a pleasant thought. I wonder how they met.'

'By chance, I should imagine.' I cut a wedge of bread and topped it with cheese. 'Actually, I've only ever seen the other Alice in her own world. I wonder if she *can* step through.'

'Does it matter?' Esther sneaked a piece of cheese, murmured in appreciation. 'I once travelled with you between worlds – surely she could be brought back and forth by *our* Alice?'

'I suppose so. But there's still too much unexplained. Why, for instance, leave the child alive to raise the alarm?'

Esther cut off a corner of bread with the knife Tom had brought; she must be feeling a great deal better. 'Perhaps that was the point. The murderer *wanted* her to raise the alarm.'

'In heaven's name, why?'

Esther mused. 'Suppose this *Richard* – or whatever his name is – wanted Alice to be trapped in the house and blamed for the killings. He roused the child then ran out of the front door, thinking Alice could not escape.'

'But there's still the rope,' I protested. 'Alice knotted the rope *in advance*. Why?'

We sat in silence for a moment. I was thinking that Esther's theory worked the other way round too, that Alice could have roused the child to trap her lover. Damn it, which of them had done the killings? Did this Richard really exist or had Alice been cleverer than I thought, and persuaded me to believe exactly what she wanted. No, there was indeed a man involved – the one stealing the antiquities. Was that Richard, or someone else entirely? And what about the Alice from the other world? What was her part in all this?

I drew the curtains against the chill evening; the room became warm and cosy in the candlelight. 'Charles,' Esther murmured, 'Why don't we just have a quiet evening at home and talk? It seem such an age since we simply sat together.'

She was regarding me with her mischievous smile and I wanted to sink down on the sofa, banish the servants, and pretend the Gregsons had not been killed.

'I have to go out again,' I said wearily. 'Heron wants to see me. Something I said this morning has given him pause, evidently.'

Esther sighed. 'I suppose there won't be much time until this matter is settled. Afterwards then?'

'I promise.'

'I won't let you forget,' she said, still smiling. 'I presume you won't have time to see Mrs Fletcher? She was here this morning, trying to get information out of me. She said to tell you particularly that she wants to know *everything* that is happening.'

'She'll have to wait until tomorrow.'

As I bent to kiss her farewell, Esther raised her hand to caress my cheek; I angled my head to rub against her fingers. She laughed softly. 'Send Heron a message saying you cannot come tonight.'

I was tempted, very tempted, but shook my head. 'He'll only blame Fowler for not making the urgency of his request clear.' I kissed her palm. 'Besides, he may indeed be able to help me clear this matter up – and the sooner I can do that the better.'

She hesitated, then nodded. 'Take care.'

For the second time that day, I tramped up Northumberland Street. In the dark this time, although it wasn't particularly late. It was bitterly cold and I shivered all the way despite my greatcoat. The last snowfall hadn't come to much, and what remained lingered only at the sides of the street; carts had worn the snow in the middle to dirty slush and, in some places, to nothing at all. On Heron's lawns, however, the snow still lay in a thick layer, pristine white except for a line of prints made by a cat.

The butler showed me into Heron's study again at the back of the house. In the candlelight, the heavy wainscoting and tall bookcases lurked in shadows. Heron was standing in front of the fire with a glass of wine in his hand; a salver on the table held another unused glass. When I was announced, he nodded dismissal at the butler and turned to pour me wine. He said, 'It is time to put an end to this matter.'

My heart sank at once; that brisk tone never portended anything good.

'This man is plainly collecting all the antiquities found in the mercer's shop,' Heron said. 'He has already made one attempt to get into this house. I suggest we encourage him to make another.'

I'd been right to be concerned. 'You mean we should set a trap for him?'

'Exactly.' Heron gestured at the tall windows that, if I remembered correctly, led out on to a terrace overlooking the garden at the back of the house. 'We will leave a window unlocked into this room. Then we will keep watch and when he walks in we will apprehend him.'

How easy it sounded. But I'd done something similar myself about a year back and knew that things didn't always go to plan. 'We?'

'Myself, you and Fowler.'

Well, I had no faith in my own ability in a fight, but I'd seen Heron at swordplay and wouldn't like to have to face him. The real difficulty would be keeping Fowler from shooting the thief, if he thought he'd anything to do with Ned's death. He boasts he never misses.

Heron was raising an eyebrow at my hesitation; I said, 'There are so many things that can go wrong.' Knowing already I'd never talk him out of it.

'Nonsense.' He stepped briskly across to ring for the butler again. 'There is no need for complicated arrangements. We will simply hide ourselves here and wait for the man's arrival.' The butler came and he gave orders that Fowler should be sent for. He glanced about the candlelit room. 'Fowler and I will hide behind the curtains on either side of the window. You can crouch down behind the sofa.'

I looked at the furniture in question. Heron's taste in sofas, unluckily, does not run to the substantial; it would offer very little protection.

'Of course,' Heron said, 'you had better send word to your wife that you may be home very late tonight.'

I was shocked. 'You want to do this *tonight*!'

Fowler came silently into the room, wearing Heron's livery of blue; his gaze flickered to me but he didn't otherwise acknowledge my presence. 'You wanted me, sir?'

'You and your pistol both,' Heron said, looking around the room again. 'We are going to set a trap for this murderer.'

Fowler looked at me again. I shook my head, but he merely said, 'Certainly, sir.' There was, of course, nothing else he could say. Not if he wished to keep his place. 'At what time do you require me?'

'The house usually retires at eleven,' Heron said, more to me than to Fowler. 'We will behave as usual, but as soon as everyone is in bed, we will keep watch here.' He glanced at the clock. 'It will be three hours yet.' He looked Fowler up and down. 'Wear something darker.'

'Yes, sir.' Fowler bowed and retreated.

'And now,' Heron said to me, 'you may give me another violin lesson to pass the time.'

Single-minded as ever, Heron tackled his pieces with his usual cool efficiency and not a hint that he was distracted by what was to come. I was the one distracted. I'd sent a message to Esther, saying merely I was following up something Heron had told me, and would be late home; knowing she wouldn't worry was all the consolation I had. How could Heron think this plan would work? We'd no proof the thief would try to get into the house again; how could he possibly know that tonight would be a good time to try? Would he not be suspicious when he found both the garden gate and a window unlocked? Why should he try this room in preference to any other that gave on to the terrace? Though admittedly it was the first one he'd come to.

And was the thief the murderer? Heron assumed he was. But what if it was someone else entirely, someone unconnected with the Gregsons' deaths? That would be a coincidence, but couldn't be discounted entirely. Even if thief and accomplice *were* the same, and a man (rather than the Alice from the other world), that man was Kane, and Kane was in Shields, no doubt on a boat destined for the Colonies. We'd probably sit here all night without anything happening. I hoped we would.

Events gathered a momentum of their own. Heron dismissed the servants to bed and went off on his usual rounds, making sure the doors and windows – with one exception – were locked. Fowler came down while Heron was absent. He was dressed completely in black, and looked pointedly at my light brown and green coat. 'Not the best clothes for a midnight expedition,' he said with a trace of malice.

'I didn't know I was going to be indulging in a fool's errand when I came out,' I retorted. 'And if anyone does come through that window,' I added, 'don't kill him!'

Fowler smiled.

'He might be able to tell us what happened in that shop,' I pointed out. 'And exactly what part Alice Gregson had in it.'

'I know what part she had in it,' Fowler said. 'She killed Ned.'

'This fellow might be the only witness to that.'

He said nothing, but I saw he'd taken in what I said.

Heron came back; he too was now dressed in dark clothes. I vowed to stay well hidden. Let Heron and Fowler deal with any rough stuff; I wanted to get a good look at the face of any intruder. Even if he got away, I wanted to be able to identify him. I still thought, hoped, that nothing would happen.

Heron unlocked a cupboard and lifted out a wooden box; he unlocked this too, and took out a soft bag that chinked. He emptied coins on to the table, and took down a volume from the bookcase behind the table, opening it at some illustrations. A number of coins were sketched on the page; Heron arranged the coins and the book as if he'd been comparing the two.

He stood back and studied the effect. It looked suspiciously obvious to me; surely any collector would make sure his precious antiquities were locked away when he went to bed. But there was plainly no reasoning with him. He arranged us too. Fowler hid behind the curtains to the left of the window, one of his pistols in his hand and the other pushed into the waist of his breeches; I crouched down behind the sofa in just about as uncomfortable a position as I've ever been in. Heron blew out the candles and stood on the other side of the window behind the harpsichord.

My eyes slowly adjusted to the darkness. A red glow from the banked-down fire glinted on the coins. Heron had arranged the curtains to leave a tiny gap through which an intruder could peer; through that gap came a gleam of cold white light, reflected from the snow outside. The other pieces of furniture were indistinct hulks. I wondered if even Fowler could hit his target in the dark.

And there we stayed, for what seemed like forever. I wondered idly why Heron had not moved the harpsichord to the side of the room, out of his way. Perhaps he thought the fellow would blunder into it. Presumably he was confident he himself would not fall over the music stand when he came out of hiding. And that Fowler would not get tangled in the curtains. Come to think of it, the one thing I could be certain of was that Fowler wouldn't get tangled in the curtains; he'd far too much experience in these matters to make such a childish mistake.

Perhaps Heron thought my calf muscles wouldn't start trembling and shaking.

I put out a hand to shift my balance, went down on one knee. The rug was deep and soft but after a few minutes was just as uncomfortable – the floorboards beneath seemed to bore into my flesh. This was a ridiculous idea! I shifted again – and heard the window-latch click.

A draught of freezing air washed over me as the window opened, then eased as it was pulled to again. Soft footsteps, a thud and an oath as the intruder bumped into the harpsichord. A man, definitely a man, although I couldn't identify his voice from the little I heard. Then he tripped over the harpsichord stool, and Heron said sharply, 'Stand still or I'll shoot.'

There was a silence, then the stool went over with a crash. Fowler shouted. A shot. Then two more, close together. Someone grunted in pain and went down. A shadow passed in front of the window. The cold air blew in again.

I scrambled to my feet. The window was wide open, and in the light reflected from the snow outside, I saw two figures. One lay prone on the floor in darkening blood, the other leaned over him.

'Damn it,' Heron said, in a rage so thick I hardly recognized his voice. 'Get the servants. Get the barber-surgeon. Damn it, do something!'

Fowler had been shot.

Thirty-Two

Never offend a gentleman – he will not forget.
[Letter from Louis de Glabre to his friend Philippe
Froidevaux, 23 January 1737]

The servants were barging in at the door; I leapt for the open window and the terrace behind the house. Instantly, I skidded on soft snow. Arms flailing, I caught at the swinging window.

There was sufficient light, reflecting from the snow, to show me the eerie expanse of garden, the clumps of bushes and trees. I knew that a high wall surrounded the garden and the only gate was to the left. A line of shadowed footprints led in that direction.

I ploughed into the snow, taking care not to tread on top of the footprints. The drifts lay undisturbed here; I found myself at once ankle deep. Bushes loomed ahead, evergreens that had kept their leaves and were thick and concealing. I slowed. If I were the intruder I'd rush on regardless to the gate, but he hadn't been far ahead of me . . .

A shot crashed out. I ducked, put my hand down in the freezing snow to prevent myself falling. I was an easy target. But the intruder had shot at least once in the house and now another shot out here . . . Even if he had a pair of pistols, he'd now have to reload, which gave me the advantage. I ran for the bushes. The glimpse I'd had of the intruder in the house had been of someone slight and about my own height. Someone I could tackle with a reasonable hope of overpowering. I plunged into the undergrowth . . .

At the last moment, I sensed movement behind me, swung in time to deflect the downward blow of the pistol. The blow glanced off my left shoulder. My arm went numb. I stumbled back and the fellow struck out again.

Heron crashed through the bushes, bellowing in rage.

The intruder took off. I caught a glimpse of him as he plunged into another thicket of trees and bushes. Heron stopped, took calm aim and fired.

The fellow ran on. Heron cursed. I plunged after the intruder, labouring through the deep snow. Behind, Heron shouted to the servants. Twigs clawed at my face; bushes whipped back into my eyes. The wall loomed up.

The gate was swinging open.

I ducked out into a narrow alley at the side of the house, glanced both ways. To my right was a dead end; to the left, the alley led back on to Northumberland Street. New footprints in the snow. And a dark spot or two that might have been blood . . .

Gasping for breath, I ploughed down the alley, following the prints. The intruder was already too far ahead of me; on Northumberland Street there'd be people, and a good chance of losing himself amongst them. I skidded to a halt at the point where alley met street. The footprints, so clear in the alley, headed out into the middle of the street where the snow was trampled into nothing, and were lost.

I looked around. Several huddles of drunken miners blundered up the street, singing loudly; a carter led a horse pulling an empty cart; a couple of whores talked to a customer. A travelling preacher crossed the street to talk to accost the drunken miners. Any one of the men might be the intruder – or none of them at all. He'd probably just dashed straight across the street into one of the alleys on the other side.

Heron came to my shoulder, breathing heavily. When I glanced round, his face was set in an ugly mask of anger.

'He's gone,' I said. 'He could be anywhere.'

Without a word, Heron turned and strode back down the alley. I took one last look across the street and followed him.

I checked the gate as I went back into the garden. Raw gashes in the wood showed palely in the snow's glow; the intruder hadn't bothered to check whether the gate was locked or not – he'd forced it open. Inside the garden, a line of footprints cut off from the gate along the line of the wall under some shrubbery; I ducked under the low branches and followed the prints. They kept to the line of the wall until level with the house, then turned towards to the terrace. This must have been the way the intruder came; two very clear footprints told me he'd had worn boots – hardly surprising – and had large feet. And he'd stepped more heavily on the heel, particularly of the right foot; the impressions were deeper there than at the toe.

So now all I had to do was persuade every villain I could find to step in the snow and compare the footprints.

Or . . .

I pondered. *Could* it have been a woman? A woman may fire a pistol as well as a man, as Esther can prove. The intruder had been rather tall for a woman, but the second Alice – the one I'd met briefly in that other world – *she'd* been tall.

I stood in the chill night, with the snow gleaming around me, and cursed. No further forward, and Fowler was hurt. Not a good night's work. And all the worse for being predictable.

When I pushed the window open into the house, servants were milling around. Fowler, half-conscious, was propped sitting against a chair, and the only person acting with any sense was a middle-aged housekeeper in nightgown and robe, with a grey braid of hair down her back, who was directing the other servants with confident authority. A bowl of reddened water lay at Fowler's side; the housekeeper was pressing a pad of blood-soaked cloth to his left shoulder, close to the junction with his neck.

My arm was taken in a vice-like grip; Heron pulled me aside. 'Did you get a good look at him?'

Reluctantly, I shook my head. 'About my height, slender, young, I think.' I told him about the footprints. He listened with that look of detached coolness settling back on his face. In front of servants, Heron would never be anything but the calm, restrained master; there would never be even a moment's weakness displayed.

Gale arrived and took charge, examining Fowler, then insisting he be carried to his bed. Heron disposed of the milling servants with a few curt words. We were left alone in the library, and Heron poured brandy into two large glasses and threw back one of them in a single draught.

I bent to pick up Fowler's pistol which had fallen behind a chair. I'd heard three shots, one alone, then two close together. From my position behind the sofa, I'd been able to gauge the different directions of the shots; I turned, trying to remember exactly what I'd heard. The first shot had been close to me; that was the intruder. Then the other two shots close together; that was Fowler and Heron. Fowler first from the left, then Heron. By that time, the intruder had already been running back towards the window.

I held up a candle to the wainscoting behind the curtain to the left of the window. It took some time to find where the shot had hit; I dug around in the hole with the letter opener and prised out a flattened pistol ball. The intruder had missed Fowler. Then I stood where Fowler had and looked across the room, aiming an imaginary pistol. And dear God, there was Fowler's shot – embedded in the back of the sofa behind which I'd been hiding! Blood smeared across the satin upholstery. Fowler's boast was good; he'd not missed, even though he had not incapacitated the intruder.

All of which meant that the third shot, the one that hit Fowler . . .

Heron had been watching me, bleakly. He poured himself more brandy. 'The fellow was heading back towards the window when I fired,' he said. 'I missed him.' He spoke with a curious blank finality.

I reached for my brandy. Heron tossed back his second glass. I was desperately trying to think what to say. *These things happen? You weren't to blame?* Neither was true, nor untrue. Accidents do happen, but this had been a risky business from the start.

'And for what?' Heron said bitterly. 'Nothing. He got away.'

Fowler's blood was sticky underfoot. 'For the moment,' I said. Tomorrow I'd ride out to Shields. I'd probably be too late but in this weather there must be a chance that whatever ship Kane had found had not yet sailed.

Heron poured still more brandy. He didn't look at me. 'You had better go. Mrs Patterson will be worried.'

I hesitated. Leaving Heron alone at this moment seemed the most unwise thing I was ever likely to do, but I couldn't find a good reason to stay, or anything to say that would in the slightest console him for what had happened. I nodded. 'Send me a message to let me know how Fowler does.'

He said nothing and I let myself out of the house.

Thirty-Three

They are great ones for correspondence, which I particularly appreciate. I have any number of correspondents, some of whom write to me every day. And that is only the ladies . . .
[Letter from Louis de Glabre to his friend Philippe
Froidevaux, 23 January 1737]

Snow was falling in a silent still cloud, flakes drifting down around me, muffling sounds and blurring the houses on either side of Northumberland Street. The whores had taken themselves indoors and only a couple of drunks stumbled along in the snow, arms affectionately around each other. St Nicholas's church clock struck midnight.

I walked down the central strip of road, where a thin veil of snow was beginning to settle on top of the cobbles again. The intruder must have cut out into the middle of the street so his footsteps couldn't be seen, but there was a chance he might have taken a side turning, into one of the alleys where the snow was thicker. I looked for fresh prints as I passed each alley, hoping perhaps to see a trace of blood as well – but there was nothing.

Northumberland Street became Pilgrim Street and sloped down towards the river. It was more exposed here; the old snow had lingered longer and there were several tracks. Two sets of foot-prints close together – a small pair and a larger – turned into Silver Street going towards All Hallows' church. Two other sets of larger prints went past Silver Street, and headed down Butcher Bank.

The steep slope of the Bank was treacherous. Under the newly falling snow, the old slush had frozen. Twice my feet went out from under me and I skidded, arms flailing, before regaining my balance. One of the sets of footprints stopped at a house door; there was a muddled patch on the threshold as if someone had stamped his feet to get the snow off his shoes before going indoors. Which left one more set of prints going on down the Bank, towards the Sandhill.

Where, of course, the passing of carts had obliterated all the previous snow, and no footprints at all were visible.

The flat Sandhill was easier to negotiate than Butcher Bank, even with the new snow falling. On the far side, the Guildhall was a dark hulk; beneath its columns, the open fish market was deserted. Behind the Guildhall was the slope up to the bridge and as I paused to draw in a long breath of icy air, I realized the bridge wasn't deserted. Faint lantern light shimmered through the snow, and touched a figure staring at the Gregsons' shop.

As I came up to him, Balfour looked round. He was huddled in his greatcoat, hands in pockets. 'I suppose Demsey told you I'd walked out on the Directors?' he said, straight away, with some belligerence. 'I couldn't face another meeting about those damn Rooms. I wish I'd never accepted the commission.' He shifted his shoulders in his coat as if trying to make himself comfortable. 'I can't get out of my head what happened here last night. The spirit was so angry . . .'

I repressed a feeling of impatience. After all that had happened – was happening – Balfour could think of nothing but himself. 'Like your father, no doubt?'

'He insulted my mother all the time – allowed her no peace at all. And I was constantly told in no uncertain terms what a fool I was and how I'd never amount to anything! Yet, if anyone called, he'd be the most courteous and gracious of hosts. I think that was the worst thing – that no one else understood what it was like.'

I was shivering violently in the cold. 'Go home,' I recommended.

'What time is it?'

'Gone midnight.'

He laughed in amazement. 'I'd no idea I'd been here so long! Did you come to look at the house?'

I wasn't sure what I was doing. Perhaps I *had* deliberately come here without realizing it. I remembered Ned saying Alice had been eager to look at Gregson's letter book, into which he'd copied his letters to the lawyers in London. If there'd been a lover in the offing, perhaps something might have been said about him. I fished the key out of my pocket and whispered for Ned. The spirit came at once and was pathetically pleased for the company. 'He's still upstairs,' he whispered. 'Hasn't said a word for hours.'

He was less happy about the idea of my coming in but I promised to be as quick and quiet as possible. I lifted down one of the lanterns, so I didn't have to spend time lighting the candles in the shop, and gave it to Balfour to hold as I fumbled the key with my cold fingers.

'Do you think there'll be something about the accomplice's identity in the letters?' Balfour whispered.

'I know his identity,' I whispered back, 'but some solid evidence would be helpful.'

'You know who he is!' He started at the sound of his own voice, and guiltily lowered it again. 'Who?'

I pushed the door open. 'The thief-taker from London.'

His mouth formed a soundless whistle. 'Have the Watch got him?'

'Unfortunately he's run off.'

The room was like an ice-house; light from the lantern flickered over the shutters, the pale walls and the battered once-elegant furniture, reflected from the fragments of glass that still littered the floor. Ned's spirit was on the counter, just sliding over the other edge.

There were no sounds from upstairs.

I wasn't going to linger here any longer than I had to. I hurried round the counter and saw the spirit hovering on one of the thick ledgers on the shelf below. 'This one!' it whispered. The book was at the bottom of a pile of three ledgers; I lifted them off, opened the letter book at random on the top of the counter. 'Bring the lantern closer.'

Obediently, Balfour held the lantern over my head and peered at the book with me. 'That's dated last year – January.'

I rifled through more pages: April, June, September. When was any correspondence likely to have taken place? I turned to the last entries in the book and started to work my way backwards. Most of the letters were to customers, dealing with the cost of wallpaper and fabrics, of shipping furniture from London. References to orders and payments. Ned's spirit hung on the edge of one of the ledgers and I wondered whether to say anything about Fowler. The lad was bound to hear of it sooner or later from the spirits' network; if I told him now I could at least re-assure him that Fowler wasn't badly hurt.

If only I knew that for certain. Even flesh wounds can turn bad.

I found a letter to the lawyers at last but it was un-informative.

> Further to my letter of 21st inst. November, I agree to your terms. Under protest. Send the wench home.

Balfour muttered in protest. 'How can any man write that of his own daughter?'

The letter of 21st November was not much better.

> I have received your letter of the 10th inst. and your enclo-sures. I'am not surprised to hear that her aunt will not have her to stay any longer; she's an expensive fool. I am not

made of money, sir – she'll have board and lodging, why should she want an allowance as well? I won't do it and you may tell her so.

I had to go back to September to find another letter about Alice, and this was even briefer and less sympathetic.

So my brother's dead, is he? Well, I suppose his wife will have some peace now.

'He didn't like his brother,' Ned explained unnecessarily.

I shut the book up and walked away. 'This is useless!'

'No, no.' Balfour opened the book again. 'There must be *something* here!'

He leafed through the pages. I paced about the room, rubbing my arms against the cold. Gregson had been uncompromising in his dismissal of his daughter's expensive habits – surely he'd have said something equally cutting if an unsuitable lover had been in the offing. It would be a rare father who would forgive his daughter an illicit alliance, and Gregson was not that father. Moreover, he had another daughter on the verge of making a good match; he'd not want anything to reflect badly on her.

The broken shutter was hanging loose and I went across to anchor it more firmly. The door had been left ajar and I opened it. The snow blew in. 'We'd better go.'

'No!' Ned whispered piteously. 'It's so lonely here!'

And then it happened again. One moment, it was pitch black outside, the next it was daylight – a thin strained light under heavy cloud. As I shivered, I saw a man driving three sheep across the bridge, a dog dancing at their heels to keep them moving; outside the house opposite, a carter was loosely holding the reins of his horse and chatting to an attractive young maid. I was in the other world again. And watching a woman trying to negotiate the narrow gap between cart and sheep, apparently in a hurry.

I only saw her from behind but I was certain it was the same woman. Tall, elegant, dark hair dressed fashionably. I called out, 'Miss Gregson! Alice!'

The woman hesitated, then hurried on. The carter turned to give me a knowing look. I started after her, feeling a sense of time repeating itself. This was how it had been on Sunday, when I'd walked out of the shop. I called again, tried to dodge the sheep. Another woman was waiting at the end of the bridge: a slighter woman, with white skirts showing beneath her cloak. Blonde hair in ringlets, with ribbons and lace threaded through the curls. The other Alice – *our* Alice – and she had the audacity to raise a hand and wave cheerfully at me!

The sheepdog snapped at my feet; I was ready to kick it out of the way but its master called it off.

When I looked up, the women had gone.

Cursing, I rubbed my eyes. It was clearly afternoon in this world, but it was the early hours of the morning in my own world, and I'd been up too long. I needed sleep. Tomorrow I'd get up early and see if I could get through the snow to Shields. If I could confront Kane with what I already knew, perhaps I could get a true story out of him.

I straightened, aware of a smell of burning. Smoke seemed to drift around me. If there was a fire, chaos would break out and I certainly didn't want to get involved in something like that. Not in *this* world. I took a step back, reaching for my own world. Night folded around me; snow drifted into my face . . .

Someone violently knocked me aside. I slipped, grabbed at the wall of Fleming's shop. There was chaos *here*, in *this* world, people milling around, shouting, yelling for action. Buckets of water were being tossed from man to man – one slopped its contents over my feet. Smoke billowed over me. I started choking and coughing—

The Gregsons' shop was on fire.

A furnace of heat blew out of the open door; flame belched from the windows. A woman yelled a warning; we all scattered. Someone grabbed my arm. Hugh. I yelled above the roar of the fire and the shouts of the firefighters. 'Balfour was in there!'

Hugh shook his head. 'Behind you!'

I glanced round. Balfour was hanging over the edge of the bridge, coughing and spluttering, gasping for breath. 'Spirits told me where he was!' Hugh shouted. 'He was already out of the shop when I got here.'

Balfour saw me, started gesticulating wildly, still coughing. Tears streamed down his cheeks; soot streaked his face. 'Greg— Greg—'

'Gregson did this?'

He nodded and hung over the edge of the bridge, retching.

All the neighbours had turned out and were ferrying buckets of water in chains along the bridge. Fleming, in his nightshirt, was directing operations, no doubt afraid the fire was going to spread to his shop. Women shepherded excited children out of danger.

I grabbed a bucket of water from a boy and threw it over the fire, reached for another. Then there was a great shrieking, rising above the shouting of the crowd. A woman's scream. A roar so loud it seemed to come from hell itself. Everyone froze in panic; Fleming shouted, 'The spirits. On the roof!' We all stared up.

Two spirits clung to the roof slates. Flames leapt up around them; they looked like stars fading in the face of a full moon. The screaming went on and on, the roar seemed to merge with a great rumble—

Hugh hauled me back. An empty bucket clattered in his hand. 'The house is going to go!'

He was right. The walls were leaning at an alarming angle, tilting back, away from the road, over the drop to the river. Roof slates started to slip. Great cracks shot down the façade of the building; a chunk of masonry fell in a flare of flame. The crowd scattered.

Two spirits on the roof – where were the other two? I scanned the facade of the house, yelled for Ned. Then I saw him, a faint gleam, low down, on a brick to the side of the door. The door was ablaze and the frame around it; old mortar crumbled, bricks flaked and blackened in the heat. The flames leapt up and for the moment I couldn't see the spirit.

Slates cascaded down, bricks exploded and burst out at us. Then the walls toppled backwards and we heard a roar as the back of the house tumbled over the edge of the bridge. Water slapped up, drenching the crowd. Steam fountained. Then the rest of the house went, smashing down as the crowd scattered for safety. I heard the spirits scream.

And at the last moment, I leapt forward, wrapping my hand in the skirts of my greatcoat, and grabbed up a fragmenting brick and the pale gleam on it.

Thirty-Four

The night is almost as busy as the day!
[Letter from Louis de Glabre to his friend Philippe
Froidevaux, 23 January 1737]

Even through the thickness of my greatcoat, I felt the scald of the brick and almost dropped it. Fleming seized a bucket of water from a neighbour; I dropped the brick in. The water fizzed and sizzled; steam blossomed.

The top corner of the brick poked out of the water. The spirit slid to the dry point. 'He did it!' he yelled. 'He did it.'

'The others are gone,' Fleming said, staring at the ruins of the house.

The fire began to die down, smoke billowing and intermingling with the falling snow. The crowd formed chains again to throw water on what remained. Fleming was right – I could see nothing of the other spirits. At best they were amongst the wreckage at the bottom of the river, but I suspected that they'd evaporated in the flames. Fire is one of the few ways to be rid of a spirit before its natural dissolution takes it eighty or a hundred years after death; in a way, Gregson had just committed suicide, and taken his wife and daughter with him.

At least Ned had survived. Fleming was giving his apprentice instructions to keep the brick and bucket safe, but as soon as the lad tried to walk into Fleming's shop with it, he staggered and almost dropped it. 'It's got heavier! I can't carry it!'

Fleming took it from him and could barely lift it. I seized the handle too and between us, we dragged it back towards the burning house. It grew lighter with every step. We put it down on the street, in contact with one of the fallen piles of bricks from the shop.

'A spirit can't leave the place the living man died,' Fleming said, in a low voice so Ned couldn't hear. 'But I thought the brick would suffice to represent the whole, so to speak. What are we to do?'

'Build the brick into the wall of the new building, I suppose. Do you know what happened?'

Fleming shook his head. 'My apprentice woke me. He'd heard Ned shouting for help. Between them, they probably saved the entire bridge.'

I pushed through the crowds to Balfour. He was still hanging over the edge of the bridge, hacking and retching, bent double with his hands at his throat, white as the ice on the river, with smudges of soot across his cheeks. One hand was scorched and reddened. He whispered, 'The door handle was hot . . .'

I gave Hugh a look and, between us, we got Balfour off the bridge and out of the crowd. Even the movement of walking made him cough and by the time we reached the end of the bridge, it was obvious he couldn't get to his lodgings. We sat him down on the step of a house and waited until the coughing eased.

'What happened?' I asked when I thought he could answer.

'The moment you were out the door.' Balfour retched, dragged his handkerchief to his lips. 'Came shrieking in.'

'Gregson?'

He nodded. 'Told the boy off for bringing in strangers – shouted – the boy was scared. I said I'd go . . .'

'But he didn't let you?'

'Ranted and . . . raved.' He was recovering. 'Knocked the lantern over. It broke. The oil flooded on to the books. Went up—'

'The place was full of paper,' I said. 'Ledgers, letters, wallpaper samples. Cloth too.' And one of the shutters had been broken and letting in a strong draught to fan the flames.

'I saw the spirits,' Balfour said, 'in the flames, burning . . .' He buried his head in his hands. Hugh gave me an exasperated look which I thought was unfair. 'All of them lost . . .'

At least I could reassure him on that point. 'We managed to save the apprentice's spirit.'

He stared at me, obviously confused. 'The boy was saved?' He seemed to slump. 'That's something, I suppose.'

Exhaustion abruptly overwhelmed me. Men milled around us, shouting for more water. One of the church clocks struck a single resounding note. 'We all need some sleep.'

'I couldn't,' Balfour protested.

'I could,' Hugh muttered.

'I *couldn't* sleep,' Balfour repeated. 'I can't stop thinking . . .'

He couldn't let anything go, worried at every detail like a terrier at a rat. But I saw salvation approaching: Gale, obviously dressed in a hurry and bearing his bag. He spotted us at once, frowned at Balfour's coughing, and headed our way in a business-like manner. 'Smoke,' he said briskly. 'It gets inside you and clogs you up. Now—' And he opened his bag and started sorting through the powders and potions.

Hugh and I took our chance to escape, Hugh sniffing at his greatcoat. 'Damn it, my clothes will stink of smoke for weeks.'

'I'm going home,' I said wearily. 'Walk with me up Westgate.'

We trudged together through the silent snow, hearing it crunch beneath our feet. We passed St John's church; Hugh said, 'It's been a trying day.'

'Balfour?'

'He's refusing to do anything with the plans. Says they'll have to be accepted as they are, or not at all. Walked out of a meeting with the Directors this evening. I had to spend hours calming them, then more time tracking him down.'

We were the only people in the street; behind the dancing snowflakes, the house windows were dark.

'Fowler was shot,' I said. 'Heron shot him. And the intruder got away.'

Hugh stopped to stare at me. He shook his head. 'No, I'm too tired for this. Tell me tomorrow. Is Fowler dead?'

'Shoulder wound.'

I left Hugh at his rooms and went on home alone. The house was silent as I let myself in but George slid down the banister, whispering, 'Is the fire out, Master?'

Of course he knew already; given the efficiency of the spirits' message system, every spirit in town would know by now.

'Nearly.'

'And the spirits are dead?'

'All but one.'

'Yes, the apprentice. I'm glad about that, Master. People say all sorts of things about apprentices and it's unkind.'

Having been an apprentice himself when he died, George knew what he was talking about.

I heard a footstep and looked up. Esther, in her nightgown and robe, hair loose about her shoulders, stood at the top of the stairs. She looked both anxious and relieved at the same time. George made a strangled, embarrassed noise and slid away into the inner recesses of the servants' quarters. I went up the stairs; Esther cupped her hand against my cheek and kissed me softly. The weariness slipped out of me; I sighed with relief.

In the bedroom, I stripped off my filthy coat and related everything that had happened, from the disaster at Heron's house to the fire on the bridge. In the light of a single candle, Esther propped herself up against the pillows in bed and listened carefully, occasionally posing a question or two when I was too terse.

'You never saw the face of the intruder?' she said at last.

I shook my head.

'A pity. So still all you have is Alice's word that this accomplice is Kane.'

'Not even that,' I admitted. 'That's merely my supposition, although in view of the fact he's left town, I think it's a good one.'

She trimmed the guttering candle. 'Oh, for an independent witness!'

I was about to pull off my shirt – I paused, stared at her. 'An independent witness?' In the way that often happens when you're tired, my mind skittered off in quite a different direction. Those antiquities. Hugh's ring had been stolen and the widow living below had seen the fellow, even though she didn't know what he'd done. I myself had seen the intruder at Heron's house; I had my own evidence that I'd been attacked in the street.

But what evidence was there of the theft in Balfour's room?

Esther said, 'Charles? What is it?'

I cursed. 'I should have known there was something wrong – how could a casual thief find his way through that warren of rooms and passageways in the George! And nothing belonging to the George was damaged – the fellow didn't even turn the mattress over. What kind of thief leaves the mattress untouched? More than that, we only have Balfour's word there *was* a coin to steal!'

'Balfour?' Esther echoed, startled. 'You think *he's* the thief?'

'The intruder at Heron's house was about the right size.'

'But then—' Esther shook her head. 'He cannot have killed the Gregsons, Charles! Think of his own family background – his father's death!'

'But we only have his word for that too. Although, admittedly, I'm inclined to believe it.' Something else occurred to me. 'Mrs Fletcher showed me a letter Alice's lover wrote – it was a dreadful scrawl. And he's refusing to redo the plans!'

'Charles,' Esther said severely. 'You are rambling!'

'I found some cuttings in Alice's trunk. Where the devil did I put them . . .'

I scrabbled through the bits and pieces on the dressing table. Somewhere I'd put those cuttings – heavens, almost a week ago! Here they were; I disentangled dog-eared corners and crumpled folds, angled the paper to catch the feeble candlelight. Esther stretched to read over my shoulder. 'This refers to something Balfour built in Deal in Kent – *small assembly rooms – delightful design, the chandeliers sparkling wonderfully . . .'*

I turned the cutting over. A scribbled note on the back said simply *Gazette, 20 July 1717.* 'Twenty years ago. How old would you say Balfour is? Thirty? Would he be designing buildings at the age of ten? He's an impostor!'

I paced about the room. 'According to Heron, Balfour initially refused to come north. That was the *real* Balfour. Then he purportedly changed his mind. An elderly man – or middle-aged at least, if he was working on his own twenty years ago. What if this fellow – Hitchings or 'Richard' or whatever his name is – found out that the real Balfour wasn't coming and seized the opportunity to impersonate him?'

'So he could follow Alice, presumably.'

'As for the fire tonight,' I said. 'We've only Balfour's word that Gregson started it. Balfour did it himself!'

'Why?'

'The letter book,' I said. 'Balfour was looking through it when I stepped through to the other world. Maybe he found something in there about his alliance with Alice.'

Esther was shaking her head. 'You do have an independent witness to the fire, Charles. The apprentice's spirit. *He* said Gregson did it.'

I stared at her in the flickering candlelight. Thinking of the moment Ned's spirit had slid to the top of the brick and shouted: *He did it, he did it.* 'He was referring to Balfour,' I said, and then the horror of it properly struck me. 'If Balfour *did* set that fire, then Ned's the sole witness to what happened! And I've left him alone on that bridge!'

I grabbed my coat and ran.

Thirty-Five

A villain will never allow himself to be apprehended, if he has any other choice.
[Letter from Louis de Glabre to his friend Philippe Froidevaux, 23 January 1737]

I got a stitch running down Westgate and had to slow to a limping walk. I was right, I *knew* I was. I remembered how cheerful Balfour had been after the inquest, how he'd gone out and got drunk, and whored all night – he must have been relieved Alice was officially blamed for the murders, and no one suspected there was an accomplice!

The snow was drifting down in a half-hearted fashion. I turned into the Side, tried to run down the slope, slipped and had to grab hold of a window sill to keep myself upright. I might be too late already. Perhaps I should find a spirit and send a warning to Ned. But he was stuck on one small brick in a bucket and there was nowhere for him to go – how could he defend himself?

Hugh and I had left Balfour on the bridge an hour or more ago. More than enough time to hurt Ned. But there'd still been people around, making sure the fire was out. That would take some time. Even after that, someone would probably be stationed in front of the shop to keep watch in case the fire broke out again. But would anyone stay outside long in this dreadful weather?

I tottered on, down the Side. What would Balfour do? What *could* he do? Tipping Ned into the river would ensure he lay isolated and unheard for the rest of his eighty or hundred year sojourn as a spirit – assuming no one dredged him up again. But carrying the bucket with Ned's brick in it had been almost impossible – Balfour wouldn't be able to lift it over the bridge's parapet.

It would be easiest to toss the brick into the rubble of the shop in the hope it would burn up. But no one would leave until the fire was pretty much extinguished so Balfour would have to stir up the embers into a blaze again, and that would put the residents of the bridge at risk. Would Balfour go to such lengths to protect himself?

If I was right about him, he'd already killed four people here, and two in Kent. Why should he hesitate over a few more?

Near the bottom of the Side, I heard the uneven clip clop of a horse's hooves and was so distracted I nearly went head over heels. I grabbed at a post to support myself and wrenched my left arm badly. The one that had been hit in Heron's garden. Pain shot through me. Cursing, I tottered across the slippery cobbles into the Sandhill—

And came face to face with Joseph Kane.

He was covered in snow, in a thick layer over his greatcoat; his hat was pulled over his face and he had his head down. But I knew it was him by his voice; he was swearing at the horse he was leading, which was lame.

He must have heard me, glanced up. 'Damn horse,' he said viciously, 'damn town, damn snow, damn night.'

Only this morning I'd suspected him of running for his life and now he was back – and just in time. Two of us ought to be able to tackle Balfour.

'Been to Shields again?'

'And that's a hole of a place,' he said sourly. 'Two houses, twenty taverns and a couple of broken-down old ships.'

So he'd got through. 'Didn't find your man there?'

'Go to the devil,' he said and started walking towards the Fleece.

'I know where he is.'

He turned back, staring. 'If you're playing some kind of gentleman's trick—'

'He set fire to the Gregsons' shop to destroy the letter books. And he's gone back to get rid of the only witness – the apprentice's spirit.'

Kane dropped the horse's reins and abandoned it. 'What the devil are we waiting for!' And he was off running for the bridge.

Even slipping and sliding, I caught and overtook him easily; too many late nights and too many tankards of beer had taken their toll on him. I was first on to the bridge. The lights in the shops and houses were out; a thin line of smoke curled into the drifting snow from the Gregsons' shop. And one shadowy figure, barely touched by lantern light, was in front of the ruins, bending to pick something up.

I almost called out his name but there was no point in giving him warning. I started towards him, slipping in the snow, Kane puffing and panting behind me. I saw the figure try to straighten; something metallic scraped on cobbles. The spirit's voice called out in alarm, 'What are you doing? Put me down!'

The figure dragged what it was carrying on top of a heap of bricks. In an errant flicker of light, I saw the glint of the bucket, the pale oval of Balfour's face. The bucket began to tip . . .

'Balfour!' I roared.

He started, dropped the bucket. It hit the ground with a crash and a splash and he leapt back. For one brief moment, he stared—

He took off running. I leapt over the bucket and the brick that had fallen out of it, and went after him. Kane shouted. 'Stop or I fire!' More guns. And I knew how perilous it was to shoot in the dark.

Balfour leapt for the parapet of the bridge, hauled himself up on to it. I made a lunge for him. My fingers grazed the skirts of his greatcoat.

He jumped.

There was a moment's silence. Then we heard the splash below.

Thirty-Six

It is no good expecting a villain to tell you the truth; the English villains are as inventive in this regard as the French.
[Letter from Louis de Glabre to his friend Philippe Froidevaux, 23 January 1737]

Kane let out a roar and ran for the Key. Halfway down the slope of the bridge, his feet slid out from under him and he crashed down on his back. His pistol flew out of his hand, hit the ground and fired with a crack that resounded through the night. A dog close by started barking furiously.

I reached to help him up. He shook me off. 'Get after him!' There was no point in arguing; I went after Balfour.

Not that I expected him to be alive. The river was still flowing freely in the middle and would be icy cold; he'd probably been swept away already. But if he was dead, I wanted to see his body, to be sure of it.

By the time I skidded off the bridge on to the Key, lights were glimmering on a ship moored at the wharf. A man stood on deck, with a lantern held high to give his fellows light to launch a rowing boat. The dog, a lithe ugly brute, was barking at his side.

I clambered aboard the ship; the deck was icy and I clung on to various bits of rigging to keep my feet. The man glanced round as I came up behind him. 'Jumped or fell?' he asked laconically.

'Jumped.'

He spat into the water. 'Not worth picking out then.'

The rowing boat, another lantern swaying at one end, was struggling to make the channel of water, oars battering against the fragments of ice that littered the river. Balfour had disappeared but I could see the widening ripples where he'd gone in. Then a head broke the surface, and a floating trail of greatcoat skirts. Someone in the boat yelled instructions.

'They've got him,' the sailor said, with a sneer. 'They'll take him to the landing steps. If he's dead, we want the contents of his pockets, mind.'

'Fair enough.' They deserved something for their efforts. Although I intended to look closely at the items before handing them over.

I struggled off the boat again, on to the Key. My arm ached where I'd wrenched it in my near-fall on the Side; I was rubbing it when I met up with Kane limping through the snow. 'They're bringing him to the landing steps.'

Cursing, he turned round again and we made our way past the bridge to the steps on the other side, where Alice Gregson had stumbled ashore early last Sunday morning, after the murders.

The rowing boat came through the dark water, gliding slowly into the steps. Kane was clenching his fists in delight, swearing he'd escort Balfour to the noose himself. I didn't share his exultation. I believed Balfour was the killer, but he hadn't committed the crimes the way Alice had claimed; she was all sweetness and light, all mischievous innocence – and totally untrustworthy.

While they were struggling to get Balfour out of the boat and up the steps, I found a spirit on a nearby house and asked it to send for Abraham McLintoch and the Watch. When I went back to the landing steps, one of the sailors had dumped Balfour face down on the Key and was thumping his back with a meaty fist. 'Full o' water.' He thumped again; Balfour convulsed and spewed. I went back and asked the spirit to send for Gale as well.

The sailors were unsympathetic. They dragged Balfour unceremoniously up the steps to the shelter of the Fish Market beneath the Guildhall, more to get themselves out of the desultory snow than to find him shelter. They went through his pockets, found a few coins and a button; I recognized the button at once as Hugh's. And one of the coins was the ancient artefact Balfour claimed had been stolen.

'I'll give you a sovereign for the button and the old coin,' I told the sailors. 'You can take the rest.'

They accepted the offer with grunts and nods, and went off with Balfour's money, his handkerchief and his cravat besides. If he'd drowned, they'd probably have taken *all* his clothes.

By this time, the landlord of the Fleece had turned out, presumably alerted by the boy who kept watch there overnight; he brought brandy and offered it to Balfour at cut-price rates. Kane took it off him and drank most of it himself without paying. A couple of watchmen came up and said McLintoch was following.

Balfour was shivering uncontrollably. I took the brandy from Kane and made Balfour drink. He spluttered, and vomited most of it up again.

'Don't waste good brandy on the likes of him!' Kane said, contemptuously. Snow drifted in under the columns of the Fish Market as he bent to slap Balfour's face. 'Know who I am? I'm the fellow who's going to take you back to London to hang for those two you killed in Kent.'

'He's going nowhere until I know what happened,' I said sharply. Balfour protested incoherently; I was far from sure he knew where he was.

McLintoch came up in the company of Gale, who was looking weary. Kane begrudgingly stood back to allow Gale room to examine Balfour. 'I'm taking him back to London,' he insisted.

'He doesn't fit the description you gave me,' I pointed out. 'Big, burly, middle-aged, you said.'

'Devil take it, I never saw him – how the devil do I know what he looked like!'

Well, I should have known not to trust anything Kane said. Although perhaps if he'd not been so dogmatic about the man's appearance, I might have considered Balfour earlier.

Gale stood up. 'He needs dry clothes and his bed.'

'He's going to a prison cell,' Kane said stridently. 'And then back to London.' He squatted in front of Balfour and shouted. 'Tell me how you killed them!'

McLintoch said, 'Mr Patterson, is he the one as killed the Gregsons?'

'I believe so.'

'Then *I* want him.'

Balfour was trying to sit up against the wall of the Fish Market. The landlord of the Fleece came back with an armful of blankets, and between us we got Balfour's saturated greatcoat off. I was putting it aside when I felt a stickiness on my fingers, and looked down to see a tear in Balfour's shirt sleeve. Underneath was a long thin scratch along the forearm, still bleeding. I thought of the smear of blood on Heron's sofa and the drops in the snow. Here was proof positive that Fowler had not missed his target. No wonder Balfour had kept his hands in his pockets when I saw him earlier; the blood must have been running down his fingers.

We wrapped Balfour in the blankets. By this time, Kane and McLintoch were shouting at each other, each demanding custody of the prisoner. Gale pressed a folded paper into my hand. 'If you ever get him indoors,' he said, 'Give him that powder. I've just come from a pious woman who's dying, and I'm in no mood for suicides and murderers.' And he stalked off across the Sandhill, passing, on his way, Claudius Heron.

Heron was at his most sombre. Snow dusted his shoulders; his sword disturbed the lie of his greatcoat skirts. He looked down on Balfour expressionlessly. 'A spirit sent a message to Fowler to say the killer had been found.' He gave me a measuring look. 'I suppose this is all to do with the apprentice.'

Which was tantamount to admitting he knew of Fowler's *inclinations*. I nodded. 'How is Fowler?'

'Sleeping.'

'The shooting,' I started, but Heron immediately interrupted me.

'Has he said why he did it?'

I'd been intending to say something consoling, something to the effect that it had been dark and that Heron wasn't to blame for Fowler being hurt. But of course Heron was right to interrupt. Banal platitudes, and untrue ones at that, were not to the point. We both knew that Heron's obsession with those coins had for a short while overwhelmed his reason.

'He hasn't said anything yet.'

'Then perhaps you had better start questioning him before he dies of cold,' Heron said dryly.

The landlord was still plying Balfour with brandy and had his reward when Heron pressed coins into his hand. I squatted down beside Balfour.

'I want to know what happened.'

There was colour in his cheeks again. 'I didn't kill them.' His voice was hoarse; the effort of speaking made him retch. 'I told you – my father – blood.' He said, with bitter self-pity, 'I'm haunted by violent death.'

I laid a blanket on the floor of the Market and sat down. It was obvious that if Balfour had to talk a great deal he'd tire easily. And thanks to Kane, he was aware of the danger he was in – he'd deny what he could, as long as he could. I decided to take a roundabout route and hope to gradually persuade him to talk. '*You* set fire to the shop last night,' I said, 'not Gregson. You found something in the letter book and decided to destroy it. I assume you didn't think of the ledgers when you broke in last Monday after attacking me in the street?'

A moment's silence. Balfour shook his head.

'Of course,' I said, 'once you realized the apprentice had survived the fire, you had to get rid of him, or sooner or later he'd make us understand what had really happened.'

'What's one more killing?' Kane said contemptuously. 'Four here, two in Kent.'

'Not in Kent,' Balfour protested feebly. 'I didn't kill them!'

Kane laughed.

'They came after me,' Balfour said. 'One of them drew a pistol. It exploded – killed him.'

'And the other?' I asked. Kane was muttering in disbelief.

'Fell in a ditch. Drowned.'

'Pushed, more likely,' Kane said. 'Look here—'

Heron took one step towards him, hand on sword hilt. 'No,' he said softly. '*You* look here. Either you keep quiet or I will personally throw you in the river and leave you to take your chances. Do I make myself understood?'

Kane stiffened, face white. McLintoch, apparently suddenly realizing he was in the presence of a gentleman, whipped off his hat and stood bare-headed in the snow.

'I presume you went up to London looking for bigger and more attractive game,' I said to Balfour. 'You met Alice there. You originally intended to rob her uncle's house, I presume?'

He nodded. There was a dull, resigned look on his face.

'But then the uncle died and Alice was summoned back to Newcastle, so you transferred your attention to her father. And when Alice told you that some of the money in the cellar was ancient coinage, that only made the theft more attractive, didn't it?'

'Yes,' he said, almost inaudibly.

'Which leads us to your imposture as John Balfour, architect.'

He pulled the blankets tighter. 'My master,' he said hoarsely.

'What, the one that took you to Italy?'

He nodded. 'Saw him in London. He's old, ill. When I said I was coming north, he gave me the plans, To bring with me.'

'All neatly drawn and annotated,' I said. 'No wonder you were in despair when the Directors wanted new ones. Your scrawl would have given away that you weren't the original architect. And I wager you didn't finish your apprenticeship, so you didn't have the expertise needed.'

He nodded again. 'Inherited money from my father, went off to enjoy myself.'

'And the money didn't last long. Did the trip to Italy give you a taste for antiquities?'

'Better than people,' he said bitterly. 'Good solid gold and silver don't change. Never argue, never shout.'

I wondered what kind of a childhood he'd had. My own had been strict and cold, as far as my father had been concerned, but always impeccably well-mannered. 'So you took my coin and Hugh's ring, and staged the robbery in your own rooms. And then you tried to rob Mr Heron's house.'

Heron was standing over me, blocking out most of the light from the lanterns carried by the watchmen. Odd shadows fell across his face; he was at his most impassive. The epitome of a fashionable man. And dangerous.

'Had to rush it,' Balfour said with a trace of bitter amusement. 'Should have waited, wooed a maid to get the key. Wanted to be able to get out of town quickly, when the snow stopped.'

'So,' I said. 'We come to what happened on Saturday night.'

Balfour said nothing.

'I know what led up to it,' I said. 'Alice came to Newcastle on the Tuesday, you followed on the Thursday. All that seasickness was faked so you could keep to your lodgings. That ensured as few people as possible saw you. If things had gone right, you'd have carried out the robbery on Saturday night, ridden out of town and got away almost unnoticed. Did you intend to marry Alice?'

He shook his head.

'Well,' I said, 'she was planning to double-cross you too, so you're even on that score. Of course, as far as the robbery was concerned, each of you was counting on the other to keep quiet for fear of being apprehended.'

He set his head back against the wall behind him. His face was white, his body still trembling with cold.

'You managed to have a word with Alice,' I said, 'perhaps with the help of the female spirit who hated Gregson. Alice told you to come to the door of the shop at a certain time and she'd let you in. So what happened then?'

He turned his head to look at me in silence. Kane started to say something; McLintoch seized his arm.

Balfour took a deep breath.

'I didn't kill them,' he said, obstinately.

Thirty-Seven

I was in love the other day, you know, but alas, there was
already another, younger, man in the field before me.
[Letter from Louis de Glabre to his friend Philippe
Froidevaux, 23 January 1737]

He slid his knees up, embracing them with his arms. Water ran
off his hair and down his face. He looked around his audience,
his gaze lingering on Kane. 'I'll tell you what happened,' he said,
'but only if you promise I'll not go back to Kent.'

'You'll hang,' McLintoch said. 'Here or in Kent, what's the
difference?'

'Not if I didn't kill them,' Balfour said. He was regaining a
little of his old confidence, I thought, which was not altogether
a good thing. 'Promise me I won't hang and I'll bear witness
against her.'

'And she'll bear witness against you,' Heron said dryly, hand
on sword hilt. 'Which one of you are we supposed to believe?'

'I won't say a word unless you promise me,' Balfour said
doggedly.

'There's no point in going through all this rigmarole!' Kane
exploded. 'There's evidence against him in Kent. I'm taking him
back.'

Balfour stared at me. I simply looked back. The snow fell
around us. Kane shifted impatiently. Balfour's eyes dropped; he
said, 'She let me in the shop door.'

'Go on.'

'The apprentice was snoring, behind the counter. I didn't know
there was an apprentice till then – she never said.' He coughed
briefly and McLintoch offered him what was left of the brandy;
he shook his head. 'She said the coins were in the cellar but the
box was too heavy for her to lift. She said to go down and get

it, while she went upstairs for her bag. So I did. I found the box easy enough – it was on the table, open, and a bag beside it. It was full,' he said almost reverentially, 'full of ancient coins.' He paused for a moment to catch his breath. 'There was a scrap of paper there too, I didn't look at that. I pushed the coins into the bag – it took some time.'

He started to smooth down the blankets that lay over his knees, regular, slow, almost obsessive movements. 'I knew something was wrong as soon as I went back up into the shop, only I couldn't decide what. Then I realized the apprentice wasn't snoring. I was worried maybe he'd woken up, so I looked round the edge of the counter.' The rubbing action speeded up. 'And I saw the blood—'

'The boy was alive when you went down into the cellar,' Heron said, 'but not when you came up again?'

Balfour nodded. 'Then I heard a noise upstairs. I panicked.' The rubbing action slowed. 'I thought I'd be found with the body. Alice had left the key in the door so I simply ran out. And I'd hardly taken four or five steps when the child screamed.' He looked at me. 'I *had* to stay in town – all that snow. What choice did I have but to brazen it out?'

No wonder he'd looked ill on the Sunday. Or that he'd gone back to the house that afternoon. Perhaps he'd been trying to convince himself it had never happened.

'Anyway,' he said. 'I could keep an eye on what was happening, try and distract attention from myself if need be.'

'According to this version of events,' Heron said. 'The girl must have killed the apprentice before she went back upstairs.'

I nodded. 'And she had already killed the others before coming down to let Balfour in, because she knew she wouldn't have time later. That's why the knife was downstairs, near the boy. He *was* the last one killed.'

'But why go back up again? Why not simply walk out of the front door?'

'She had to wake the child,' I said, 'so the alarm would be raised. And the rope was to give credence to her story of running in panic from a murderer.' I glanced at Balfour. 'She must have planned to come out of hiding immediately, when you were caught. But you were too quick for her – you got away, and that left her the only suspect. What excuse did she give you for not doing the robbery on the Sunday, when the house would be empty and everyone out?'

'She said her mother was ill and wouldn't be going to church.'

'She had to have some excuse,' Heron said, 'because she *wanted* to kill her family.'

'But *why*?' McLintoch said, with more passion than I'd heard from him. 'A lass like that killing the parents that bore her? What could bring her to do anything so unnatural?'

Balfour laughed bitterly. 'I don't know. Why did my father pick the quarrel that killed him?'

I heard that self-pity again in his complaint. But I believed Balfour, nevertheless – his was a detailed account, not vague like Alice's. *She* was the killer. But, in one way, we were still no further forward. There were two Alices. *Which one of them had done the killing?*

McLintoch said, 'It's the old story – we need to find the lass.'

'Don't care about that,' Kane said. He reached down, grabbed Balfour's arm and dragged him up. 'I'm having you.'

'No,' McLintoch said. '*I* am. And I'm the one with two watchmen here, and I'm sure Mr Patterson and Mr Heron will give me a hand if I need it. We're taking this fellow off to jail and no one's getting their hands on him until Mr Patterson here says so. Mr Patterson,' he said to Kane with an air of triumph, 'is standing in for Mr Philips, so I does what he says. Come on, my lad.'

And the watchmen, with distinct pleasure, bore Balfour off into the snow, followed by a cursing Kane.

The landlord of the Fleece, with an ostentatious sigh, retreated, cradling his sodden blankets and empty bottle. Heron and I were left alone under the Fish Market with snow floating around us. I said, with some annoyance, 'I forgot to ask Balfour where he hid the coins.'

'Leave them hidden,' Heron said. 'I wish they had never been found.' He gave me a long hard look. 'So what now?'

I got up with some difficulty; one foot was numb and my left arm still ached. 'We go and talk to Alice.'

His head lifted. 'You know where she is?'

'Yes,' I said, 'Balfour told me.'

Heron raised an eyebrow.

'He said that staying in the town helped him to keep an eye on what was going on,' I pointed out. 'That was exactly what *Alice* decided to do. And she's done more than keep watch,' I added angrily. 'She's been manipulating me, encouraging me to think there might be an accomplice, then that the accomplice might have been the killer. Giving me letters from him. Trying to mislead me by claiming jewellery had been stolen . . .'

I smiled bleakly on Heron. 'She's been right under our noses from the beginning. Mrs Fletcher.'

Thirty-Eight

I have tried to relate my experiences as honestly as I can, my dear friend, but there is always something I forget. Never mind, we will gossip about it when I am back home.

[Letter from Louis de Glabre to his friend Philippe Froidevaux, 23 January 1737]

The snow drifted down; the dog on the boat barked once and was quiet. 'Mrs Fletcher is dark,' Heron said. 'All the descriptions of Alice Gregson say she is fair.'

I nodded. 'But there's another Alice from the other world, and she's dark.'

He listened grimly as I explained my recent encounters with the two women. 'Our Alice was the one acquainted with Balfour,' I said. 'She let him in the house. Mrs Fletcher is the Alice from the other world. But which killed the Gregson family? I've met both Mrs Fletcher and Alice Gregson – and Mrs Fletcher is by far the more ruthless woman.'

'You will never find out,' Heron said. 'If this is a conspiracy, they will protect each other.'

'I don't think I care which one did it,' I said. 'They planned this together, they acted in concert and killed at least two innocents. That's unforgivable. I want both of them.' And so I did, though if I could find out which of them struck the blows, I would.

We walked briskly across the snowy Sandhill to Butcher
Bank. We were probably already too late to capture either of the
women; the business with Balfour would have spread on the
spirits' message network, and the spirit of Letitia Mountfort would
make sure it got to Alice's ears. But I was determined to at least
try.

On the steep slippery slope of Butcher Bank, the scents of
meat and blood were thin but distinct in the freezing air; over
our heads and the tops of the houses loomed the squat tower of
All Hallows' church. We strode up a deserted Pilgrim Street and
came to the door of Mrs Mountain's lodging house on the corner
of the High Bridge. A light shone in a downstairs room; I knocked
on the window and after a moment, the curtains parted and the
lady herself, fully dressed, peered out. She looked surprised,
though not alarmed; she signalled to us to wait, and came to
open the front door. She beckoned us into her room with a
finger to her lips.

'You're lucky to catch me up, gents,' she said cheerfully. She
was a rotund elderly woman and even walking to open her front
door had made her breathe heavily. 'Waiting for one of the
comedians to arrive, I am. Supposed to be here tonight but don't
suppose he'll make it in all this snow. There'll be no dashing
villain at the theatre this week! Was you looking for someone?'

'One of your lodgers.'

'All asleep,' she said fondly.

'I think you'll find this one isn't,' I said.

We knocked on Mrs Fletcher's door. There was no reply. Mrs
Mountain hovered encouragingly on the stairs. 'Knock again, sir.
She often has visitors late, her cousin comes to see her.'

Heron turned; Mrs Mountain took an uncertain step back at
his expression. 'A fair-haired girl? Flighty and insolent?'

'That's her, sir,' Mrs Mountain said.

'Like the one the whole town is looking for?'

Now she was seriously alarmed. 'I'm sure I didn't – I never
thought. One girl's just like another . . .'

'You may go,' Heron said coldly. Mrs Mountain retreated
instantly.

I knocked again and this time heard footsteps. The door opened,
and there was Mrs Fletcher, in her outdoor clothes and boots,

looking faintly amused. I thought how like her counterpart she was: taller and darker in colouring, but with very similar features. I'd put the resemblance down to the family connection of course.

'Alice Gregson?' I said.

'I'd an inkling you'd discover us sooner or later,' she said, ignoring Heron as if he didn't exist. 'Alice's tale set you on guard, of course.'

I nodded. 'Why did she tell me so much?'

'I love her dearly,' she said, in a flat resigned tone. 'But she has no common sense. I knew there'd be trouble if I left her kicking her heels while I took care of things. She was bored and my methods were too subtle for her. She told you everything, of course?'

'Not quite everything. Her story was only convincing up to the point where she let Balfour into the house. What happened then?'

She considered me for a long moment, then said blandly, 'I don't have time to talk. You've picked an inconvenient moment – I was just on my way out.'

I laughed. 'At two in the morning? Letty Mountfort's spirit has told you Balfour's in custody, I suppose. Why don't you just step through to the other world – surely that would be your quickest escape?'

She grimaced. 'I can't. Only Alice can do so – she takes me with her when she comes and goes. And Alice is at the moment in my lodgings in that other world, *my* world, blissfully asleep, no doubt, and doesn't have the least notion I'm in any danger.' She stood back. 'Very well, if you must know, come in before you wake the whole house.'

She held the door open. Heron gestured me in front of him, came behind, hand on sword hilt. It was a large room, comfortably, if shabbily, furnished for sitting. Mrs Fletcher – Alice – strolled to the table in the middle of the room, where a book lay open, beside the remains of her supper of bread and cheese on a plate. I glimpsed an unmade bed through a half-open door; she must have been sleeping when the spirit's warning came.

'And when I've told you everything,' she mused, toying with the plate. 'What then? Will you let me go?'

I hesitated.

'No,' she said, 'I thought not.'

She swung round. I caught a glint of metal in the candlelight. Heron shouted; his sword sang out of its scabbard. But it was too late – Alice had an arm round my neck and a knife at my throat.

I choked, more from fear than from the pressure of the cold metal against my skin. Alice was a tall woman, and her arm round my neck dragged me back, and down. Her voice was close to my ear.

'Put the sword down! Now! Or he dies.'

From my uncomfortable position, I could just see Heron, in the doorway, sword at the ready. He stood for a long, frightening moment, before lowering the sword point to the floor. Without taking his eyes off us, he closed the door behind him. He sounded almost conversational. 'If you hurt him, *you* will die.'

'We'll see,' Alice said grimly.

I could hardly talk for the pressure on my throat. 'While – while we're here, why not tell us—'

'Only if you guarantee our freedom.'

'You have that guarantee already,' Heron said. 'Even if we put you both in prison, you can easily escape to that other world.'

She nodded. The knife twitched unpleasantly at my throat; my back and knees ached from bending over backwards. My awkward position sent a stab of pain through my bruised shoulder.

'We want freedom to come and go as we please, in both worlds.' Mrs Fletcher – Alice – laughed softly. 'Why should we suffer for what Balfour did? That patronizing, condescending idiot! *So* careful not to tax puny female brains! And Alice liked him!'

The old doubts resurfaced. Had Balfour been telling the truth? Or was he the killer after all?

I gestured feebly. 'I can't breathe . . .'

She shook her head. 'You don't fool me that way. You talk like this or not at all.'

Struggling for breath, trying to crane back away from that knife blade, I managed, 'If you're innocent of the killings, why didn't you just tell me about Balfour, and what happened that night? Instead of all this complicated plotting and planning?'

'Would you have believed us?' she said. I had to admit I probably would not. 'Besides, you're a dangerous man, Mr Patterson.

You can step through between worlds. We didn't want to be looking over our shoulders the whole time, wondering if we'd see you in hot pursuit. We had to make sure you were so convinced of Balfour's guilt you didn't even attempt to look for us – which meant allowing you to come to your own conclusions.'

'So you posed as your sister from Bristol.' Heron was calm again, cool. I knew that look – he was waiting his opportunity. He'd sheathed his sword but still had his hand on its hilt.

'Dear Sophia.' Mrs Fletcher nodded. 'I've derived a great deal of satisfaction from offending people in her name – we've never got on. Of course, I mean in my own world.'

'Nor with the rest of your family, I suppose,' I said.

'My father was a brute,' she said roughly. 'The only decent thing he ever did was die and leave me an allowance. A paltry allowance, it has to be said, but enough to guarantee genteel independence.'

'So robbing another Samuel Gregson in this world was an attractive prospect.'

Heron was very still, but I've seen him leap into action in the fraction of a moment. I fixed my eye on him, ready to react, to play my part if he decided to act.

'Very attractive,' she said. 'But we're not fools, Mr Patterson – neither of us wants to hang.'

She hadn't denied the charge, I noted. 'I don't believe Balfour killed them,' I said. 'He can't stand the sight of blood. His father was killed in front of him and he has never forgotten it.'

'He killed in Kent,' she pointed out.

'He says the deaths were accidental.'

She said nothing. There was no sense in holding back now; I said. '*You* killed the Gregsons. You or the other Alice. Which one?'

A long, long silence. I tried to ease my aching back but she tightened her grip. Choking, I put up my hands to my throat but she kicked at my ankle. I nearly went down. The knife point pricked my throat and I felt the warm trickle of blood.

Heron never moved.

'The more you know, the less likely you'll get out of here alive,' Mrs Fletcher said softly. 'Think twice, Mr Patterson – do you really want to know the truth?'

She'd already told me too much to let me go. I was staking my life on Heron. I was frightened, but knew how good a swordsman he was, and how unflinching. 'Yes, I want to know. Tell me.'

'Really, Mr Patterson,' she said, and laughed. 'You've no concern for your own safety at all, have you?'

She pressed the knife in harder. Heron started forward but she shouted at him and he jerked to a halt. Hot blood ran down on to my coat.

Oddly, there was no pain. 'What exactly happened?' I felt her warm breath on my cheek, heard it quicken and catch. Then an infinitesimal relaxation of her arm.

'Why not?' she said, as if to herself. 'Very well, I'll tell you. Alice came for me about an hour before Balfour was due to arrive. She brought with her the box of coins from the cellar. Not the old coins but the recent takings of the shop – there was fifty pounds or more there. Then we came back to the shop in *this* world.'

She paused; I said encouragingly, 'And then?'

'Alice went downstairs to wait for Balfour to arrive while I killed the people upstairs.' Her voice was steady but I felt the hand with the knife tremble. 'You have no idea how many years I have wished to lay hands on Samuel Gregson.'

So many years that she killed another man: a man with the same name, but a different person nevertheless.

'When Balfour came,' she continued, 'Alice let him in, and told him where the coins were. He went down into the cellar, I came downstairs and killed the apprentice; we'd left him alive until then so Balfour heard his snoring and was reassured. Then Alice took me back to my own world.'

She took a deep breath; I felt the knife turn slightly against my throat as she took a firmer grip. 'Alice came back to this world to leave a trail. It had to look as if she was fleeing for her life, so she slid down the rope to escape. She was to go to the derelict house to wait for the furore to die down; when the spirit told her Balfour was captured, she'd have run out and told her story.' She added wryly, 'She'd have told it very well. She's extremely good at wheedling and winning her own way.'

I thought of the girl I'd encountered in the alley. Mrs Fletcher spoke of her with some exasperation, yet when we had arrived, she had said she loved her dearly.

'Just before she slid down the rope, she woke the child so the alarm could be raised,' Mrs Fletcher said. 'Unfortunately, Balfour was more alert than we'd anticipated, and escaped. Which left Alice the only suspect.'

My back and leg muscles were beginning to twitch from the unnatural position. 'I can understand why you killed Samuel but what about the others? The girl, Sarah, and the apprentice? Why did they have to die? And then you attempted to blame the boy for the killings!'

She laughed harshly. 'Oh, don't have any sympathy for them! Sarah was going to marry a man four times her age just for the money. And the boy was no saint – he was always creeping out to some girl or other. Well, he should have crept out that night, or not come back so early.'

'So it was *their* fault you killed them.'

She was still holding on to me firmly; Heron was watchful but I knew there was nothing he could do, unless I could break Mrs Fletcher's hold. And there was only one way to do that – to make her careless with anger.

'You want us to believe *you* killed them,' I said. 'You know – I don't believe you. I think the other Alice did it.'

'Don't be stupid,' she said roughly. The knife shifted at my throat. 'I've told you the truth.'

'Nonsense. You're an intelligent woman; you're not foolish enough to think you could get away with something like this. But the other Alice – she's a silly impetuous child, acting on impulse, without thinking of the consequences.'

'*I* did it!' she said. 'Not Alice.' And her anger broke the surface. 'Can't you understand, you stupid fool!'

Her weight shifted, the knife quivered. Her grip on me loosened.

I kicked backwards.

I caught her shin. She shrieked. Heron was already halfway across the room, lunging forward, sword coming up. Mrs Fletcher struggled to get a firmer grip on me; we stumbled sideways, fell against the table, toppled it over. It crashed down—

Mrs Mountain's voice floated up from below. 'What's going on! Mr Patterson! Mr Heron!'

It was only a momentary distraction but Mrs Fletcher seized her opportunity. She pushed me. I stumbled against Heron; he whipped the sword away with a cry of alarm – and then Mrs Fletcher was out of the door.

Mrs Mountain screamed as Mrs Fletcher went headlong past her, knife in hand. She was standing where the stair took a turn on to a second flight; she grabbed at my arm as I stumbled against her. 'Mr Patterson – oh, dear God – blood!'

Heron vaulted over the banisters, landed awkwardly on the lower flight of stairs, regained his balance and rushed on. Mrs Mountain whispered, 'Blood . . .' and crumpled in my arms.

I dumped her unceremoniously on the floor but the door to the street was already slamming back. I leapt down the stairs, fumbled with the lock, pulled it open, skidded as I stepped out on to ice. Snowflakes stung my cheeks.

The street was empty.

I yelled for a spirit. One came with alacrity and didn't even ask what I wanted. 'Left at the end of the street!' it shouted. 'Then into the alleys on Pilgrim Street!'

'Damn!' Once she was in those alleys there were a dozen ways she could go. I dashed out into Pilgrim Street, ran for the nearest alley – and met Heron coming back towards me.

He shook his head.

Thirty-Nine

Odd how the unexpected ought always to be expected. And the lady was so charming, too.

[Letter from Louis de Glabre to his friend Philippe Froidevaux, 24 January 1737]

I woke with a burning pain at my neck; instinctively, I put up a hand to touch the raw flesh. There was the smell of . . .

Chocolate.

I opened my eyes. Esther was sitting on the edge of the bed, in a haze of candlelight, a dish of hot chocolate in her hands. She was still in her diaphanous nightgown, her blonde hair in a braid down her back, and she was looking at me with such an enigmatic expression . . .

'It really wasn't my fault,' I said.

She shook her head. 'George has had the entire story from one of the spirits at Mrs Mountain's. Admittedly, I think he probably exaggerated the swordplay but judging by what I can see, and the blood on your coat and shirt, I would say he has the story generally right.'

'It's just a scratch,' I said. 'Heron said it wasn't anything to worry about.' It didn't feel like a scratch; it was very painful. More painful than it had been at the time.

She said nothing.

'It probably was a mistake to try and apprehend Mrs Fletcher,' I admitted, 'but I thought she'd escape to the other world.'

She shook her head. 'I know you too well, Charles. You didn't think at all.'

I sighed and heaved myself up against the pillows. The candle flames fluttered wildly. 'No. But I did have Heron and his sword with me.'

'Oh, I'm sure he would have caught her if she'd killed you,' Esther said sarcastically. 'Charles . . .'

She pushed the dish of hot chocolate into my hands. It was so hot I nearly dropped it over the bedding.

'I know better than to think I can stop you trying to unravel these puzzles,' Esther said. 'I even admire you for it – after all, someone should bring such people to justice. But . . .'

An odd, uncharacteristic hesitation. As the silence lengthened, I started to say that I'd take more care in future, but she interrupted me. 'I wish you would not put yourself in danger, Charles. It is important to me.'

My heart contracted; I looked down into the dish of chocolate.

'And,' she said, with an air of great determination, 'to our child.'

I stared at her. At the candlelight gleaming on her pale hair, the fine strands escaping from the braid to curl against her neck.

At the flush on her cheeks, the wary look in her grey eyes. I should have known, of course I should. Her recent erratic health, her lack of appetite and unusual longing for sweet things . . . I'd been so tied up in the mystery of the Gregson's deaths that I hadn't paid any attention to what was going on in my own house!

And my principal feeling was – fear.

Esther was watching me closely. 'Yes,' she said. 'It is alarming, isn't it? Particularly with the ladies agog over stories of Alice Gregson's misdeeds, relating the endless ingratitude of sons and daughters, saying how impossible it is to control even young children.'

I'd like to see any child disobey Esther. I cleared my throat. 'I disliked my father,' I said. 'Very much.'

'I loved mine,' she said, and gave me a careful, tentative smile.

Forty

I am in the middle of my preparations to come home and I find I have left my belongings and scattered halfway across the country, in inns here and there.
[Letter from Louis de Glabre to his friend Philippe Froidevaux, 24 January 1737]

We had an enormous argument after that. I wanted Esther to go back to bed, and not overtire herself. Esther insisted she had to finish the Norfolk estate accounts. I said she must leave all that to me now. She burst out laughing. In the end, of course, she had her way, and we breakfasted in amicable silence, broken only by sneaking looks at each other and giggling like two young girls.

'Well,' Esther said, as I finished my coffee. 'What do you plan to do today, Charles?'

This was plainly dangerous territory – she was still smiling, but a trifle fixedly. I didn't pretend to misunderstand her. 'There's no point in trying to find Mrs Fletcher again. She'll have met up with *our* Alice and stepped through to the other world by now.'

'You don't propose to go after her there?' Esther said lightly.

I shook my head. 'Searching that world would be as big a task as searching this one. I thought I might look at Balfour's rooms, and at Mrs Fletcher's. I think we have to admit the murderer – whichever Alice it is – has escaped us, but we may be able to clear up what mystery remains. We don't know, for instance, where Balfour put the hoard of coins or Hugh's ring.'

'Ah,' she said, with some annoyance. 'I forgot to tell you. George has had an exchange with one of the spirits in the watchmen's hut. Balfour is apparently recalcitrant; he refuses to divulge the location of the artefacts.'

'I suppose I could talk to him,' I said doubtfully.

'I knew you'd forget, Mistress,' George said, startling us both by sliding up the table leg on to the edge of a used plate. The gleam of the spirit was bright – he was evidently happy today. 'I've got another message now. From Mr Heron. He says to tell you Mr Fowler has left the house and is wandering about the town and if you see him, will you please tell him to go home again, or Mr Heron will dismiss him, and he really means that.'

I doubted that last bit. I sighed. 'Fowler will be looking for Alice. He's always been convinced she killed the Gregsons.'

'He was right,' Esther pointed out, and raised an eyebrow. 'He must have been a good friend of the apprentice to take such pains over hunting his killer.'

I felt myself reddening. 'I believe so.'

My throat was on fire as I went out into the cold air in the square. The cuts, as I'd seen in my mirror, were indeed not deep or long, and when I was dressed they were hidden beneath the folds of my neckerchief. Unfortunately, the cloth chafed the cuts horribly. At least the pain in my arm was now only a dull distant ache.

New snow had come down overnight and covered up all the old footprints; servants and carters had laid down new tracks. Looking up, I saw the sky covered in a greyish layer of cloud; in the east, the grey was darkening to pewter. I walked briskly out of Caroline Square, towards Westgate Road. One of the church clocks struck eleven. Hugh might well be teaching, but if he wasn't, he might come with me.

He was indeed teaching; I heard the screech of his kit fiddle as I climbed the stairs, and the heavy thump of feet on floorboards. That sounded very much the way I danced. The dancing school-room door was ajar and I poked it open cautiously. Hugh had a little cluster of eight young ladies, none of them older than four-teen, partnering each other in a country dance, with their mamas – allegedly chaperoning them – chattering away to each other over a glass or two of what was almost certainly sweet wine.

The lesson was plainly coming to an end, and the young ladies were doing their best to remember the steps, although there was a great deal of pushing and shoving as the better dancers tried to remind the worse ones which way to go. I lounged in a corner for a moment, until one of the mamas signalled to me and I went across to talk. I only heard half she said; I was looking at the young ladies and thinking that in a few years time my daughter might be thudding away at her dance steps. If she turned out to be anything like me, she would have two left feet.

Or it might be a son, of course . . .

The young ladies were dismissed, swooped into their mamas' arms and ushered out. As I stood back to let them pass, I slipped on a stray piece of orange peel and nearly fell. Ridiculous; I was going to be a father and I had suddenly become accident-prone.

'Hugh,' I said, when the room was empty, 'I was wondering . . .' and instead of asking him whether he wanted to come and search Balfour's room for his missing ring, I said, 'Esther is with child.'

I hadn't meant to say it in such a doom-laden voice. Hugh burst out laughing. He slapped me on the back. 'Congratulations, Charles! A family man, at last! I want to be godfather, mind.'

Dear God, I hadn't thought of complications like that. My own father had been judicious in his choice of godparents, picking out the rich gentlemen who were his patrons with an eye to future advantage. He couldn't have predicted that my own wealthy godfather would die in a fall from his horse within three months of my birth and prove of no use at all.

Hugh was grinning from ear to ear. 'Is it common knowledge, or am I to keep quiet about it?'

'Hugh,' I said. 'I'm not fit to be a father. I get myself in scrapes every other day. I nearly got myself killed last night . . .'

Of course, he wanted to know all about it and took me off

to the nearest tavern so I could have plenty of time to explain. He regretted missing the excitement at rather too great length but did say that he thought Heron had probably been more use than he would have been. Not that Hugh isn't a good swordsman too; dancing masters usually are. He was only too eager to come with me to Balfour's room, having no more lessons until the afternoon.

'Mind you,' he said, 'there'll be no more gallivanting for you. You're a respectable family man now, Charles. You'll be reading books of sermons to the servants next!'

'Never!' I said fervently.

I wished he wouldn't grin so much.

Balfour's room had been left untouched; possibly the people at the George didn't yet know he was in custody. We stood in the doorway for a moment, looking about. His travelling trunk stood under the window; a coat and waistcoat were laid neatly on the bed, as if put out to wear. The plans for the Assembly Rooms were tucked down between the table and chair; I pulled them out and unrolled them. The loose sheets of paper on which Balfour had been writing fell out of the roll; one was covered in the almost illegible writing of the letter Mrs Fletcher had shown me. I could make out hardly any of it, except for one sentence, which was underlined: *Why did you do it?*

The room yielded no clues. There were no other letters, no hidden store of money, and certainly no ancient coins or ring.

We went on to Mrs Fletcher's rooms – a bedroom and a sitting room – which we searched to the accompaniment of Mrs Mountain's indignant requests for reparations. Heron had evidently got his sword tangled up in her best curtains, or so she said, and there was a great slit in them. She wanted the cost of new curtains. She went very coy, however, when I asked to see the damaged curtains and said she'd show them only to Heron. I recommended her to do so and shut the door on her. Leaving her, no doubt, to go for her scissors to slit the curtains.

Mrs Fletcher's rooms were not as tidy as Balfour's. She seemed to have made herself very much at home, with her own teapot and dishes, and a caddy full of an expensive blend of tea. She had a drab selection of dresses, in keeping with her role as a widow, a novel or two, and a copy of the latest *Courant*.

'There's a box here,' Hugh said, picking it off the mantelshelf. 'It's locked.' He broke it open with a pocket knife before I could protest. 'Letters.' He turned them over. 'Addressed to *Miss A Gregson* at an address in London.' He laughed. 'I don't know what Alice told everyone but this is not a fashionable address. Heron would turn up his nose at it.'

I took the letters. He was right; the address was in the sort of street that's patronized by people who make their living from trade. The letters were dreadfully written but I eventually deciphered enough to see that Balfour had not been cautious or wise. He referred to *that little plan I put to you concerning your father* and added that . . . *no need to be careful of his feelings – he's not been careful of yours.* In another letter, he said: *does your father keep much money in the house?* Something, something, something illegible, then . . . *won't miss it* . . . *always make more.*

All of which suggested that Balfour had indeed been the one to suggest the theft. I turned on my heels in the middle of the room, musing.

'Do you believe her?' Hugh asked. 'Mrs Fletcher, I mean. Do you think she committed the murders?'

I looked at the cosy, everyday objects. Owned, and used, by her own admission, by a murderess.

'She's certainly strong enough, and determined enough, to have done it. And all the planning bears her stamp. The other Alice is a creature of impulse, not careful preparation.'

'But?' he prompted.

'I still don't know,' I admitted.

'Maybe they *both* did it?'

'They certainly planned it together. But which wielded the knife—?'

'I suppose it doesn't matter,' he said. 'They were accomplices – they'll both hang if we catch them.'

'It matters to me.' Particularly after last night.

From Mrs Mountain's lodging house, we went to the Old Man Inn on the Key in search of Fowler. The serving girls swore he'd not been there. I asked several spirits if they knew where he was. They didn't.

'He can't get far,' Hugh pointed out as we came back out on

to the snowy Key. 'He has a hole in his shoulder. Any exertion will probably send him into a fever.'

'Something will have to be done,' I said, 'And quickly. As long as Alice is at large, Fowler won't let this matter rest. And I shudder to think what he might do if he gets desperate. I wouldn't put it past him to try and get at Balfour, for instance – he'll probably know exactly which watchman to bribe to let him into the cell. And if he does something stupid, like killing Balfour—'

'He'll hang too.'

'Besides,' I said. 'I object to being manipulated, and laughed at, and being made the object of a girl's silly spoilt wiles! I want them, Hugh!'

'They're certainly in the other world by now.'

'We could tempt them back . . .' I stared at the ships at the wharfs, in the icy water, outlined against the bank of bare trees on the Gateshead side of the river. The sky was growing darker; more snow was certainly on the way.

'Charles,' Hugh said sharply. 'You promised your wife you wouldn't get in any more trouble.'

'I promised her I wouldn't get myself hurt.'

'I'm not sure that would be *her* understanding,' Hugh said. 'What are you planning, Charles? Charles!'

I swung round, heading back along the Key towards the Printing Office.

'Charles! Where are we going?'

'To talk to Balfour,' I said.

The watchmen's hut was hot as a furnace as usual, and full of smoke both from the fire and from the four watchmen who were smoking in there. McLintoch was holding forth to his subordinates on his own courageous behaviour in apprehending Balfour and wasn't in the least embarrassed to realize we'd overheard as we came in.

'I was wondering if I could speak to Balfour,' I said. 'I need his help in finding Alice Gregson.'

'Won't talk, sir,' McLintoch said philosophically. 'Tried every way I know and he just sits there dumb.'

'Can you take me to him?'

He was shocked. 'Certainly not, sir! A gentleman like you oughtn't to go in a place like that. I'll bring him up here.'

He went off with two of his men; another two hurriedly put out their pipes and talked loudly of going off and doing their duty. Before they could be driven to such desperate straits, however, McLintoch came back with Balfour. The watchmen were bristling with pistols – two each – and Balfour's hands and feet were manacled. He was pushed down into a chair and regarded me resentfully. His clothes were filthy and he smelt badly.

'I'm glad to see you haven't taken any ill from your soaking in the river,' I said.

'Oh, yes,' he said. 'I'll be well enough to hang.'

The watchmen laughed cheerfully.

'I've had a talk with Alice,' I said, suddenly realizing how awkward this was going to be. Balfour had no idea there were two Alices and the watchmen couldn't be given any such suspicion. 'Unfortunately, she escaped.'

'I heard about that,' McLintoch said. 'Mr Heron sent me a message. Pity.'

'She did at least make it clear that *she* killed the family.'

Balfour gave me a sharp look. I said, 'She killed most of them before you got there but left the apprentice alive because he snored, so you'd be reassured everything was well. When you went down into the cellar, she killed the apprentice, ran upstairs, and slid down the rope – she had to make it look as if she was fleeing from you in panic. But you were too quick and escaped before the neighbours came on the scene.'

He laughed bitterly. 'It's good to know I put one spoke in her wheel.'

'You may yet put another,' I said.

'Charles,' Hugh said uneasily.

'We can set a trap for her.'

'No!' Hugh said sharply.

McLintoch took his pipe out of his mouth and said, 'Don't like the sound of that, sir.'

'You wrote to her?' I said. 'Did she ever reply?'

'Of course she did,' Balfour said contemptuously.

'And you kept the letters?' He hesitated. I said, 'You're a thief by nature, Balfour, you want money and you want as much as possible. You'd keep any letter Alice sent you. If the plan to rob her father never came off, you might be able to use those letters for a little blackmail.'

He said nothing.

'I don't care whether I'm right or not about the blackmail,' I said. 'Were Alice's letters indiscreet? Do they incriminate her in the plot to rob her father?'

After a moment, he nodded. 'But they're in London. Somewhere safe.'

'It doesn't matter. We have the basis of a plot.' I glanced up at McLintoch. 'Can we use your spirits to spread a message? We need Letty Mountfort's spirit in the derelict court to think Alice's letters are in the hiding place Balfour's used for the coins.'

'Easy done,' McLintoch said, nodding. 'You reckon she'll try and get her hands on them? And we keep watch on the hiding place and apprehend her when she does.'

I shook my head. 'Alice is too clever for such a ploy. We need something more subtle.'

I told them my plan. None of them liked it.

Forty-One

Alas, all is at an end. I must return.
[Letter from Louis de Glabre to his friend Philippe
Froidevaux, 24 January 1737]

The snow came down steadily, unceasingly, leaving a thick layer of new powder on top of the slush and ice of the previous days' fall. In the porch of the little chapel at the end of the bridge, a cold breeze teased our ankles and stirred the skirts of our great-coats. The clock of All Hallows' struck eleven. Only a week ago, we had been laughing over a glass of wine at home, proposing an outing in the snow. Only a week ago, Samuel Gregson and his family had been alive, and Fowler's Ned . . .

Kane was not happy. I gathered he'd spent an hour last night arguing with McLintoch over the custody of Balfour and then another hour drinking away his sorrows in the Fleece. He'd not slept well and woken with a hangover which still lingered. From the moment he'd stepped into the porch of the chapel, he'd talked of nothing but his maltreatment.

'Damn it, Patterson! I was the one who told you about this fellow! If it wasn't for me, you wouldn't have your hands on him now!'

I resisted pointing out that his description of Balfour had been very wide of the mark and had misled me – I didn't have the energy for an argument. I wasn't feeling particularly happy myself. Esther had said nothing when I told her about tonight's expedition but she'd plainly indicated she didn't wish me to get involved in dangerous matters. It was undeniable that both Alices were potentially very dangerous. The thought of never holding my child, of never even seeing it, was enough to make me want to walk away from here directly, straight home to the warmth of the house in Caroline Square.

But I wouldn't leave those two women to enjoy themselves travelling from world to world, secure from justice and punishment. If they succeeded in getting away with these crimes, who knows what havoc they might try to wreak? No, I had to have one more try to catch them. They'd want those letters, to make sure nothing hampered their freedom of movement. They'd want Balfour too, because he was the only one who could definitely tie them in to the murders. And perhaps they'd want me too . . .

Through the thickening snow came the hoot of an owl. Assuming it wasn't a real owl, it was the signal McLintoch had promised me, from his watchmen stationed along the Key. 'Balfour's on his way,' I said.

'Letting him out of prison!' Kane grumbled. 'The fellow will just run away.'

'He knows this is his only chance of cheating the noose.'

'He *should* hang!' Kane said vehemently. 'He killed in Kent and he killed here! He shouldn't have been promised anything else.'

I sighed. 'Transportation isn't exactly an attractive alternative. He won't have an easy life in the Colonies.'

'He should hang,' Kane said obstinately.

I contemplated the driving snow, the silent street, the dark buildings. I was putting Balfour at risk and deliberately using him as bait, knowing he might get injured or killed. And the fact that he had no alternative if he wanted even the possibility of escaping the hangman's noose, hardly made it better.

I brooded, letting Kane grumble on, not looking for answers, merely indulging his sense of grievance. I set my head back against the chapel walls, admitting to myself that I had a certain amount of admiration for Mrs Fletcher. She'd a great deal of courage to stay right under our noses, spying on us, gathering information. And to fearlessly take on two men, one of whom was armed . . .

Of course, by her own admission, she was a murderer. If I believed her. Which I didn't. That complicated tale she'd spun of Alice stepping backwards and forwards between worlds, letting Balfour in, going upstairs, taking Mrs Fletcher back to the other world, coming back again to slide down the rope . . . It couldn't be done. Given the differences in time between the worlds, stepping from one to the other so precisely simply could not be guaranteed. And there was too much to fit in, in too short a time.

If Mrs Fletcher was not the murderer, then Alice Gregson must be. *Our* Alice. All fashionable clothes and demure manners, her disarming looks and impish glances, sweet pleas and delightful vivacity. So innocent. On the surface. She'd killed probably for no better reason than spite, because she hadn't been allowed to stay in London. Yet Mrs Fletcher had said she loved her dearly, and she'd plainly entranced Balfour, if only for a short time.

A figure coalesced out of the blizzard: Heron, shaking the snow from his hat and brushing it from his shoulders. He took not the slightest notice of Kane, and said without preamble, 'Fowler is still missing. But at least we have some idea as to the reason. One of the spirits in the house passed a message on to him from the apprentice's spirit, about the fire and Balfour's attempt to dispose of him.'

'Dear God,' I said. 'Fowler is looking for *Balfour* now?' At any moment Balfour, apparently free and happy, was going to be walking through the streets; if Fowler saw him and didn't realize we were setting a plot, if he took a fancy to shoot him, the plan would crash to the ground and the real murderer go free. I'd cursed Fowler for persisting in his suspicions of Alice, and now, at just the wrong moment, he changed his target!

'I am still trying to find him,' Heron said grimly. 'But he is not in any of the obvious places.'

I thought of the apprentice's spirit. 'Ned can get a message to him, tell him what is going on, and ask him to stay his hand. He'd listen to the boy.'

'Any message might come to the ears of the spirit in the derelict court,' Heron pointed out, 'And she will warn Alice we are trying to trap her.'

I swore. Heron nodded. 'The only choice is to walk the streets looking for him.'

'Hugh's in one of the chares off the Key,' I said. 'He's supposed to follow Balfour after he leaves the prison but there are plenty of watchmen doing that. If two of you are looking for Fowler, you'll have a better chance of finding him.'

Heron's mouth twisted wryly. 'I would not place a wager on that.'

Kane stared sulkily after Heron, as he walked away into the snow. 'You gents think a lot of yourselves, don't you? Think you can just ignore the likes of us lower folk.'

Considering Heron was desperately trying to find a sick servant who was intent on running his head into a noose, Kane was decidedly wide of the mark. He lapsed back into silence and so did I. Thinking again of Esther and the child. Of Alice and her father. Of Balfour and his. Of mine. Dear God, I wasn't ready for this.

Another owl hoot. This one sounded closer – halfway along the Key perhaps. Balfour was clearly heading this way. So far, so good.

It was surprising that Balfour still would not reveal the location of the coins, even after agreeing to our plan; he must think there was still a chance he could get away with them. The hiding place must surely be relatively near the bridge. Balfour hadn't had long to hide the coins after the murders – he must have been panicking and would have wanted to get them off his hands as soon as possible. A pity he wouldn't talk; if we had known exactly where the hiding place was, we could have stationed watchmen there and increased our chances of catching Alice.

I wondered what I'd say to Kane if *both* Alices turned up.

Snow drifted into our faces; Kane swore and wiped his cheeks with the sleeve of his greatcoat. The chapel was tiny and the porch hardly worth the name; by putting out the lanterns at this end of the bridge, however, we'd created deep shadows and were tolerably certain Balfour wouldn't see us. More to the point, *Alice* wouldn't see us.

A dog bounded along the Key, paused to sniff at the foot of a post and to raise its leg. It trotted off. A moment later, a figure loomed out of the snow. Balfour.

He was huddled in a greatcoat, hugging himself as if he was cold, shuffling along in the snow like an old man; I wondered if the manacles he'd been wearing over the past few hours had chafed. I had little sympathy, but I did want him to last until this trap was sprung. As he passed, I caught a glimpse of his face under his hat; his expression was bleak.

Kane started to move out into the snow to follow. I pulled him back. 'Wait!'

Moments passed. The snow fell silently. Then another figure. A woman. Tall and cloaked, walking upright and proud, as if she had every right to be there. She glanced in our direction as she passed the chapel; Kane caught his breath and froze. I did not move. I saw Mrs Fletcher's expression, and it was a hard mask of pain.

She *knew*. She knew we were there; she knew this was a trap. *What was she doing?*

We let them get a few steps ahead and then followed. Kane was quiet; I had to admit he knew how to follow someone without being seen, even though we were forced to keep closer than I'd have liked because of the limited visibility. The footprints in the snow gave me the oddest sense of repeating what I'd done last Saturday night: the fresh prints of the dog, the man's prints and the woman's . . .

Balfour paused, looking about him as if checking there was no one watching. Kane and I instinctively slid into the shelter of a doorway.

A spirit whispered in my ear and made me start. 'Message from Mr Heron, sir. He says the gent he's been looking for has been seen heading this way.'

'Damn!'

Balfour seemed to straighten and walked on with more

confidence, heading for the ruins of the town wall which jutted out into the street. Last week, Alice – our Alice – had run straight past these ruins, on along the Key and into the derelict streets beyond; tonight, Balfour was keeping to the inner side of the wall. Houses were built on to the side of the wall and a narrow alley ran in front of them; I thought Balfour must be heading for the alley, but he went straight to the place where the first house jutted from the town wall. The wall was tumbledown here; stones had fallen away or been robbed out. There was even a suggestion of what might once have been a small fireplace.

Balfour had his back to me; I shifted until I could see him in profile. He was removing stones from the wall at the bottom of the fireplace niche; bricks crumbled in his hands. And from behind the stones, he lifted out a large bag.

It was obviously heavy; he seemed to weigh it in his hands. He brought it to his chest as if he was cradling it, like something precious.

Kane said, 'What the devil . . .?'

Mrs Fletcher was strolling towards Balfour, although he had his back to her and hadn't yet noticed her. But Kane was looking at the space beside Mrs Fletcher, at the shimmer forming in the air.

I've always tried to *step through* where there are no people around, precisely to avoid causing the kind of stupefaction Kane was obviously experiencing. Alice plainly didn't care. We saw the girl solidify. She was wearing a cloak but it swung open, and underneath she had only a white dress in some flimsy floaty material. Her golden hair and bright ribbons drifted in the breeze.

Mrs Fletcher was plainly not expecting her. She stopped, said, 'Alice! No!'

Balfour turned. I couldn't see his face, but he seemed to clutch the coins even tighter. I had a sudden panic: we should have retrieved the bag earlier, put some papers in it to look like letters – if one of the women looked now they'd know this was a trick.

But I remembered Mrs Fletcher's expression as she passed the chapel. *She already knew . . .*

Alice danced forward. 'Dear John, thank you so much. It's so kind of you to give us those letters back.'

'Alice!' Mrs Fletcher said sharply. 'Go back! Now.'

Alice paused, laid a hand on her arm, smiled up at her mischiev-ously. 'Dear Alice, you always treat me like a child. I've told you – I can look after myself.'

'No,' Mrs Fletcher said. 'You cannot. Go back!'

Alice ignored her, darted at Balfour. He let the bag go without protest. I heard the breath sigh out of him.

'She's right,' he said. 'This is a trap.'

Kane cursed. We both leapt forward at the same time, and both, like idiots, went for Alice. We collided; thrown off balance, I slipped in the snow and went down. Alice shrieked, Mrs Fletcher shouted and Balfour went off like a hare.

There was chaos. Someone yelled. Watchmen ran from every direction and piled into Balfour; he crashed to the ground under their weight, struggling wildly. Kane headed for Mrs Fletcher, seized her—

Alice stepped backwards, staring wildly. I tried to scramble up, but my feet went out from under me again. Alice retreated, clutching the bag of coins. The panic was gone from her face, and she was looking around in a calculating way. Frightened but in control. And the shimmering started again.

She was going, abandoning Mrs Fletcher. And Mrs Fletcher was calling to her to do it. Kane saw it too; he tried to disen-tangle himself from Mrs Fletcher but she clung on to him. She was sacrificing herself, letting Alice get away, and the girl wasn't arguing in the least. She was even smiling as she went.

I struggled to my feet. Mrs Fletcher shouted, pushed at Kane. He fell. Mrs Fletcher barged straight into me, just as I reached Alice. I stumbled, hit the ground again with a crash that knocked the breath out of me.

The shimmer took both women . . .

Someone was at my side. I looked up into Fowler's white, strained face. He said nothing. He was aiming at the shimmer, at the thinning figures of the women. He fired a single shot. I saw one of the women sag and fall.

The shimmer faded. There was nothing but an empty street.

The watchmen hauled Balfour out of the snow, looking exceed-ingly pleased with themselves. They started to look round for the women, demanding to know what had happened. McLintoch limped up, out of breath and cursing. Kane was staring, shaking his head, already beginning to disbelieve what he'd seen.

I dragged myself to my feet and took hold of Fowler's arm.

'I killed her,' he said, swaying. 'She killed Ned and I killed her. Only fair. She killed Ned. For no reason.'

I took the pistol from his loose grasp. 'Yes,' I said. 'You killed her.'

There was no body, and therefore no prosecution to face. I'd tell everyone the women had run off, persuade Kane he'd been imagining things – he was already halfway convinced anyway, going off with watchmen to search the surrounding streets. Fowler could go home in safety.

And I wouldn't tell him I thought he'd killed the wrong woman.

HISTORICAL NOTE

Every effort has been made to be geographically accurate in a depiction of Charles Patterson's Newcastle. In the 1730s, Newcastle upon Tyne was a town of around 16,000 people, hemmed in by old walls, and centred on the Quay where ships moored to carry away the coal and glass on which the town depended. The single bridge across the Tyne, linking Newcastle with its southern neighbour, Gateshead, was lined with houses and shops, a chapel and even a small prison; from the Quay, the streets climbed the hills to the more genteel, and cleaner, areas around Westgate and Northumberland Street. Daniel Defoe liked the place when he visited in 1720, but remarked unfavourably on the fogs and the smells that came drifting up the river. Places such as Westgate, High Bridge, the Sandhill and the Side did (and still do) all exist, although I have added a few alleys here and there to enable Patterson and his friends to take short cuts where necessary, and invented a stylish location for Esther's house, Caroline Square.

Musically, Charles Patterson lives in an atmosphere that the residents of Newcastle in the 1730s would have recognized instantly. The town had one of the most active musical scenes in England, after London, Bath and Oxford. From 1735, inhabitants could hear music in a weekly series of winter concerts (and occasionally during the summer too), listen to music in church (plain simple music if you went to St Nicholas, much more elaborate and 'popular' music at All Hallows), attend the dancing assemblies in winter, and listen to the fiddlers, pipers and ballad singers in the street. Nationally and internationally famous soloists often visited but sadly, there is no evidence to support the story that the most celebrated musician of the period, Mr George Frideric Handel, ever visited Newcastle.

A number of real people fleetingly appear in Charles Patterson's world. Solomon Strolger, organist of All Hallows for 53 years, is one, as is another organist, James Hesletine of Durham Cathedral. Thomas Mountier, the bass singer in *Broken Harmony*, was a singing man at the Cathedral for a short while until drink intervened; James Fleming had a stationer's shop on the Tyne Bridge. The Jenisons and Ords were real families with a particular interest in music but the specific individuals who appear in these books are fictional. The Gregsons are also fictional; Samuel's profession of upholsterer was what we would nowadays call an interior designer – he would have dealt with all aspects of decoration, including painting and wallpapering as well as furnishings.

There were indeed new Assembly Rooms in the Groat Market in the late 1730s although, as Patterson points out, they were designed for dancing, and far from ideal for concert-giving; there is no evidence, however, that a London architect was brought in to design them. Esther's comment about stylish new rooms in York refers to the Assembly Rooms in Blake Street, which still survive and give some idea of what the Newcastle Rooms might have looked like.

The relationship between London and regional cities such as Newcastle was always fraught with ambiguities. The inhabitants of Newcastle prided themselves on being up-to-date with the latest fashions, and boasted of obtaining new publications, new entertainments and popular performers from the capital with great speed. At the same time they could affect a snobbish disdain for anyone who suggested that London was in any way superior to Newcastle, and Defoe himself, a man who was hard to please, admitted that the Tyne Bridge was almost as impressive as London Bridge. Alas, the bridge came to a sorry end, washed away in dramatic floods in 1771.

Charles Patterson is entirely fictional, but the difficulties he finds in making a living would have been entirely familiar to musicians of the time. If he has an *alter ego*, it would be Charles Avison, a Newcastle-born musician and composer who was extremely well-known in his time and who dragged himself up by his own efforts from obscurity to wealth and respect. If Patterson's career follows the same path, he will be extremely happy.